THE
PAPERWHITE
NARCISSUS

———

THE
PAPERWHITE
NARCISSUS

CYNTHIA RIGGS

THOMAS DUNNE BOOKS
ST. MARTIN'S MINOTAUR
NEW YORK

THOMAS DUNNE BOOKS.
An imprint of St. Martin's Press.

www.minotaurbooks.com

ISBN 0-312-33983-6
EAN 978-0312-33983-8

First Edition: May 2005

10   9   8   7   6   5   4   3   2   1

FOR

DIONIS COFFIN RIGGS
POET

1898–1997

ACKNOWLEDGMENTS

When I told fellow Vineyarder, fisherman, and mystery writer Phil Craig that I'd never driven along the slender barrier bar that separates Katama Bay from the Atlantic, he said, "We'll take you there!" He and his wife Shirley spent half a day driving me around a part of the Island I'd never seen before. He also explained how the currents at Wasque might carry a body where I wanted Victoria to find it, and reassured me by saying, "You can write anything you want."

Dr. David Finkelstein, Victoria's, Katie's, and my eye doctor, is a fisherman first. He gave me advice on surf casting and bluefish behavior, then read the manuscript to make sure I got the fishing parts right.

Nurse Christine Flanders Fielder, whose Vineyard roots are as deep as mine, checked the passages involving hospital procedures and poison reactions and treatment. "You do realize," she scolded me, "that we would *never* divulge information the way Hope does." She grinned. "But I guess you can write anything you want."

Members of my two writers' groups have kept me going. Among them are Carolyn O'Daly, Wendy Hathaway, Linda Shumway, Lois Remmer, Brenda Horrigan, Jackie Sexton, Jeanne Hewitt, and Shirley Mayhew. Thanks to Alvida and Ralph Jones, Ann and Bill Fielder, and William Stewart for critiquing the manuscript.

Special thanks to Nancy Love, my agent, and Ruth Cavin, my St. Martin's editor. The best in their fields, both of them.

And thanks, as always, to Arlene Silva, who got me started, and Jonathan Revere, who kept me going.

THE
PAPERWHITE
NARCISSUS

———

CHAPTER 1

The breeze blew off Nantucket Sound, past the lighthouse that guarded the entrance to the harbor, past the freshly painted captains' houses lining North Water Street, past white picket fences laden with yellow, pink, and white roses. The breeze whispered through the screened front windows of the *Island Enquirer*, carrying the scent of honeysuckle, roses, and the sea.

Ordinarily, Victoria Trumbull wallowed in the newness, richness, and sensuousness of a June day like this.

But not today.

She didn't hear the tidy sounds of hedge clippers and lawn mowers. A boy painting the trim around the newspaper's windows called out, "Hey, Mrs. Trumbull," and she paid no attention. The boy shrugged, and dipped his paintbrush into his pail again.

Victoria opened the gate in the picket fence, strode up the walk, heedless of the way her lilac-wood stick jabbed the bright green moss that bordered the uneven bricks, marched through the open front door, and stopped at the reception desk.

Faith Norton, the receptionist, greeted her with a broad smile. "Good morning, Mrs. Trumbull. Nice day."

"Where is he?" said Victoria.

"Mr. Jameson? I think he's back by the press. Want me to call him?"

"That won't be necessary." Victoria pushed her way through the inside door that opened into a room with a dozen desks. She ignored the greetings of several people who looked up from their computer screens as she passed and continued through a second inner door that led to the far back room. There, the huge old press was churning out a steady stream of this week's edition of the *Island Enquirer*.

A short man with too-dark hair spun around as Victoria pushed the door shut behind her.

"What are you doing here, Victoria?" he shouted over the noise of the press. He was wearing a white shirt with broad blue stripes, the sleeves rolled up to his elbows, and a tie that Victoria recognized as his prep school tie, loosened at his throat.

"I need to talk to you, Colley Jameson," Victoria shouted back.

"Hell of a time." The editor gestured at the press, which was spitting out pages of the real-estate section. "Call and make an appointment."

He spun back to the press, his jowls quivering, his tie flying out in an arc.

Victoria got as far as shouting "Appoint—!" when the press snatched up the end of Colley's tie along with the ads it was printing. Colley tried to free his tie from the jaws of the press, but the press ran on and his tie tightened around his neck.

In that instant, Victoria threw down her walking stick, flung herself at the giant red button on the side of the press, and slammed it with her gnarled hand.

The press stopped with a shudder. Except for Victoria's heavy breathing and Colley's muffled oaths, the pressroom was deathly quiet.

"Well?" Colley mumbled, his mouth pressed into the photo of a water-view trophy home.

"Do you want me to cut your tie? I'll have to find scissors."

"Jee-sus Christ," Colley mumbled. "Do something!"

Victoria found a pair of long editorial shears in the composing room next door and returned.

"Careful!" Colley mumbled as she snipped close to his nose.

Reporters, photographers, rewrite people, the ad sales team, the keeper of the morgue, the receptionist, swarmed into the room, drawn by the silence of the press.

Once freed, Colley glared at the crowd that had gathered

around him. "What the hell are you gaping at! Get back to work, all of you."

There were a few snickers and Colley's face flushed a dark, unhealthy red.

Someone said, in a stage whisper, "What's black and white and read all over . . . ?"

"Get out!"

Colley loosened what was left of his tie and pulled it off over his head. Everybody but Victoria had gone. She handed the cut-off tie ends to Colley, who put them in his shirt pocket.

"It would be polite to say thank you," she said.

"The hell I will," said Colley. "If you hadn't distracted me . . ."

Victoria pointed a knobby finger at the sign on the wall that stated, in ultra-large letters, NO TIES OR LOOSE CLOTHING AROUND THE PRESS.

Colley took a handkerchief out of his pocket and wiped his hands.

"You'd better wash your face, too, before the ink sets," Victoria said. "I'll be in your office."

Colley's office was on the second floor of the old building, separated from the reporters' desks by a waist-high partition topped by a clear glass window. As Victoria walked down the aisle between desks, she was met with grins and thumbs up and a salute.

A few minutes later, a freshly scrubbed Colley, his striped shirt open at the neck, walked between the desks. On either side, reporters' fingers flew over keyboards.

The editor shut the door, glared at Victoria, who was waiting in his visitor's chair, and sat at his desk. Victoria, facing the bright June sunlight that streamed through the window behind him, couldn't see his expression.

Her back was straight. She held both hands on her stick. Her beaky nose was high, her eyes were hooded. Her wrinkles were set in an expression of disapproval.

Colley opened the bottom drawer of his desk, brought out an

3

ornate silver flask, unscrewed the top, and took a deep swallow. He tightened the cap and put the flask back in his drawer. He wiped his mouth with a blue-bordered handkerchief that had matched his tie, refolded it neatly, and returned the handkerchief to his pocket.

Victoria said nothing.

Colley swiveled his chair left and right, left and right. "You have to keep up with the times, Victoria. The *Enquirer* needs a new look. More youth appeal."

"That's why you fired me?"

"I didn't fire you. I suggested that you retire. There's a difference." Colley fiddled with a beach stone holding down a stack of papers on his otherwise tidy desk. "You've been writing that West Tisbury social column for, what, fifty years now?"

"News column, not social column. I've been writing the West Tisbury news column since the year you were born."

"Forty-nine, then. It's about time you retired. Give younger writers a break."

"Bah," said Victoria. The sunlight coming from behind Colley was making her eyes water and she dabbed at them.

Colley looked down and toyed with the beach stone paperweight.

"You know, don't you Colley, there are laws that protect workers against age discrimination."

"*You* don't need protection, for God's sake," Colley snapped. "You *are* ninety-two, after all."

"Exactly my point." Victoria withdrew a crumpled letter from her cloth bag. "Do you plan to defend this in court?" She tapped the edge of the letter on Colley's desk.

Colley sighed.

"Can you afford to lose another discrimination suit?"

Colley swiveled his chair and looked out of the window at the street below.

Victoria waited.

Finally he turned back to his desk. "Stop tapping that damned letter, will you?"

There was a knock on the door and Faith, the receptionist, entered with the mail. She glanced at Victoria, then stepped behind Colley's desk. "Didn't you notice, Mr. Jameson? The light is right in Mrs. Trumbull's eyes." She lowered the shade.

Victoria said, "Thank you," and Faith dropped the mail on Colley's desk and left.

Colley picked up the top envelope and slit it open with a silver-handled letter opener. Victoria was still in the same position, her expression unchanged, when he finally looked up. He pushed the remainder of his unopened mail to one side.

"What the hell do you expect me to do, Victoria?" Before she could answer, he went on. "I get nothing but crap from everybody." He flicked his hand at the mail on his desk. "Letters from every damned environmentalist on this Island. All riled up because I support the golf course. The affordable housing types are furious because I accept upscale real-estate ads. Open space people are angry because I back the idea of a mini-mall. Do any of these do-gooders buy ads? Hah!" Colley stood up, raised the blinds again, and glared out of the window.

Victoria started to say something, but Colley went on. "They don't believe me when I say that I'm as much of an environmentalist as the best of them." He tapped his chest. "I'm the one defending the piping plovers. By sticking up for the damned birds, now I've outraged all the fishermen."

"Only the surf casters," Victoria said. "But . . ."

"The damn fishermen run their buggies all over the dunes. I write one editorial supporting the birds and look at the mail I get. Shall I go on?" He sat again.

"You asked me . . ." Victoria started.

Colley continued. "Readers cancel subscriptions because I accept too many ads. Advertisers cancel because they don't like my editorials. I get sued for harassment, sex discrimination, and now age discrimination. How does anyone expect me to pay the bills?" He grunted. "I've got four ex-wives to support, for God's sake." He jabbed his finger at his chest. "I have to have armor-plated skin to publish this goddamned newspaper."

"I see I'm wasting my time." Victoria tucked the crumpled letter back in her cloth bag, stood, and headed for the door.

As she opened the door, Colley said, "You never told me what you expect of me."

Victoria turned. "You're right. I didn't."

CHAPTER 2

The clerk at Al's liquor store gave a thumbs up to J. Ambler Fieldstone. "Don't let those green types get to you, Mr. Field-stone. There are plenty of us Islanders who want that new golf course of yours." He lifted the case of sauvignon blanc that Fieldstone had purchased. "I'll carry this to your Outback for you."

"Thanks, Dave. And thanks for your support." Fieldstone wrote out a check for the wine, and when the clerk returned from the parking lot, slipped him a twenty-dollar bill.

"Thank *you*, Mr. Fieldstone, sir."

Fieldstone then drove across the road to the Stop & Shop and parked next to a Ford pickup. The pickup sported a bumper sticker printed with Day-Glo orange letters that vibrated against a blue background. It read GOLF COURSE NO! Fieldstone frowned and went into the store.

Like most Islanders, he was dressed in a frayed plaid shirt, worn jeans, and scuffed boat shoes. He was in his early fifties, medium height, medium build, and medium looking except for his intense blue eyes and profuse, prematurely white hair.

He stopped at the gourmet section of the store and selected an assortment of cheeses and crackers. He added white grapes, a roasted free-range chicken, freshly ground Costa Rican coffee, and fresh orange juice. He put together a salad for two at the salad bar, and chose warm-out-of-the-oven breakfast pastries at the bakery.

The woman at the checkout counter slid the Brie and cheddar past the scanner, and the scanner beeped. "Looks like you and the wife are going out on your boat for the weekend, Mr. Fieldstone." The pâté and the crackers and the smoked bluefish went past the scanner.

"Something like that," Fieldstone replied vaguely.

"It's supposed to be nice this weekend. My husband and I went out last week on my day off, but it was still kind of cold. Plastic or paper?" she asked, referring to the grocery bags.

"Paper. Got to protect the environment. Did you catch anything?" he added politely.

She shook her head. "The blues were feeding. You could see them. But they weren't taking our lures."

Fieldstone nodded.

She loaded the final item into the last paper bag and rang up Fieldstone's credit card. "My husband says you'll give Islanders a break on club membership. Is that right?"

"That's the current thinking," said Fieldstone.

"He plans to vote for your golf course." She ripped the credit-card receipt from the cash register and handed it to him. "Me, I haven't decided yet."

"I hope you vote to approve it." Fieldstone signed his receipt and loaded the grocery bags into the cart.

"I always read the *Enquirer,* especially letters to the editor. Some people say there'll be too much fertilizer."

"Doesn't have to be that way," said Fieldstone. "A lot of people are misinformed. Tell you what, next time I come by here, I'll bring you some brochures."

"Give me several and I'll hand them out."

Fieldstone made a note to himself on the back of his receipt.

"Whether I vote for your golf course or not, I know you're a good man, Mr. Fieldstone, whatever people say."

Fieldstone glanced at her name tag. "Thank you, Sarah."

He wheeled the cart out to his car and stowed the grocery bags in the back. The pickup truck that had been parked next to him was gone. He thought briefly about what he could do to counteract the effects of the bumper stickers that were appearing all over the Island and the anti–golf course letters to the editor. As he closed the tailgate he decided the best tactic was to keep quiet. Let Colley Jameson write his pro-golf editorials and screen his reporters' articles. The *Enquirer* was still respected by Islanders, although lately Colley seemed to be losing some of his influence.

Fieldstone returned the cart to the shelter of the store's overhang, then drove to Oak Bluffs along the narrow strip of land that separated Sengekontacket Pond from the sound. On both sides of the road wild roses bloomed profusely, and he breathed in the heady scent. He felt younger than he had in years. This promised to be a good weekend.

He kept his boat, a forty-foot Hatteras sportsfisherman, in the Oak Bluffs harbor and as Sarah at the checkout counter had guessed, he was going out for the weekend, but not with his wife. Audrey was off Island, attending a garden club meeting in Boston.

Two dock stewards, high school kids he remembered from last year, helped him unload the wine and the groceries onto his boat, and he tipped both of them.

"Thanks, Mr. Fieldstone. Thanks a lot," said Chuck, a tall muscular blond.

"Need anything else, Mr. Fieldstone?" asked Curtis, short, stocky, and dark.

"That'll be all, thanks. I'm going out with a fishing buddy, a woman friend."

"Yes, sir, Mr. Fieldstone. Good luck." The two dock stewards sauntered down the boardwalk that led to the harbormaster's shack and disappeared from sight.

Fieldstone stowed the groceries below deck, a couple of bottles of wine in the ice chest along with the perishables, the rest of his supplies in lockers behind the galley sink. He filled his stove with propane and stored the container underneath. He checked the bedding in the V-berth. Freshly laundered sheets, a queen-size fleece blanket, and a new double sleeping bag, in case the weather turned cool.

He was checking the head to make sure the stewards had cleaned it thoroughly and had replaced soap and toilet paper when he heard her low voice calling from the dock.

"Anyone on board?"

Fieldstone scrambled up on deck to greet her, a tall elegant woman in her forties with shiny dark hair cut short in back, longer in front. She wore no makeup. She didn't need it. Her face was milky pale, and her dark almond-shaped eyes seemed huge. She, too, was wearing boat shoes and jeans, and she carried a canvas satchel.

"Permission to board?" She smiled and handed the satchel up to him. "What an awful name, *S'Putter*."

"Welcome on board," said Fieldstone. "What better name for a boating golfer?" She took his hand and clambered gracefully over the transom.

"I'll stow your gear below," Fieldstone said. "Did you have any problem getting away?"

"I'll never understand that man," she said, after they'd climbed down the ladder and were below decks. "The world revolves around him. I could run naked down Main Street and he wouldn't notice."

"A lot of other people would," said Fieldstone, holding out his arms to her.

She snuggled against him. "And you?" Her voice was muffled in his shirt. "What did you tell Audrey?"

"The truth. That I was going out for the weekend with a fishing buddy. She's in Boston."

"I like that. 'Fishing buddy.'" She laughed. "Was I supposed to bring worms?"

"For this weekend, I have high-tech lures."

She broke away from him with another laugh. "I'll help with lines, or will you handle lines and let me run your boat?"

"I'll take her out of the harbor. Then you can steer."

"I can run your boat as well as you can."

Fieldstone put an arm around her again. "Probably better. But I want to take her out."

"Where are we going?"

He laid a chart book on the navigation table. She looked over his shoulder as he paged through the charts. He glanced at her. "How about Block Island?"

She held her hair away from her face as she leaned over. "Can we get there and back in three days?"

"We'll see how far we get." He left the chart book open on the table and went above to the wheelhouse, where he started up the engines, one after the other. The diesels cut in with a rumble.

She undid the stern lines and the spring lines from the boat, flipped them neatly onto the dock, hung the bow lines on the pilings with the boat hook, turned and saluted him. "Lines off, Captain."

While Fieldstone and his fishing buddy were leaving the Oak Bluffs harbor, Candy Keene, who'd just moved into her new house in West Tisbury, pranced into Town Hall in a haze of perfume. She confronted Mrs. Danvers, the town secretary.

Candy Keene, who was pleasingly plump and a well-preserved forty-something, had bright blond hair permed in a way that had to have been done off Island. She was wearing high-heeled boots and jeans faded in an oddly unnatural way with a pale starburst that drew attention to her crotch.

Mrs. Danvers looked up from her computer screen, her mouth drawn down. "May I help you?"

"I'm Miss Keene, and I'd like to talk to whoever's in charge."

"I know who you are." Mrs. Danvers stood, a tall, reed-thin woman. She examined Candy Keene from her boots to her jeans to her hair, and then to her carefully made-up face. "I'm the one in charge," she said.

"How do I file a complaint?"

Mrs. Danvers paused before she answered. "It depends on the complaint. A dog attacking your chickens goes to the animal control officer. Oysters and clams to the shellfish warden. Bad smells to the health department." She sniffed, then opened a desk drawer and extracted a form. "Fill this out. I'll see that it gets to the right person. Exactly what is your complaint?"

"I want that gas station out of there. We don't need a gas station in a residential area. Right next door to me."

Mrs. Danvers folded her arms over her chest and stared, her eyes magnified by her glasses. "That gas station has been there for seventy-five years. Before then it was a blacksmith shop catering to horses. Same family. Same idea." She handed the form to Candy Keene, who stuffed it into her purse but didn't move.

Mrs. Danvers looked down at her. "Is there something else?"

"Somebody's shooting in the field next to me."

Mrs. Danvers sat down again and turned to her computer. "That goes to the chief of police, Mary Kathleen O'Neill."

"A *woman*?"

"A chief of police," Mrs. Danvers replied. "She's at the police station. Will that be all?"

Candy Keene shrugged, swiveled on her heels, and headed for the door. She checked her face in the glass door panel, wiped lipstick from the corner of her mouth with the little finger of her right hand, opened the door, and went down the brick steps to the paved area in front of the building.

As she started across the road, a car slowed to let her pass, then turned into the gas station. She made a face at the back of the car and scowled at the man who was pumping gas. He lifted his hand to her with a smile, but she thought she detected a wiggle of his middle finger.

She was not going to walk to the police station in these boots. She got into her BMW, drove the quarter-mile to the tiny station house on the other side of Mill Pond, and parked in the oyster shell area in front.

Casey, which was what everyone in town called Chief O'Neill, was typing something into her computer when Candy entered. Casey turned away from her work and lifted her coppery hair away from the collar of her uniform shirt. "Can I help you?"

"Are you the police chief?"

"Yes, ma'am," said Casey. "And you're Ms. Keene, aren't you?"

"*Miss* Keene. Someone's shooting in that field next to my house."

"Yes, ma'am. We know about that. A father and son. They've got permission from the landowner, they're shooting into an approved target, and they're the required distance from any dwelling."

Candy stepped closer to Casey's desk and pounded a soft fist on the desktop. "I want you to put a stop to that shooting. I don't feel safe."

"Won't you sit down?" Casey indicated the wooden chair where her deputy usually sat. Candy looked at the chair and wiped the seat with her handkerchief before she sat down.

Casey hid her smile with a slight cough.

"It's outrageous to have gunmen right in the middle of town like that."

"You're entitled to file a formal complaint if you'd like." Casey opened a desk drawer.

"Formal, schmormal. All I'm getting in this supposedly friendly town is a runaround," Candy said. "I moved here for peace and quiet. Now I find I'm living next to a shooting gallery."

Casey took a blank form out of the drawer. "I understand your concern. But I've checked out the father and his son. They practice for only an hour, two at most, on Thursday afternoons after school."

"Give me that form, then." Candy snatched the paper out of

Casey's hand, filled in the blanks quickly, and tossed it on the desk. Each *i* was dotted with a circle.

"If I don't get action, you'll hear from me."

"I'm sure I will," said Casey.

Chapter 3

The phone was ringing the next morning when Victoria came into the house from her garden, her arms full of purple iris and pink peonies. She dropped the flowers into the sink, and left her secateurs on the table. The caller was Colley.

"Very funny, Victoria."

Victoria brushed the dirt off the knees of her gray corduroy trousers and sat down in her chair in the cookroom, the small room next to the kitchen. "What are you talking about now, Colley?"

"Your clever little obituary."

"What obituary?"

"You needn't play dumb with me, Victoria. It doesn't become you."

"Colley Jameson, I have no idea what you're talking about."

"Get yourself in here and I'll show you," and with that Colley slammed down the phone.

Victoria arranged her flowers in the two amber glass vases on the parlor mantelpiece, emptied the compost bucket onto the compost heap, and straightened up the kitchen. She scribbled a note for her granddaughter Elizabeth, who was at work, gathered up her cloth bag and walking stick, and went around to the front of the house where she stood by the road, intending to hitchhike into Edgartown. The bus came along first and stopped for her. The driver was a man from church whose name she could never remember.

"Mornin', Miz Trumbull. Nice day. Going to the paper?"

She nodded. She was about to drop four quarters into the coin box, but the driver held his hand over the slot. "Over sixty, you ride free. You're over sixty, right?"

Victoria smiled weakly at the intended compliment, thanked the driver, who was quite an elderly man, and sat up front, where she could imagine she was driving.

"I hear you saved the editor's neck the other day. Almost got chewed up by the press, did he?"

"News travels fast," said Victoria.

"Can't keep a secret on this island."

Victoria was the only passenger until they reached the youth hostel, about a half-mile from her house. Two young women lifted their rental bicycles onto the bike rack on the front of the bus, climbed on board, and sat behind the driver, across the aisle from Victoria. They unfolded a map and she could hear them discuss the best bike routes.

She leaned over to them. "Is this your first time on the Island?"

"This is the first time we've stayed overnight. We live in Hyannis," the dark-haired girl closest to her said. "We're here looking for summer jobs."

"The restaurants need a lot of summer help," said Victoria.

"We were hoping to, like, find work on a newspaper or magazine," the dark-haired girl continued. "I want to be a writer, and she," pointing to the blonde next to her, "wants to get into advertising."

Victoria thought for a moment before she decided to tell them about the *Enquirer*. "The editor often uses summer interns," she said. "In fact, I'm going to the paper now to talk with him. He doesn't pay much."

"Actually, we mostly want the experience."

The other girl, the blonde, said, "We just need enough to, like, pay for a place to stay."

Victoria nodded.

The bus followed the straight-as-an-arrow West Tisbury–Edgartown Road that Wampanoag Indians had established as a trail long ago. Every couple of miles, the road dipped into one of the valleys that drained into the Great Ponds lining the south shore.

The bus driver slowed at the outskirts of Edgartown and turned right onto Main Street. He spoke over his shoulder. "You girls watch yourselves around Colley Jameson." He pulled the bus over to the side, got out, and helped unload the bicycles. "Here you are, ladies. Take care, now."

The three of them walked the block and a half to the *Enquirer,* the girls wheeling their bicycles along the brick sidewalk beside Victoria. They leaned the bikes against the picket fence, releasing a sprinkling of rose petals, and went into the building with her.

Victoria told Faith that the girls were looking for jobs, and the receptionist gave them forms to fill out. "You can sit at the desk in the other room. Mr. Jameson will be with you after he meets with Mrs. Trumbull."

Victoria went upstairs, past the reporters, and into Colley's office. He beckoned her to the seat in front of his desk.

"What obituary are you talking about, Colley?" Victoria demanded.

He shifted some papers from under the beach stone and pulled out a letter typed on heavy cream-colored deckle-edge paper. He flipped it across the desk. "You want to explain this?"

Victoria picked up the letter. A neatly drawn black border framed the text.

She looked from the paper to Colley. "This is the obituary you called me about?"

"You know damned well it's the obituary."

Victoria glanced at it. The text began: "The body of Colley Jameson, fifty-five, editor of the *Island Enquirer* and well know *bon vivant*, was found by a reporter last night, hanging by his school tie from a beam in the newspaper's morgue . . ." Victoria laughed. "So, I've been writing my column for fifty-five years, not forty-nine." She set the obituary back on Colley's desk. "Shaving a few years off your age, Colley?"

17

"Very funny, Victoria." He pointed at the letter. "I suppose you thought that would alarm me?"

"Alarm you? What are you talking about? Surely you don't think I wrote that. Is this why you called me in?"

"Same kind of notepaper you use."

"Everybody on this Island uses deckle-edge paper for condolences and thank-you notes."

"Typed?" said Colley. "You're the only person on this Island who still uses a typewriter."

Victoria pursed her lips. "I'd never use my typewriter for a social note. When did you get the letter?"

"In this morning's mail."

Victoria folded her arms over her chest. "Have you shown the letter to the police?"

"An obituary isn't a threat."

Victoria reached across the desk and picked up the letter. "It's either a threat or a bizarre practical joke. Who's upset with you? Besides me, that is."

Colley took the letter and slapped the back of his hand against it. "You didn't write this?"

"Don't be ridiculous. You called me in here just to accuse me of writing that note?"

"I couldn't imagine anyone else," Colley said.

"We might have settled this over the phone. I had nothing to do with it." Victoria rose from her chair. "What do you intend to do now?"

"Nothing," said Colley. "Bill me for your carfare." He slung the obituary into his wastepaper basket.

"May I?" Victoria reached over and reclaimed it.

"Suit yourself." He added, "You will anyway."

Victoria tucked the cream-colored note into her cloth bag, left the editor's office, marched between the reporters' desks, and headed down the narrow stairs.

The two girls, both fresh and pretty and awfully young looking, stood as she went by the receptionist's desk.

"Thanks, Mrs. Trumbull," the dark-haired one said. "Keep your fingers crossed for us."

Victoria smiled.

She caught the bus returning to West Tisbury and got the same driver. He waited until she was seated. "I hear somebody's been sending Jameson his own obituaries, is that right?"

"Good heavens! How did you hear that?"

"It's in the air," said the driver. "You want off at your place or at the West Tiz police station?"

"The police station," said Victoria, settling back into her seat.

The bus driver leaned forward and looked up through the windshield. "Looks like we might be in for some weather."

Victoria hadn't noticed the thunderheads that had been building up while she was at the *Enquirer*. From her seat in the front of the bus she could see the flat anvil tops of the clouds spreading rapidly. Lightning flickered.

By the time the bus stopped in front of the police station, the wind had picked up. Victoria climbed the steps to the front door and pushed it open. She set aside her walking stick and sat down in the chair Candy Keene had vacated the day before. Victoria unzipped her light jacket, the silky bombardier's jacket her niece had given her, and fanned herself with the sides.

"The seat is nice and clean," Casey said. When Victoria looked puzzled, Casey laughed. "Candy Keene—*Miss* Candy Keene—needed to dust your chair with her lace hanky before she would sit down."

"You know who Candy Keene is, don't you?"

Casey nodded. "She bought the Captain Rotch house and has the whole town in an uproar because of the renovation."

"Renovation!" Victoria stopped fanning herself. "She tore the house down and built that monstrosity in its place."

"She left one wall of the old place," said Casey. "That makes it a restoration. She claimed the house was in pretty bad shape."

"That house was a classic eighteenth-century sea captain's house. Historic."

"Seems like the trend these days." Casey leaned her elbows on her desk. "Everybody wants four bathrooms and a sauna."

"Did you know she's one of Colley Jameson's ex-wives?"

Casey sat up straight and took her elbows off the desk. "The *Enquirer* Jameson? He was married to her? She doesn't seem his type. The present Mrs. Jameson is classy."

"Calpurnia is wife number five." Victoria settled back in the chair. "His first wife was his college sweetheart. That lasted about five years until he met Candy, who was an ecdysiast in a New Jersey nightclub."

"A *what*?"

"Ecdysiast. A stripper. Ecdysis is what snakes do when they shed their skins."

"How do you learn this stuff, Victoria?"

"I've been around," Victoria said, fanning herself again. "H. L. Mencken came up with the term 'ecdysiast' in the 1940s to describe striptease artists. But that's not why I'm here." She handed Casey the obituary she'd retrieved from Colley's wastebasket. "Colley got this in the mail today."

Casey examined the note. "What am I supposed to do with this?"

"He thought I'd written it," said Victoria, sitting forward. "It looks to me like a threat."

"It's not." Casey flicked her fingers against the note. "This may be somebody's idea of a joke, but it's not a threat in the legal sense. He got his tie caught in the press and someone's making a joke out of it."

Victoria sat forward. "It's not a joke. It's a threat."

Casey sighed. "Even if it were a threat, Jameson lives in Edgartown, not West Tisbury. The Edgartown police have jurisdiction, not me."

Victoria retrieved the note and got to her feet. "I see I'm wasting my time here, too."

"Where are you going?" Casey pushed herself away from her desk.

Victoria zipped up her jacket. "To see William Botts."

"What does William Botts have to do with this?"

"He's the editor of the *West Tisbury Grackle,* of course."

Casey looked confused. "The what?"

"West Tisbury's newspaper. A competitor to the *Island Enquirer.*"

Casey laughed. "Oh, *that.*"

"I wouldn't dismiss the *Grackle,* if I were you," Victoria said stiffly, as she headed for the door.

"Wait," said Casey, getting up from her chair. "I'll drive you there. It's about to rain and I need to check on something out that way."

William Botts, founder and editor of the *West Tisbury Grackle,* was in his office in what had once been the hayloft of a barn. He was a gnomelike man with disheveled gray hair and a puckish expression. The *Grackle* was a one-page sheet Botts ran off on the library's copying machine and sold for ten cents a copy from boxes posted outside the senior center and Alley's store. He was eating a peanut butter and jelly sandwich when Victoria mounted the rickety stairs that led up from the horse stalls. He looked up as she hoisted herself onto the floor of the loft.

Botts, who was at least twenty years younger than Victoria, set the remains of his sandwich on the rim of his coffee cup, wiped his hands on his tan pants, and arose from his editorial seat. "Mrs. Trumbull," he said. "To what do I owe the honor of this visit?"

Victoria perched on the edge of an overstuffed chair, avoiding a broken spring that showed through the upholstery. "I wanted to talk with you."

"Sorry about that chair." He tugged a brightly colored Mexican serape out from under a large graying black dog, who moaned and got unsteadily to his feet. William shook out the blanket and laid it over the seat cushion behind Victoria.

"Thank you," she said.

Botts returned to his seat behind the desk, which was piled high with paper. "So that egomaniac fired you, eh?"

"That's what it amounts to," said Victoria. "I'm here to apply for a job on the *Grackle*." She settled back in the overstuffed chair with its now-covered spring and waited.

Botts folded his arms on top of his piled-up papers and eyed Victoria over his half-frame glasses. He, too, waited.

Finally Victoria said, "Colley got an obituary in the mail this morning. Reporting his death."

"His own?" Botts raised his shaggy eyebrows.

Victoria nodded. "The obituary said he was found in the newspaper morgue, hanged by his prep school tie."

"I heard you saved him yesterday."

"He thought I'd caused the accident. Now he's convinced that I sent him the obituary."

Botts leaned forward. "I don't suppose you did?"

Victoria peered at him through half-closed eyes and ignored his question. She fished the note out of her cloth bag and handed it to Botts, who studied it, then looked over his glasses at her.

She waved a knobby hand at the note he held. "That letter is clearly a threat. Yet neither Colley nor our chief of police seems to be taking it seriously."

"I must say, Victoria, I agree with them." Botts handed the note back to Victoria.

"Our police chief plans to do nothing." Victoria smoothed her white hair. "If you hire me, William, I'll get to the bottom of this. You'll have a scoop for the *Grackle*."

Botts shook his head. "I only report West Tisbury goings-on and I don't pay salaries."

"The money is not important. It's a matter of principle," said Victoria.

Botts leaned back with his hands behind his head. The black dog looked up at him, then put his head down and closed his eyes.

Victoria eased herself out of the deep, uncomfortable chair. "I'll give you time to think it over, William. When you hire me, you'll have an experienced newspaper correspondent and a new angle on stories. You won't have to pay me a cent. At least, not right away." She stood, bracing herself on her walking stick. "It's time the *Enquirer* had some competition."

"From a one-page broadsheet?" Botts muttered. "With a circulation of fifty?"

"It's a start," Victoria said. "You don't happen to be driving my way, do you? It's beginning to rain."

Matt Pease was waiting outside Colley Jameson's office with his camera bag when Colley returned from lunch. Rain was coming down heavily. The waterproofing of Matt's raincoat was long gone and when he took his coat off, the shoulders of his gray sweater were darkly wet.

Colley gestured Matt into his office. He removed his tweed hat and his own raincoat and hung them on the coat rack in the corner of his office. He checked his reflection in a mirror behind the coatrack and ran a comb through his hair. Then he turned to Matt.

"Have a seat, Matt. Quite a storm we're having. Can I offer you a warmer-upper?" He reached into his bottom drawer and brought out his silver flask and two silver shot glasses.

"No thanks," said Matt.

Colley poured himself a small drink and put the flask away. He downed the drink, wiped his mouth and his shot glass with his handkerchief, and put the glasses back in the drawer. "Just what's needed, day like today." He refolded his handkerchief and put it in the breast pocket of his blazer.

Matt leaned forward in his chair. "Mr. Jameson, I wanted to talk to you about my summer hours."

Colley's expression changed slightly. "There's not much to discuss, Matt." He leaned back in his chair.

"The baby's due next month and I need the money."

Colley assumed a sympathetic expression. "I understand how difficult it is for you, Matt." He straightened his tie, lifted his chin, and stretched his neck.

"When I drop below twenty hours a week, I lose health benefits."

"I have to tell you, Matt, I never have guaranteed a permanent position on the *Enquirer*. I have young photographers lining up for their chances during their summer vacation." Colley straightened the pile of papers on the side of his desk. "In fact, I interviewed two young women just this morning."

"It's not right to cut back hours of year-round staff like that."

Colley cleared his throat. "If you don't like the way I manage the *Enquirer,* Matt, move on. Work for one of the off-Island dailies where the pay is better." He smiled. "I'll give you a good recommendation."

"This Island is my home."

Colley shrugged. "What can I say? I'm not in the business of providing charity. You want to stay on the Island, get yourself a summer job. Plenty of openings this time of year. Wedding photos. Great market."

"I've been with the *Enquirer* for five years now. Even before you took over. I believe I've proven myself."

"Indeed you have," said Colley. "I have no intention of letting you go. Come September, you'll get your full forty hours again." He leaned back in his chair. "But think for a minute. There are good jobs off Island. Cheaper housing, cheaper cost of living, the whole nine yards."

Matt stood. "You're firing me, aren't you?"

"Not at all. I'm in business to make a profit for the paper and, while I'm at it, to train young newspapermen. And women, of course. Staff salaries are my biggest expense. It's in my interest to cut back hours of the higher-paid staff for the summer. Not what I'd call a big deal."

"Mr. Jameson, I was born on this Island. My dad was a Linotype operator when your dad bought the paper. I want to raise my kids here, not off Island. I'm not asking you for a handout. You need additional photographers during the summer. I can train them. Please, I beg you. Don't cut my hours right at this time."

Jameson stood up, too. "I hear you, Matt. You've made your point."

"Will you at least consider my request?"

"I have considered your request. You have choices, Matt. I don't." Colley came out from behind his desk. "Now, Matt, if you'll excuse me, I've got catch-up to do."

Matt got to his feet, scowling.

Colley walked over to his door and opened it. "Thanks for stopping by, Matt. Have a good weekend."

CHAPTER 4

Friday's thunderstorm had left the Island freshly washed. The restaurant on the Gay Head cliffs was open for Sunday brunch. The Menemsha bicycle ferry had started its summer runs across the narrow channel. In West Tisbury, the bell in the Congregational church steeple was ringing for ten o'clock service. Geraniums and white petunias lined the sidewalk in front of the Bunch of Grapes bookstore in Vineyard Haven. Rain had knocked petals from the roses that covered the picket fence in front of the *Enquirer*, which was closed on Sunday. Boats were arriving in the Oak Bluffs harbor from Falmouth to spend the day. This was the last weekend before boaters would need reservations.

The Hatteras sportsfisherman slowed and entered the harbor between the jetties at the entrance. The yacht turned and backed slowly into its slip.

A dock steward raced from the harbormaster's shack along the boardwalk to help with lines.

When the stern was within a foot of the seawall, the dark-haired woman, who'd been standing at the transom, leaped ashore and strode off, swinging her canvas satchel.

Fieldstone, at the controls in the tower, yelled out, "Hey, get my lines, will you?"

The woman ignored him. She continued down the seawall, head high. She stopped at a silver Toyota parked parallel to the seawall, unlocked the door, got in, started the engine, backed out, drove off with a skid of sand, and disappeared down the road that bordered the small pond across from the harbor.

"I've got your lines, sir," the dock steward called out. "You're looking good."

Fieldstone left the controls, scrambled down the ladder, muttering "Damned bitch," and caught and fastened the stern lines. He then went forward with a boat hook and snagged the bow lines from the pilings. He was breathing hard. "Thanks. Chuck, isn't it?"

"Yes, sir," the steward said.

"I'm back sooner than I expected to be. Would you see that the boat is cleaned?"

"Yes, sir."

"Linens laundered. Stow the wine where it won't get shaken up. Food. You dock attendants can have the food."

"Thank you, sir."

"I'll probably be going out early next week. Can you have her shipshape by then?"

"Yes, sir."

Fieldstone gathered up his gear, handed Chuck a fifty-dollar bill, and headed toward his Outback.

"Thank you, sir!" Chuck called out.

Fieldstone lifted his hand in response, got into his car and, in a screech of tires, drove in the opposite direction from his erstwhile fishing buddy.

Fieldstone's wife, Audrey, came home a day early from Boston. The club president's husband had suffered a stroke and the weekend seminar was cancelled.

Audrey was driving past the Oak Bluffs harbor when she saw the Hatteras coming in between the jetties. She parked her car by the Steamship Authority wharf, unwrapped a stick of chewing gum, popped it into her mouth to freshen her breath, and walked toward her husband's slip. She was just in time to see a long-legged, dark-haired woman leap off the boat as it backed into the slip. The woman landed on the dock and strode away, swinging her canvas tote angrily, got into her car, slammed the door, and drove off.

Audrey recognized the woman immediately. Colley Jameson's wife, Calpurnia.

Audrey had watched through narrowed eyes. Calpurnia was tall and slim—skinny, really—and almost flat-chested, whereas she, Audrey, currently a redhead, had a voluptuous figure, large high breasts, a slender waist, nice full hips, and shapely legs. Her thighs were a bit heavy, but she was working on them.

J. Ambler Fieldstone was Audrey's second husband. Her first marriage had never been legally terminated, although she'd lost track of Buddy years ago. She'd never told Fieldstone she'd been married before, of course. She had almost forgotten that she was still Buddy's wife as well as Fieldstone's.

Audrey ducked into the doughnut shop on the corner. She sat on a stool by the window where she could continue to watch. She saw the dock steward take the lines, saw her husband's white hair and angry red face, saw him hand the kid a bill, saw him get into his Suburu and drive off in the opposite direction from Calpurnia.

"Can I get you anything?" The boy at the counter lowered his eyes to her chest and looked up quickly. Audrey watched him with a slight smile. "Coffee? A doughnut?"

"No thanks." Audrey got up from the stool and pushed through the door, stalked to her car, and drove directly to her attorney's office in Edgartown. She parked in the lot behind the building and went upstairs.

Martha Jo Amaral, the attorney's secretary, a solid woman with graying hair, looked up from her computer keyboard and said brightly, "Good morning, Mrs. Fieldstone. Mr. Fox is with someone right now. Can I get you some coffee?"

"How long will he be?" Audrey demanded.

"Maybe ten or fifteen minutes?" Martha Jo replied.

Audrey paced to the end of the reception area and back. "You can get me a good stiff drink," she said.

"Certainly, Mrs. Fieldstone." Martha Jo left her desk and reappeared with a tumbler half-full of scotch. Audrey took the drink and flounced onto one of the pale leather chairs in front of Martha Jo's desk.

Audrey had grown up in Secaucus, New Jersey, where her father was a farmer. When she was seven, she had sworn a mighty oath to herself that when she grew up she would get away from pig farms and pig smells. When she turned sixteen, she married Buddy.

While she was musing on how far she'd come since Buddy, Al Fox came out of his office with his client, a man Audrey had seen around the Edgartown Yacht Club. The man nodded to Audrey and shook hands with Fox.

Fox was totally hairless. No eyebrows, no eyelashes, no shadow of a beard. His scalp shone in the bright morning light. "You don't need to worry about a thing, Fred," the attorney assured his client. "I'll take care of all the details." He turned to Audrey and held out his arms. "How can I help you, my dear?"

Audrey brushed past him. "Let's go into your office."

Before Fox joined her, he paused at the door. "Hold my calls, will you please, Martha Jo."

"Certainly, Mr. Fox."

As he was shutting the door, Audrey blurted out, "I want a divorce."

Fox led Audrey across the thick carpet overlaid with oriental rugs to a leather armchair that faced another leather armchair across a glass-topped coffee table and at right angles to a leather couch.

"Have a seat," he murmured.

Except for a slight paunch, Al Fox had the build of an athlete, a tennis player or a swimmer.

"I want to get that two-timer for every cent he's got," said Audrey, still standing, her eyes glittering.

When she stopped, Al Fox said quietly, "You recall, don't you, that you and J. Ambler signed a prenuptial agreement? He didn't believe in divorce, and, as I seem to recall, you didn't either." He smiled.

Audrey perched on the edge of one of the soft chairs, and Al Fox sat behind his desk. "I didn't expect that bastard to run around on me with that woman."

"We went over the prenup in detail," Fox said. "I doubt if we can break it. I'll do what I can, but I think you'll have to be satisfied with a modest settlement. A very modest settlement, I might add. He and you had top legal advice when you signed that document." He cleared his throat and played with the letter opener on his desk. "I wouldn't make too many waves, if I were you."

"That agreement should be invalid if . . ." Audrey didn't finish.

Fox smiled. "It should, shouldn't it?" He steepled his hands and put the tips of his fingers under his chin.

Audrey stood, started to say something clever and smart-ass and cynical, decided she'd better not, and stormed out of the office instead, slamming the door behind her.

When Colley arrived home that evening, he found Calpurnia upstairs in their bedroom with the door closed. The bedroom was hers now. Colley had been banished to the guestroom since last Easter.

He knocked.

Calpurnia's voice was muffled. "Go away."

"I'm fixing drinks, darling."

"I don't want to talk to you."

"Come down when you're ready. I'll light the fire." Colley went downstairs into the long, narrow front room that overlooked South Water Street and the harbor. Fog had set in and the evening was chilly. The house smelled of damp old wood. Somewhere in Nantucket Sound a foghorn moaned.

Colley moved the fire screen aside and held a lighted match to the paper underneath the logs. Then he mixed two drinks at the bar at the end of the room, scotch for him, bourbon for Calpurnia.

He had almost finished his first drink, sitting in one of the chintz-covered wing chairs that flanked the fireplace, reading William Bott's *West Tisbury Grackle,* when Calpurnia came into the room. Her eyes were puffy, her face swollen. She had changed from the jeans and sweatshirt she had been wearing earlier in the day into a diaphanous caftan printed with a lavender and blue floral design.

Colley straightened his tie and got up politely. Calpurnia sat in the wing chair that faced his.

"I can use that drink now," she said.

"I'm sure you can." Colley added more ice to her glass and took it to her.

"Thank you."

They said nothing more for several minutes. Colley examined the nails on his left hand and burnished them on the lapels of his blazer. He continued to study the broadsheet. Calpurnia stared into the fire. The foghorn moaned in the sound.

Calpurnia finished her drink. Colley looked over his spectacles, got up, and refilled both her glass and his.

She held her drink in both hands in front of her face. "I assume you know what I'm so upset about?"

Colley took off his glasses. "I have no idea."

"Don't be so goddamned sanctimonious." Calpurnia slipped off her shoes and drew her slender feet under her.

Colley sucked on the earpiece of his glasses.

"You knew I went out with J. Ambler Fieldstone on his boat, didn't you." A statement, not a question.

"I've known for some time that you and Fieldstone were having an affair." He straightened the crease in his trousers and crossed his right leg over his left.

"You set me up, didn't you?"

"Now, darling," Colley said.

"Don't you 'now darling' me, you . . . you pimp!"

Colley held the earpiece of his glasses and swung them in an arc. "And what does that make you, may I ask?"

"He was paying you, wasn't he? For my services. As if I were a call girl."

"A high-priced call girl, I must say," said Colley with a smile.

She set her drink on the candle table next to her chair with a thump and a splash.

"You'd better wipe that up before it stains the finish," said Colley.

"How can you be so . . . so . . ."

"So *what*, darling? You went along with the game."

"Game! Is that what you think? I cared for him, I really cared for him."

"Were you so naïve as to think he was about to leave his Audrey for you? Don't be silly. He doesn't believe in divorce. You were a diversion."

Calpurnia finished her drink in one long swallow and set her glass down again. Colley handed her his handkerchief, which she ignored. He got up, lifted her glass, wiped the spilled drink from the tabletop, and set her glass down again.

"A refill?" he asked.

She nodded.

He returned from the bar and handed her a new drink. "I suspected he'd tire of you sooner or later."

"He told me how much he was paying you."

"Yes," said Colley. "Indeed."

"I feel so dirty. To think I actually thought he was in love with me." She sipped her drink. Then, angrily, "You think I don't know about *your* affairs? All those sweet young summer interns panting for bylines?"

"You're upset, darling," said Colley.

"Goddamned right, I'm upset."

"I must say, I'll miss the income you brought in." Colley lifted his glass to her. "At least he's still planning to run his full-page ads."

Calpurnia stood up unsteadily, dashed the rest of her drink into Colley's face, and flung her glass into the fire. The glass shattered against the firebrick. Shards glinted briefly before they dropped into the flames.

"Fuck you," she said, and strode out of the room into the evening gloom.

Colley laughed.

CHAPTER 5

The next morning, Calpurnia was pacing back and forth in her kitchen, nursing a cup of strong black coffee and a serious hangover, when the phone rang. She shuddered, wet a paper towel under the cold water tap to place against her forehead, and answered.

A woman's voice said, "I need to talk to you."

"Who is this?"

"Audrey Fieldstone."

Calpurnia patted her mouth with the paper towel.

"Hello, hello," said Audrey. "Did you hear me?"

"I heard you."

"I need to talk to you."

Calpurnia paced. "I don't think so."

"You can listen, then," said Audrey. "I know about you and my husband."

"Is that what you're calling me about?"

"Indirectly," said Audrey.

Calpurnia clamped the phone between her shoulder and her cheek, walked to the sink, and rewet the paper towel. She held it, dripping, against her forehead. "I have nothing to say to you. If you're calling to warn me away from your husband, it's over."

Audrey laughed. "Don't you think I know that? Ambler's flings are always short-lived."

Calpurnia pulled out a chair and sat down. "Why are you calling me?"

" 'Why' is because now my dear husband is two-timing both of us."

"Audrey, I don't care."

Audrey murmured, "I wonder what procurer he's paying for this one's services?"

"I don't want to hear any more." Calpurnia stood up and was about to disconnect.

"Wait, don't hang up yet."

"I'm really in a hurry. Come to the point."

"J. Ambler is rendezvousing with a certain someone on Nantucket over the next couple of days. Want to guess who?"

"I don't care," said Calpurnia. "I've got to go."

"Candy," said Audrey.

"What!"

"Candy. Candy Keene. Your husband's second ex-wife. The stripper. Former stripper. A bit passé now."

"You're joking!"

"I thought that would interest you."

"Why Nantucket?"

"You should know."

Calpurnia rewet the paper towel, wrung it out, and held it against her forehead again. "What do you mean by that?"

"Come, now. You needn't be quite so dense. He's driving *S'Putter* over to Nantucket by himself and meeting her there. That cheap floozy won't step foot on a boat. She has a 'delicate stomach,' she claims."

Calpurnia, despite her own delicate stomach and pounding head, asked, "Are they staying at a hotel?"

"Ambler? In a hotel?" Audrey laughed. "You know him better than that. His floating pleasure palace, of course. Tied up at the dock. Where it's not the ocean that will rock it."

Calpurnia sighed. "How did you learn all this?"

"She left a message on his answering machine. Really bright."

Calpurnia sighed again. "You called just to tell me he's going to be on Nantucket with Candy Keene? Frankly, I don't give a damn."

"I'm proposing to call a temporary truce," said Audrey.

"No thank you."

"You're a pretentious bitch, Calpurnia. I can't stand you any more than you can stand me." Audrey's voice was sharper. "But this is one time we can work together to play a little trick on J. Ambler."

At this point, Colley came into the kitchen. He opened the refrigerator door, took out a bottle of Sam Adams, bent down to check his reflection in the polished side of the toaster, and looked over at his wife.

"I'll call you back," said Calpurnia to Audrey, and hung up.

That same day, Buddy saw the photo in an old copy of *People* magazine in a stack of reading matter the garage kept for waiting customers. Another mechanic, George Mason, saw the photo first. He was thumbing through the magazine, licking his finger to turn the pages, while Buddy was changing a tire. George showed the picture to Buddy. "I didn't know you and Audrey was divorced."

"We're not."

"Look at here."

Buddy stood up. He was holding a lug wrench in one hand. He wiped his other hand on the back of his jeans and stared at the photo and caption, which George pointed out to him. The photo was in an article about a golf tournament in Georgia and was one of several photos in a lavish full-color layout. It showed a couple at a cocktail party in glittering evening dress. The couple was identified as J. Ambler Fieldstone and his elegant red-headed wife, Audrey.

Buddy stared at the photo and caption. "Shit!" He hurled the lug wrench across the garage. It hit the metal door with a clang, left a dent, fell onto the concrete floor, and bounced. " 'Elegant'!" said Buddy. " 'Redheaded'? Gimme one of your cigarettes."

"Thought you quit."

"Shit," said Buddy again, holding out a shaking hand. "Goddamned fucking bitch."

An hour before first light the Friday after Audrey had called Calpurnia, two fishermen were surf casting at the southeastern corner of the Island.

Stars faded as sky and sea changed to predawn gray, separated by a faint horizon line. Simon Newkirk now could see where he'd been casting. A wide band of breaking waves tumbled and foamed from the near shore and swirled toward the low clouds that hung over Nantucket, fifteen miles to the southeast. The turmoil marked the tidal rip that churned up food for the bluefish that were running now.

Simon and his fishing buddy, Tom Dwyer, stood in the swash from the breakers. Both wore chest-high waders. Tom, the taller, huskier of the two, had on a bush hat and was smoking a pipe. Simon was bareheaded. They stood some distance apart to keep their lines from tangling. The roar and hiss of the surf, the wind, and the cries of gulls made it difficult to talk. For the most part, they fished without speaking.

A dozen times during the three hours they'd been here, one or the other had hooked a bluefish. Each time, Simon marveled at the way the blue struck, once cutting the metal leader on his lure. He put two of the fish he'd caught in a Styrofoam cooler. The rest he released.

To the southeast, the horizon was becoming more distinct. As Simon watched, the sky changed from gray to a glowing red. In a sudden burst the sun rose behind the clouds and the churning rip sparkled in the light.

Tom took his pipe out of his mouth. "Red sky. Storm's brewing," he shouted above the noise of breakers and wind. "Maybe hit tonight or tomorrow morning."

"How much more time do we have, Tom?"

Tom checked his watch, which was set to show the times of high and low water. "Tide should run out for another ten or fifteen minutes." He put his pipe back between his teeth. "I could use a cup of coffee about now."

Simon nodded. "I brought sandwiches and a Thermos."

"Sounds good."

Simon tugged sunglasses out of a vest pocket and put them on. "How many keepers you got?"

"Four twelve-pounders," Tom called back. "Two for Phyl, Lynn, and me, two for my neighbor, Matt Pease." He cast again, hurling the lure far out into the rip.

Simon moved closer to hear better. "Matt Pease, the photographer? I didn't realize he lived near you."

"He and his wife live two doors down. Nice kids." Tom stabbed the butt of his rod into the sand and relighted his pipe. "They're expecting a baby next month."

"Talented kid. Colley's lucky to have him."

"Jameson's cut Matt's summer hours."

"Just as we head into the busy season?"

Tom nodded. "Colley brings in summer interns. College kids. They work for free."

"That's not right," Simon said.

"Damn right it's not right. But that's Colley Jameson for you."

"I imagine he's not easy to work for."

"Unpredictable cuss. In fact, he's a goddamned bastard." Tom spit into the sand.

Simon looked at him in surprise.

Tom shaded his eyes from the glare on the water. "Tide's turning. Where's that coffee?"

They reeled in their lines and trudged back to the four-wheel-drive vehicle, which Tom had parked near the dunes. They shrugged out of their heavy waders and stowed them in the back of the car, then added their surf-casting rods to the ones already on the roof rack.

Tom opened his tackle box and removed a thin-blade filleting knife and a whetstone. "Might as well clean my fish now." He sharpened his knife, moving the blade back and forth with smooth strokes. "Colley Jameson," he muttered around the pipe stem he held in his teeth. "I'd like to get my hands on Colley

Jameson." The knife blade whispered against the stone. "Want me to clean your fish?"

"Appreciate it." Simon carried the paper bag of sandwiches and his Thermos to where they'd left their catch, unscrewed the lid, and poured coffee. "What's with you and Colley? Sounds like something more than the way he treats his employees." Simon set a cup next to Tom, who was squatted down near the swash line.

"I'll wait, thanks." Tom slipped the thin blade into a fish belly, slit the belly from tail to head, tugged out the guts, and tossed the bloody mess to the sea gulls that circled around him. He held up his hands. "Colley? You don't want to know. One of these days, though . . ."

He rinsed the fillets in the surf, stowed them in plastic bags, wiped his knife carefully, scoured his hands clean with wet sand, and joined Simon with his coffee cup.

They sat on the beach for almost an hour, sipping coffee, eating sandwiches, and talking. Simon took in the sweep of sea and sky. Far out he could see breaking waves. The line of waves gradually approached the shore as he watched. There was an ominous feeling that came with the change of tide.

"Impressive, isn't it," Tom said, "changing of the tide. Incoming, now. Like clockwork." Simon watched the waves break closer and closer. "What do you suppose that is?" he pointed to a dark object several hundred yards offshore.

Tom shaded his eyes. "Looks like a seal. You see them occasionally this time of year." He wadded up his sandwich wrappings and stowed them in the paper bag. "That tasted good. Nothing like salt air to work up an appetite."

Simon stood. "Whatever it is seems to be drifting, not swimming."

They watched the floating object and talked companionably for another half-hour as the tide carried whatever it was towards the beach. Tom relighted his pipe. "I'd better get my binoculars."

Simon could see now that the object was no seal, but he still couldn't identify it.

Tom returned with the binoculars and stood near the water. "Can't tell." He handed the glasses to Simon. "What do you think?"

The object was the size of a small seal, dark, flexible. Something trailed from it, cloth or plastic or seaweed. Each breaker brought it closer.

Simon refocused. "Looks almost like a body."

"Not big enough," said Tom. "Let me have the glasses."

A wave crested and Simon caught a glimpse of dark cloth before the breakers engulfed whatever it was. It was clearly not a person, or at least not a whole person.

"Close enough now for us to bring it ashore." As the object rose to the crest of a comber, Tom added quickly, "Forget the waders. We have to go after it."

Both men kicked off shoes, and, fully dressed, waded into the surf.

Simon took a deep breath before a breaker knocked him down, but he'd managed to grasp a handful of something that felt like jeans material. He hung on and struggled to his feet just as the next wave knocked him down again.

"You okay?" Tom reached out to Simon with his free hand and helped him to his feet. Together, the two men dragged the sodden, jeans-clad thing onto the beach.

When Simon finally registered what it was they had fished out of the sea, he let go and stared at Tom.

"Shark attack?" he mumbled.

Tom wiped his hands on his wet chinos. "Wonder what happened to the upper half."

At the *Enquirer*, Katie Bowen borrowed one of the newspaper's tape recorders, snatched up her notebook, and rode her bicycle down the hill to the small three-car ferry that shuttled between Edgartown and Chappaquiddick.

"Reporting on the body that washed up?" Captain Brad asked her once he got the ferry underway.

"My first big assignment." Katie's voice was a low husky growl. "Colley's off Island, so the assistant editor assigned me to the shark attack. All Colley gives me is stuff like the West Tisbury selectmen's meetings."

The ferry crossing took less than five minutes. More like two minutes.

"Take care," Captain Brad said, as Katie pedaled off the ferry and headed down the tar road.

The asphalt surface lasted for about two miles, then became a sand track. Katie had difficulty controlling the bike. She was short and the bicycle was a couple of sizes too large for her. Wherever the sand was not packed down, her bicycle skidded. By the time she reached Wasque, the point of land Islanders pronounced *Way'-squee*, she was hot, dusty, out of breath, and angry with the assistant editor for not letting her use the *Enquirer's* Jeep.

The small parking area at Wasque was filled with vehicles— Edgartown police, state police, an ambulance, a collection of SUVs, and a Harley-Davidson.

In the interest of safety, most fishermen came by ferry and parked in the Wasque lot. But some drove along the thin barrier bar that connected Chappaquiddick to the rest of the Vineyard, a risky route to their secret fishing spots. One of these days the ocean would cut through the barrier bar that separated Katama Bay from the Atlantic. When that happened, depending on the tide, the bay would empty into the ocean or the ocean into the bay, flushing away everything in the way.

Katie leaned her bicycle against the split-rail fence next to the Harley and headed down the steep wooden steps that led from the bluff to the beach below. The presence of the motorcycle meant that Doc Jeffers was here. He must be medical examiner this week.

A group of people had gathered at the point a quarter-mile

down the beach. Katie had never seen a body before, and certainly didn't want to see a corpse that had been bitten in half by a shark.

Doc Jeffers was bent over something. Katie edged closer. The doc was a tall, massive man wearing black leather biker's pants, black boots festooned with steel chains, and a green V-neck scrub shirt that showed a triangle of curly white hair. He was talking into a small tape recorder.

Katie recognized the two fishermen who'd found the half-corpse, Simon Newkirk, her eye doctor, and Tom Dwyer, the mystery writer. She braced herself against the wind and walked over to them.

Tom, who was well over six feet, leaned down to talk to her. "I see your byline pretty regularly these days. How are things going?"

Katie hesitated. "You know Colley."

"I know Colley, all right." Tom turned away. "Simon spotted the body."

Simon came over to her. "I can't tell you much."

Katie turned on her tape recorder, and Simon talked about hauling the half-body out of the surf. Katie tucked her blowing hair into her windbreaker collar and scribbled notes, holding the recorder and her notepad in one hand, her pen in the other.

"Anything to add, Mr. Dwyer?" she asked.

"Background stuff you might be able to use." He told her about fishing the rip, the changing tide, dawn, and the morning sky.

"Is there any clue as to his identity? A wallet or something?" Katie asked.

"You'll have to get that from Doc Jeffers," Tom said.

Katie switched off her recorder and thanked them. She'd seen Ed Prada, an Edgartown police officer she'd gone to high school with, standing on the other side of the group huddled around the body. She'd had a crush on Ed ever since she could remember, but he'd been a senior when she was only a freshman and she didn't think he had ever noticed her. He'd gone off Island to college and had returned with a degree in criminal justice.

"Any idea who he was, Ed? Or how it happened?"

Ed, too, had to lean down to talk to Katie. "Doc Jeffers thinks the body's been in the water two or three days. The top half is missing, head, arms, torso. No way of knowing who he was until the forensics people examine him. Could be a fisherman or someone off a passing boat."

Katie turned her back to the wind so she could hear better. "Can they tell what kind of shark attacked him?"

"The doc says no bite marks. He thinks it was a boat propeller that killed him, not a shark."

"*Not* a shark?" Katie scribbled in her small notebook.

Ed shook his head. "Sliced across his spine."

Katie shuddered. "Would it take a big boat to do that kind of damage?"

"Not necessarily. Could have been a fishing vessel on the way to Georges Bank. Or a freighter, although most freighters go by way of the Cape Cod Canal, not the sound. Could easily have been a smaller boat, though. The Coast Guard's checking vessel owners on the Cape and Islands."

Katie nodded toward the knot of people. "Any thoughts on how the accident could have happened?"

Ed shrugged. "The victim may have fallen overboard and got swept under the boat into the propeller. Or he might have been in a small boat that got run down by a bigger boat. Hard to tell."

"But to cut the body in half like that . . ."

"Can happen," said Ed. "Obviously did."

"Don't boats have propeller guards?"

He shook his head. "The Coast Guard says prop guards pose hazards that can be worse than open blades."

"What could be worse than that?" Katie nodded toward the body.

"Trauma and sure death if a person falls overboard and gets clobbered. Prop guards throw off maneuverability."

Katie continued to write.

Ed traced a circle in the sand with his booted foot. "Before the authorities can tell what happened for sure, they'll take the body to Falmouth for an autopsy. It would help if the upper half is found."

Katie's hair whipped loose from her collar and blew around her face again. "Is it possible that they'll find the rest of him?"

Ed shrugged again. "Never can tell. Might wash up along the south shore. Or maybe they'll never find him."

There was not much for Katie to report, aside from the fact of the half-body possibly done in by a boat propeller. When she returned to the paper she would be able to write only a bare sketch of what had happened. She couldn't begin to fill in the who, what, where, when, or why.

Doc Jeffers stood up, snapped off his latex gloves, and gestured toward the bluff and the distant parking lot.

"It's a wrap," he said. "Take him away."

Katie put her notebook and pencil back in her pocket and climbed the wooden steps to the top of the bluff ahead of Ed. "Any chance you can give me and my bike a ride to the ferry, Ed?"

"Sure thing."

Ed stowed Katie's bicycle in the trunk of the police car and fastened the lid down with shock cords.

"Haven't had much chance to talk to you, Katie, since you've been working for that psychopath," he said once he was in the driver's seat. "He been hitting on you?"

"I avoid him as much as I can."

"He can start working on the summer interns soon. I feel sorry for his wife."

"She's his fifth wife, you know. I think she's about to leave him for somebody else."

"Can't say as I blame her. An Islander?" Ed slowed for a crow in the middle of the road feeding on a run-over rabbit.

"Not exactly. Want to guess who it is?"

"Nope."

"Think golf course developer."

Ed glanced quickly at her. "Not Ambler Fieldstone?"

"Yup. J. Ambler Fieldstone. The *Enquirer*'s biggest advertiser."

"Does Colley know?"

"The guys on the paper think he doesn't have a clue. But I think he does know and doesn't care. Advertising is more important to him than a mere wife."

The road stopped at the dock. Ed parked behind another car and turned off the engine. Across the harbor, they could see vehicles driving onto the ferry.

"One of my psychology profs did his dissertation on narcissism," Ed said while they waited. "Colley Jameson is a typical narcissist. The world exists for him and only for him. He has complete disregard for his wives, employees, and associates. He's got this grandiose sense of himself—thinks he's perfect, infallible, brilliant, and immune to punishment. A lot of serial killers are narcissists. Not that Colley's a serial killer," he added quickly.

"His pro-development editorials are angering a lot of people," Katie said.

"Typical narcissist. Criticism doesn't apply to him. He doesn't hear what people are saying, doesn't care what they think."

The ferry returned to the Chappy side where they'd been waiting. Captain Brad unhooked the bow chain and a car and pickup truck drove off.

"What d'ya say, Ed," said Captain Brad. "Identify the body yet?"

"Not yet. The cops, Doc, and the hearse should be along in a few minutes. They can tell you more than I can."

Once they were back on the Edgartown side, Ed drove down the maze of one-way streets that led to the *Enquirer*, stopped in front of the paper, and unloaded Katie's bike.

"Thanks," she said. "You know what Colley's wife's name is?"

"I don't know anything about her."

"Calpurnia," Katie answered.

"Calpurnia, as in Caesar's wife?"

Katie nodded. " 'A wife beyond reproach.' "

Ed laughed. "How about a beer when you get off work? I'm through work around five."

"I'd like that," said Katie.

CHAPTER 6

Victoria stood at the west door, breathing in the morning air. Her garden could use more rain. Lettuce was up, bright green against the dark, compost-rich soil. She'd already harvested radishes and wintered-over kale.

The phone in the cookroom rang and she went inside to answer. The call was from Casey. After she hung up, Victoria nudged McCavity, her marmalade cat, out of her chair and sat with her elbows on the pine table, thinking.

In the west pasture, thin streamers of mist trailed from the tips of the cedars. Weak sunlight illuminated the white steeple of the Congregational church in the distance.

When her granddaughter Elizabeth came into the room, Victoria didn't hear her. She was absorbed in her thoughts. Elizabeth had moved in with her grandmother after her divorce, and apparently was here to stay. She had a job, now, working in the Oak Bluffs harbor.

"What's the matter, Gram?"

Whenever her granddaughter appeared unexpectedly, Victoria felt her spirits lift. Elizabeth reminded Victoria of Jonathan, her dead husband. Elizabeth had the same clear low voice, a feminine version of Jonathan's. Like Jonathan, she was tall and slender and had broad swimmer's shoulders.

Victoria brushed her hand in front of her face before she answered. "Half of a body washed up on Chappaquiddick."

"Half? How awful. Who found it? Where?"

"A man's body. Simon Newkirk and Tom Dwyer were fishing at Wasque."

"That's horrible," Elizabeth said. "Let me get a cup of coffee before you say any more. Can I get you one?"

Victoria shook her head. "None for me, thanks."

Elizabeth returned, set her mug on the table, and sat down. "Was that what the call a few minutes ago was about?"

Victoria nodded. "They haven't been able to identify the body."

"Was he killed by a shark?"

"I haven't heard any details."

Elizabeth ran her fingers through her short, sun-bleached hair.

Victoria continued. "Casey wants me to show her the way to Quansoo. She's been asked to help look for the rest of the body."

Elizabeth made a sour face. "Sounds like fun."

"Volunteers are walking along the south shore, from Quansoo to the opening, from Long Point to Oyster-Watcha, from Oyster-Watcha to Edgartown Great Pond, and from there to Katama."

"What if the rest of the body is still in the ocean?"

"The Coast Guard has sent a cutter to search off the south shore," Victoria said. "They'll send a helicopter later this morning, if we still haven't found the body."

"*We?*" said Elizabeth. "Casey wants you to go with her to find the body?"

"Naturally," said Victoria.

Elizabeth picked her coffee mug up and set it down again. "Is there anything I can do to help? The harbor is busy right now, but I can take off for this."

"The harbormaster has a scanner, doesn't he?"

"Everybody on this Island has a scanner except you, Gram. You don't seem to need one." Elizabeth glanced out the window. "Here's Casey now."

Before Victoria went to the door to greet the police chief, she set her blue baseball cap on her hair and looked at her reflection in one of the small panes in the kitchen window. The cap's mirrored gold stitching read WEST TISBURY POLICE, DEPUTY.

She gathered up her cloth bag and her walking stick from behind the kitchen door, picked up her heavy sweater, and went out to the police Bronco.

From Victoria's house, Casey drove up Brandy Brow, past Alley's store, where the regulars were basking on the porch in the warm June morning. They waved as the Bronco went by. The Quansoo Road was about a mile beyond Alley's. Casey turned left onto the sand road. "I don't know how to get there from here, Victoria. You'll have to navigate."

Victoria's grandparents had taken her to Quansoo in the horse-drawn wagon scores of times. She'd walked the road, traveled it by horseback, by bicycle, and, once she and Jonathan owned one, by car, with children and grandchildren packed inside, or standing on the running board.

That is, until Casey arrived on Island and confiscated her driver's license. Simply because she had backed into the Meals on Wheels van. Victoria scowled. The driver of the van had overreacted.

She straightened her cap. Well, she told herself, if it hadn't been for the van incident, she would probably not be a police deputy, riding shotgun with the chief.

She directed Casey through the tangle of branching roads that led off to either side. Sunlight filtered through new leaves, casting perfect sun-coins along their route. Chewinks rustled in last autumn's fallen oak leaves, sounding more like deer browsing than small birds hunting insects. Crows signaled to other crows, who signaled back.

After two miles, the overarching trees thinned out and became stunted, shorn by salt winds, then gave way to low scrub oak and bayberry, wild rose and poison ivy, then grasses. The road ended at a straight, narrow creek. Casey parked the Bronco and got out.

"Wait for me here, Victoria. I shouldn't be too long."

But Victoria had already gotten out of the Bronco and started across the wooden bridge that spanned the creek.

Casey mumbled something that Victoria ignored.

The first view of the ocean through the dunes always, always took Victoria's breath away. She'd made this trip across the creek and through the dunes how many times? Five thousand? Ten thousand? The view was never the same. Today the ocean seemed menacing. Part of the feeling came from the brewing storm. But part was because somewhere out there, or washed up somewhere on the beach, was half of a man, a person who'd been alive only a few days before.

Victoria shivered.

"Are you going to be warm enough?" Casey asked.

"I'm not cold." Victoria unzipped the heavy sweater she was wearing. "Canadian," she said, opening it to show its thickness. "From Fiona's parents."

"Fiona?"

"My granddaughter-in-law."

They walked to the edge of the swash where the sand was firm, then turned left, heading east along the straight sweep of beach.

"Take your time, Victoria. We're not in a hurry."

Victoria had marched ahead of Casey, who had to walk briskly to keep up. Victoria looked over her shoulder and slowed. She had to admit, the pace was a bit faster than she, too, cared to maintain.

A roll of dirty gray clouds was moving in slowly from the south. Far out, breakers built up, moved inshore, crested, curled over, and crashed onto the beach in a continuous roll that progressed along the beach behind them. Victoria felt the steady rumble.

Twice, Casey trudged up to the high-tide line to check on a piece of flotsam or jetsam. "Lobster pot buoy," she reported back. "Tangled in plastic netting." Or a piece of lumber, silvered by salt water and sun.

Before they had gone far, Victoria stopped and leaned on her walking stick. "The fishermen found the body three or four hours ago, just as the tide changed. Therefore, we're not likely to find anything high on the beach."

Casey grunted. "What do you mean?"

"It's likely the body didn't wash ashore on an earlier tide," Victoria said. "So we need to look near the line of breakers."

A procession of sandpipers flew down and raced along the swash line, dipping their bills in unison into the wet sand, dodging incoming sheets of foaming water.

Victoria poked her stick into a drift of seaweed and bent down to pick up a pretty stone, which she tucked away in her cloth bag.

"What's that?" Casey called out suddenly.

Victoria turned to see Casey pointing to something just beyond the surf.

"A seal," Victoria said. "You don't see them often on the south shore." She rested on her stick and caught her breath. Her sore toe was beginning to ache. She really must slow down, she thought. This might be a long walk.

Casey stopped next to her. "We're supposed to go only as far as the opening. Another team is starting from the other side." The opening was a cut in the barrier bar that let seawater flow into the Great Pond to nourish oysters and clams.

Victoria and Casey had walked about two-thirds of the distance to the opening when Victoria spotted the body.

The body was just inshore from the line of breakers. It drifted up on the beach with each breaking wave, then washed back to sea again. The head, arms, and torso flopped in a strangely life-like way.

Victoria jabbed her stick into the sand and leaned on it. She could think of nothing to say.

Casey caught up with her, stopped, and stared at the half-corpse drifting back and forth between the sea and the shore. "I was hoping we wouldn't be the ones to find him."

The flock of sandpipers took off, turned into the wind with a flash of white, and settled back on the swash line beyond the drifting body.

"Well," Victoria said, taking a deep breath. "What now?"

"I call in," said Casey. She unfastened her radio from her belt.

Victoria moved away from the ocean toward the dunes and eased herself down onto a big silvered tree trunk.

Casey finished her radio call and sat next to Victoria. "I don't suppose he'll go anywhere."

Victoria shook her head. "Not until the tide changes."

"Was it anybody you knew, Victoria? An Islander?"

"I didn't want to look too closely," Victoria replied.

Doc Jeffers recognized the body and shook his head. A patient of his and a golfing partner, he said. He refused to say more. He made a small joke about his relief that the two halves weren't from two victims.

The EMTs then carried Victoria's half down the beach, over the dunes, and across the bridge, and loaded it into the hearse. Toby, the undertaker, would be taking the body to Falmouth for autopsy. He, too, made a sly comment about the convenience of not having to make two trips off Island to convey one body.

After it was all over, Victoria and Casey returned to the police station. Victoria sat in her usual chair in front of Casey's desk while the chief finished paperwork having to do with finding the half-corpse. Victoria untied the laces of her right shoe.

Finally Casey set her pen down.

"Doc Jeffers knew who the victim was," Victoria said. "Do you suppose he'll be willing to give out the name yet?"

"I'll call him." Casey reached for the phone. When she finished, she hung up and leaned her elbows on the desk. "Lord!"

"Did he say who it was?"

"The golf course developer."

"J. Ambler Fieldstone?"

Casey nodded.

Victoria took a deep breath and sat back again.

"The Coast Guard is trying to locate the vessel that ran him down, or anyone who might have witnessed the incident."

"Cut in half," Victoria murmured. "What an awful way to die."

"The state police are notifying his widow. I'm glad I don't have to."

"Mrs. Fieldstone was talking to her lawyer about a divorce, did you know that?"

"Yeah?"

"She backed off when her lawyer reminded her of a nuptial agreement she'd signed."

"No money in the event of a divorce?"

"Something like that."

"Why did she want a divorce?"

"I believe there was some hanky-panky involving Mr. Fieldstone and the present Mrs. Jameson."

"Where on earth do you hear all this stuff?"

Victoria straightened her cap and stood up. "Will you give me a ride to the *Grackle* office?"

"Has Botts offered you the job yet?"

"He will," said Victoria.

CHAPTER 7

Victoria climbed the steep stairs to the *Grackle* office, greeted Botts, and seated herself in the overstuffed chair. She removed her shoe. Her sore toe throbbed.

He looked up over his glasses. "Out walking?"

She set her stockinged foot on the floor and sighed. "Have you heard about the body that washed up at Wasque this morning?"

"I heard about it on the scanner—half at Wasque, half at Quansoo. I gather you had something to do with finding the half at Quansoo?"

Victoria nodded. "About a mile down the beach near the opening."

Botts picked up his pencil. "The scanner didn't give his name."

"I don't suppose his identity is a secret." Victoria patted her hair. "Your newspaper might as well have the scoop over the *Enquirer*."

Botts tapped the pencil on his desk.

Victoria coughed delicately. "Did I hear you say I'm on the *Grackle*'s staff?"

"The *Grackle* only covers West Tisbury goings-on."

"The upper half was found in West Tisbury."

"Did you find out whose body it is?"

Victoria nodded.

"I told you I don't pay salaries," said Botts.

"And I told you it's the principle of the thing," said Victoria.

Botts took a deep breath, let it out in a great sigh, and

swiveled in his chair. He reached down and ruffled the ears of the black dog. With another sigh, he stood up, reached over the stacked papers, shook Victoria's gnarled hand with his own gnarled hand, and sat down again. He picked up the pencil, pulled a clean scrap of paper from somewhere in the pile in front of him, and adjusted his glasses. "Okay, Madam Reporter. Whose body is it?"

At the *Enquirer*'s emergency editorial meeting the next day, Saturday, Colley flicked his fingernails at the latest issue of the *Grackle*, hot off the West Tisbury Library's copier.

"Have you seen this?" he asked the assembled reporters. He tossed the broadsheet at Matt Pease, the photographer, who was sitting closest. Then he opened his desk drawer, unwrapped a roll of Tums, and popped one into his mouth.

Katie Bowen, who was sitting next to Matt, peered over his shoulder.

"You were there yesterday, *Miz* Bowen. You saw the body. You heard the medical examiner. Presumably, you were taking notes. Or were you taking note of that Edgartown cop? I understand he drove you back to the *Enquirer*."

Katie blushed and sat back again.

Colley went on. "So who finds the body? That hack mystery writer."

"Hardly a hack," a voice muttered off to one side. "*Publishers Weekly* said . . ."

Colley interrupted the speaker. "Anybody care to tell me how Botts managed to scoop the *Enquirer*?"

Matt turned the broadsheet over. "Did you see this?" He handed the paper back to the editor.

Colley's eyes narrowed. The masthead listed two names. One was William Botts, editor and publisher. The other was Victoria Trumbull, reporter. Colley's face turned an unhealthy red. As he reached for the phone he gestured to the reporters and staff members sitting in front of his desk. "Get out of here! All of you! Get out!"

Victoria hung up the phone and turned to Casey, who had stopped by with Victoria's mail.

"Now what?" Casey asked.

Victoria was smiling broadly, her face wrinkled in delight. "Colley wants me to come to Edgartown to talk with him. Apparently he held an emergency meeting at the newspaper after he read the latest issue of the *Grackle*."

"Everybody on the Island's read it."

"The phone's been busy all morning," said Victoria. "William had to put this week's issue back on the press."

"I didn't think the library could turn out more than twenty copies."

"Fifty," said Victoria. "That was his total press run." She shuffled some papers on the table in front of her. "Tisbury Printer is printing another fifty."

"I suppose you'd like a lift into Edgartown for your editorial meeting?" Casey asked, moving away from the doorway where she'd been standing.

"If it's not too much trouble." Victoria glanced out at the overcast sky. She eased herself out of her chair and went into the dining room in search of her cloth bag and her raincoat.

"I have to do a couple of errands in Vineyard Haven and Oak Bluffs first," Casey said, once Victoria was seated in the Bronco.

Victoria held up her crossword puzzle book. "I certainly don't mind keeping Colley Jameson waiting."

Candy answered her own phone. "Keene Realtors, keenly aware of your Island housing needs. May I help you?"

"Hi. How'ya doin'?" Nice male voice.

"How may I help you?" said Candy.

"I'm looking to rent a place for a couple of weeks while I, um, track down a friend." *Really* nice voice.

"It's awfully late to get a good summer place. When did you need it?"

"Right now, end of June."

"How large a place?"

"Just me." He laughed.

"I might be able to help you, then," said Candy, paging through her rental book. "Are you on Island now?"

"I'm at the ferry dock in Vineyard Haven."

Candy smiled. "It looks like it's about to rain. You'd better take a cab to my office, and I'll show you what I've got." She hoped he wasn't some fat old creep. "What's your name?"

"Buddy Smith."

"Will you be paying by check or credit card?"

"Cash," said Buddy.

By the time Casey finished her errands, it was raining heavily. Victoria looked up from her puzzle.

Rainwater dripped off Casey's hair and rolled down the shoulders of her blue windbreaker. "Sloppy out there," she said.

The wild roses that lined the road between Oak Bluffs and Edgartown were bright in the gray gloom. Low breakers pounded the bathing beach to their left, empty now except for a few gulls. Casey followed a slow-moving car into Edgartown and down Main Street, past the house where Victoria had been born.

"I'll drop you off in front of the newspaper and find a parking place," Casey said. "Take your time, Victoria. I have plenty of paperwork with me."

Victoria went up the brick walk, holding a newspaper over her head to keep her hair dry. She greeted Faith at the reception desk and climbed the narrow stairs to the second floor and Colley's office. Again, the line of reporters grinned and saluted her. She marched the length of the room and through the door to the editor's office.

Colley looked up with a sour expression. "You certainly took your time."

Victoria moved the visitor's chair so it no longer faced the window. "I had business to attend to," she said.

Colley scowled. "I had no intention of firing you, Victoria."

Victoria rummaged in her bag and withdrew the crumpled letter he had sent her. "Would you care to reread this?"

Colley ignored the letter. "You don't want to be associated with William Botts's scandal sheet."

"Don't I?" said Victoria.

"I'm prepared to reinstate you."

"No, thank you," said Victoria.

"How much is Botts paying you?"

"That's between Mr. Botts and me."

"I can probably pay you twice what he's paying you."

"Impossible," said Victoria.

"I can give you a raise over what you were making here."

"How much?"

"Five dollars a week more," said Colley.

Victoria got to her feet. "You're wasting my time."

She started for the door just as Charity Hall, who was in charge of the newspaper's morgue, knocked and entered.

"Mr. Jameson . . ."

"I'm busy, Charity."

"I think you need to see this, Mr. Jameson."

"Not now."

Victoria returned to her chair and sat again.

"I think you really, really need to see this, Mr. Jameson." Charity handed Colley a business-size envelope that had been slit open.

"It was mailed to the morgue, Mr. Jameson."

"I can see that, for God's sake." He put on his glasses and examined the postmark.

Charity clasped her hands in front of her. "It has an Island postmark."

Colley glared at her. "Believe it or not, I can read." He extracted the letter from its envelope and read. "Oh hell," he muttered, and tossed the letter onto his desk.

Victoria sat forward so she could read the letter upside down. It began, "The body of Colley Jameson, age fifty-five, was found yesterday, washed up on South Beach. Mr. Jameson was apparently the victim of a shark attack. . . ."

Charity waited. "What do you want me to do with this, Mr. Jameson?"

"Just go away, will you? Go back to the morgue."

Charity left the room and closed the door gently behind her.

Victoria sat back in her chair. "You'd better call the police, Colley."

"The hell I will. That's exactly what some joker is hoping I'll do."

"This has gone beyond a joke," Victoria said. "One person is dead. Not quite a shark attack, but close."

"His death and this fake obit have nothing to do with each other."

"You don't think so?" Victoria pushed her sleeve off her wrist and looked at her watch. "I've got an interview in a half-hour."

"An interview, eh? Goddamned cub reporter." Colley stood up, hands flat on his tidy desk. "For God's sake, do you expect an apology from me? Well, you won't get it."

"Certainly not."

Colley sat down again and reached into his lower desk drawer, where he kept his flask.

Victoria got to her feet and before she swept out of the editor's office, turned. "When you decide you need my help in solving the mystery of the phony obituaries, call me. I'll send you my rate card."

With that, she closed the door firmly and marched between the two rows of reporters' desks to the stairs that led down to the front office and out to the street, where Casey waited.

CHAPTER 8

The memorial service for J. Ambler Fieldstone was held at the Whaling Church at noon the next day. Rain fell steadily. The police had closed off Main Street and an overflow of mourners and celebrants waited on the brick sidewalk in the gray drizzle.

Audrey Fieldstone, wearing a nicely fitted black silk designer suit that set off her red hair, emerged from the church, followed by a stream of mourners. She held the stout arm of Toby the undertaker, who was several inches taller. They stood in the shelter of the portico. Audrey gazed at the umbrellas below her.

Katie Bowen, who was in the crowd on the sidewalk, shielded her notebook with the flap of her yellow slicker and looked away briefly while she drew the hood over her hair. When she looked up again, Colley had come out of the door of the church and was heading toward the widow. Calpurnia followed her husband.

Katie pushed to the front of the crowd and climbed the side steps of the church, where she was sheltered from the rain and could hear without being obvious.

Audrey looked up as Colley approached.

Katie moved closer.

Audrey hissed at Toby through her tight half-smile. "Get that whore out of here."

Calpurnia turned away and headed for the steps.

Colley extended his hand to the widow. "My condolences."

Audrey said to Toby, still smiling, "Get him away from me, too. Now."

Toby put an arm around Audrey's shoulder and spoke softly to Colley. "Please, Mr. Jameson. The widow needs her space at a time like this."

Calpurnia had already started down the church steps. She passed through the curtain of rain that overflowed the roof gutters and disappeared in the sea of umbrellas.

Matt Pease was waiting outside the editor's office with his camera bag when Colley returned from the memorial service. Matt had been standing outside the church.

Colley gestured Matt into his office. "I don't suppose you had a chance to develop the film, did you?"

Matt nodded. "I got a few pictures of the crowd standing in the rain. Got an excellent one of you and Mrs. Fieldstone. Nice front-page shot." Matt opened the flap on his camera bag and took out a glossy black-and-white photo.

Colley studied the photo and nodded. "Good man."

"I also got a couple of nice clear pictures of your wife and Mrs. Fieldstone at the funeral and several days before."

"Let me have them, too," said Colley.

"I don't think so," said Matt.

Colley smiled. "I suppose you caught my wife and Audrey Fieldstone glaring at each other. You can hardly blame me for my wife's expression." He held out his hand. "I'd like those photos, Matt."

"Sorry," said Matt.

Colley flushed. "Those photos belong to the newspaper."

"If you recall, Mr. Jameson, I work part time for the paper now. I took these on my own time with my own film. My darkroom. I'll bill you for the photos you use. But you can't have the ones of Mrs. Fieldstone and your wife."

Colley stood up. "This is extortion."

"Certainly not," said Matt, indignantly. "It's business."

"Let me have them, then," said Colley, holding out his hand again. "I'll pay you for the photos and negatives."

Matt lifted his camera bag onto his shoulder. "As you suggested, Mr. Jameson, I've been looking for summer work. I have an offer for these photos."

"How much are they paying you?"

"I don't think you want to know," said Matt, and left the office.

Victoria and Casey were on their way back to West Tisbury after the funeral. "He's tunnel-visioned," Victoria said. "It's not a joke when a man is killed. Yet he's determined not to involve the police." She glanced at Casey. "You're not much help, either."

"My hands are tied, Victoria," Casey snapped. "I agree that he should talk to the Edgartown cops. Whoever sent those obits definitely has a weird sense of humor. That shark obituary isn't funny."

The Bronco's windshield wipers kept up a steady *swish-slat, swish-slat.* Inside, the glass had steamed up and Victoria wiped a clear spot in front of Casey.

"Thanks," said Casey.

Victoria settled back again. "Did you hear what Audrey said to Toby when Colley came up to her?"

"I was too far away to hear anything."

"She called Calpurnia a whore, Colley a pimp, and threatened to deal with both of them."

"People say dumb things when they're under stress."

"I told you, didn't I, that Calpurnia was having an affair with Audrey's husband?"

"I don't know where you get all this stuff, Victoria. I thought it was Colley who was running around behind Calpurnia's back."

"That, too," said Victoria.

Casey shook her head. "Want me to drop you off at your place? I've got to stop by the station house. Call the Coast Guard, see if they found the boat."

"I'll go with you. Then I'd like to go to the *Grackle,* if you don't mind."

Casey smiled. "I see you got the job."

Victoria watched the steady rain slash against the windshield. "I wouldn't be surprised to learn that the boat belonged to Fieldstone."

"Run down by his own boat?"

"It wouldn't be the first time something like that happened."

At the station house, Casey called the Coast Guard while Victoria waited. She asked a couple of questions, made some notes, and raised her eyebrows at Victoria.

"They found Fieldstone's boat washed up near Tuckernuck," she said when she hung up. "Nobody on board."

"And the propeller?"

"The blades were bent." Casey glanced at her notes. "The Coast Guard says, 'Consistent with encountering a semi-submerged, body-like object.' Where's Tuckernuck?"

"It's a small island off Nantucket."

Casey put her still-damp jacket back on. "Let's go. I'll wait, if you'd like, while you talk to Botts."

"Thank you, but I'm sure he'll give me a ride home."

The *Grackle* office was a short distance from the police station. Victoria ducked into the barn and made her way upstairs to the loft.

Botts rose to his feet. "Good afternoon, Madam Reporter. How was the memorial service?"

Victoria took off her raincoat, laid it on the back of her chair, and told him what Fieldstone's widow had said to the undertaker.

"Whore?" Botts whistled. At the sound, the black dog, who'd been lying on a pile of newspapers, thumped his tail.

The scanner behind the desk crackled. Botts and Victoria listened as the communications center reported that a car had skidded on the wet road and hit a tree. No injuries.

"Go on, Victoria," said Botts.

"I'm sure Colley heard what Audrey said."

Botts looked down at his pencil.

Victoria turned and sat in the overstuffed chair. "I have another scoop for you."

"Shoot," said Botts, wetting the tip of his pencil on his tongue.

"The Coast Guard found Ambler Fieldstone's boat, and it looks as though that was the boat that ran over him."

Botts scribbled.

The black dog sighed, opened his eyes, and shut them again. Botts took off his glasses, cleaned them, and put them back on.

It was still raining. Candy examined the nails of her left hand while she waited for someone to answer the phone.

"Hello?"

"Mrs. Fieldstone?" Candy asked.

"Yes?"

"I realize this must be a terrible time for you, right after Mr. Fieldstone's funeral and all, but I have something important I'd like to discuss with you." She opened her desk drawer and took out a nail file.

"Who is this?"

"Candy Keene. Keene Realtors in West Tisbury."

"I know who you are," said Audrey. "You're right. This is a terrible time. Call me sometime next week."

Candy held the phone against her cheek with her right shoulder and filed the rough spot on the nail of her pinky while she talked. "My sincerest condolences, Mrs. Fieldstone. But I don't think you'll want this to wait."

"Can't you understand? My husband died. His funeral was just a few hours ago."

"Oh," said Candy, licking her fingernail. "Was J. Ambler Fieldstone your husband?"

There was a long silence before Audrey said, "What are you getting at?"

"I've been having an interesting discussion with a man named Buddy . . ." Candy paused.

There was a slight hesitation before Audrey said, "Where do you want to meet?"

The rain continued off and on for several days and finally stopped. The ground was still soggy. It was the Thursday following Fieldstone's funeral. Victoria was again sitting in the overstuffed chair in the *Grackle* loft when the scanner cut in. The communications center reported that a woman had been found shot near the Tiasquam Brook in West Tisbury. Botts turned up the volume. The police and ambulance were responding. No word on the woman's condition or name.

Victoria levered herself out of the chair. "May I use your phone?"

Botts pushed it toward her.

When Victoria finished speaking she handed the phone back to Botts, tugged her blue cap out of her bag, and settled it on her head at a rakish angle. "Casey will pick me up here in a couple of minutes."

"Looks as though I may have to give you a raise," Botts said.

"You want to guess who the victim is?" Casey asked Victoria, who had settled into her seat in the Bronco.

"Who?"

"Candy Keene. She's still alive, or was when the call came in."

"Colley's ex-wife," Victoria added.

"The ecdysiast." Casey avoided a large puddle and turned out of Botts's drive.

"Who found her?"

"A couple of guys, father and son. The ones who target-shoot every Thursday afternoon in the field next to the brook."

"Did one of them shoot her by accident?"

"I don't think anyone knows at this point. Miss Keene filed a complaint against them a couple of weeks ago. Ironic if one of them shot her."

By the time they reached the field that adjoined Candy Keene's house, the ambulance had arrived. Casey parked behind Doc Jeffers, who was getting off his Harley. He held up a gloved hand in greeting. "Busy week," he said. He was wearing his black leather cape with a silver-and-blue caduceus embroidered on the back, two snakes twined around a winged staff, and heavy leather boots festooned with steel chains. He lifted his black bag out of the carrier on the back of his motorcycle and clanked off in the direction of the group that had gathered in the hayfield.

Casey raised the collar of her jacket against the raw wind. "You might as well wait here, where it's warm, Victoria. I'll find out what's going on and be right back."

Victoria had tied a scarf printed with wisteria blossoms over her cap. She reached for her stick and opened the door without answering.

The father and his son were standing at the edge of the field near the thicket that edged the brook. The father was wearing a red-and-black plaid wool jacket, the son was wearing a purple-and-white Vineyarders T-shirt. The son was about thirteen, a tall skinny redhead with freckles that stood out on his pale face. His father held two rifles in one hand; his other hand was on his son's shoulder. The older man was a taller, bulkier version of the boy.

Victoria, bundled up like a peasant woman in babushka, trenchcoat, and rubber gardening boots, followed Casey, who identified herself to the father.

Three EMTs were bending over the figure on the ground near the shrubbery. They had strapped the victim onto a stretcher. While Victoria watched, they carried her to the ambulance and transferred her into the back. The ambulance started up, the siren cut in, and the flashing red lights disappeared down State Road in the direction of the hospital.

Victoria turned back to the man and boy.

"I'm Sean Michaels," the father said. "And this is my son Sean."

Young Sean was shivering. "I didn't know she was there," he said. "I didn't see her at all."

"Tell me what happened," Casey said gently. "I know you've got permission from the owner to shoot here."

The father shifted uncomfortably. "Thursday is my day off. We wanted to get in one last practice shoot before my cousin Wilfred moves his hay." He pointed to a stack of about a dozen hay bales with a bedraggled paper bulls-eye. "We set up those bales last fall."

Casey took notes.

"Are you the one who found the woman?" Victoria asked the boy.

"Yes'm."

His father explained, "We'd finished for the day. I was wiping the guns. Me and the boy planned to clean them once we got home, you know?"

Casey nodded.

"I was about to take the guns to my truck, clean up the place. But never did. Sean walked down to the brook to see if there was any watercress. That's when he found her. Just this side of the bushes."

Young Sean said, "She'll be okay, won't she?"

"The EMTs say she's still alive," Casey said.

"I didn't mean to shoot her," young Sean said.

His father tightened his grip on the boy's shoulder. "We weren't shooting in that direction, son."

"Where were you standing?" Casey asked.

The father paced about a hundred yards away from the hay bales, parallel to the brook, to a stamped-down area. "We always stand here so we don't crush too much hay. We keep our backs to the road and shoot at the target. There's no house in that direction."

"And the woman, where was she?"

The father pointed toward the brook. "Right about there, at right angles to the line of fire."

"Well away from it, looks like," said Casey.

"Yes, ma'am," said the father.

"Did you hear her call? Or cry out?" Victoria asked the boy.

Young Sean shook his head. "No, ma'am. She was just lying there, like."

"Who called the police?" Victoria asked.

"My dad, on his cell phone. He called nine-one-one. I covered the lady with my jacket." He looked at Casey, his face troubled. "Do you think I can get my jacket back?"

"I'll make sure you do," said Casey.

As Victoria walked, her boots left prints that filled in with water in the soft ground. Above them, scud raced below the higher clouds.

"Let's go to the station house to finish up," Casey said. "You can get hypothermia even in June when you've given up your jacket and you're worried."

"Thank you, ma'am," the father said.

"I'll meet you at the police station. I've got to call the state police before we leave. They'll need to check the scene."

"I didn't mean to shoot anybody," the boy said again to his father.

Sean held the boy close to him. "I think you may have saved her."

On the way to the police station, Casey said, "You know, Victoria, I don't see how the kid could have shot her. He'd have to have done it deliberately and with his father watching."

"Unless he was careless and pointed his gun in that direction and accidentally pulled the trigger."

"Not likely," said Casey. "Big Sean was teaching the kid how to shoot properly. I checked him out before I gave my okay. The poor kid. We'll know more after the state police check the ballistics."

They passed Alley's and Casey turned right down Brandy Brow. Victoria removed her scarf, shook it out, and folded it neatly.

"I'll take you home, Victoria. It's been a full day."

CHAPTER 9

Victoria and Elizabeth were eating breakfast the next morning when Casey stopped by. "I've been to the hospital," she said. "Candy Keene is still alive. The bullet didn't come from either the boy's gun or his father's."

"Is the boy all right?" Victoria asked. "Would you like a blueberry muffin?"

"No, thanks. I'd love some coffee, though."

Elizabeth went into the kitchen and Casey sat at the cookroom table. "The kid is relieved, but still worried about the woman. I took his jacket to him."

"I suppose we won't know what she was doing in the field until she can tell us," Victoria said.

Elizabeth set a mug of coffee in front of the chief. "Cream and two sugars, right?"

"Thanks. I ought to cut back on the sugar."

"Are the state police still there?" Elizabeth asked.

"They've cordoned off the hayfield and are searching for evidence. They've called the shooting attempted murder." Casey finished her coffee. "I've gotta go, but I thought you'd want to know about the bullet."

"And the boy," said Victoria.

"Why would anyone shoot her?" Elizabeth asked, when Casey had gone. "I mean, nobody I know really liked Candy Keene, especially after she tore down that beautiful old house. But that's no reason to shoot her."

"Someone must have known that the boy and his father practice there on Thursdays and decided their shots would cover the sound of his."

"Everybody in West Tisbury knew they practiced shooting then." Elizabeth passed the plate of sausages to her grandmother. "Another muffin, Gram?"

"Please."

Elizabeth helped herself to another sausage. "You knew Ambler Fieldstone kept his boat in the Oak Bluffs Harbor, didn't you?"

Victoria shook her head.

"An expensive sportfishing boat," Elizabeth said. "When he took it out that last time, he told the dock stewards he'd be gone a couple of days. The harbormaster wasn't concerned when he didn't return."

"I need to talk to Domingo," said Victoria. "Was he on duty that day?"

"It was his day off. Just two dock stewards and me. Fieldstone had two young women with him when he went out."

"Really? Who were they?"

"I'd never seen them before. From the way they were acting, they hadn't been around boats much."

"Has anyone seen them since?"

Elizabeth shook her head. "Not that I've heard."

Victoria started to butter the muffin, but set her knife down. "How old were they?"

"Mid-teens," Elizabeth answered.

"What did they look like?"

"Pretty. One dark-haired, one blond."

"I met two girls on the bus the other day who fit that description. They applied for jobs at the *Enquirer*." Victoria picked up the muffin again and put it on the side of her plate. "Fieldstone wasn't known as a rake, was he?"

"'Rake?' That's quaint, Gram. I don't think he was hitting on them."

"And no one has reported them missing?"

"Not that I know of."

"What could have happened to them?" Victoria picked up the muffin again, but still didn't eat. "Two girls on an older man's boat go for an outing. His body washes up on the beach several days later. Where were the girls when he was killed? Could Fieldstone run his boat by himself?"

"Easily."

"We've got to locate those two." Victoria picked up the muffin again. "Here you've made a nice breakfast and we're discussing . . ."

"Murder," said Elizabeth. "You think Fieldstone was murdered, don't you?"

Victoria nodded and bit into her muffin.

Victoria walked to the police station after lunch. "Murder and attempted murder. We've got to find those girls. And why did Candy Keene go to meet her killer?"

"*We* can't do anything, Victoria. The boating death is in the hands of the Coast Guard. The shooting belongs to the state police and Candy Keene's not dead. Colley's got to take his obits to the Edgartown police. Not to *me*."

Victoria started to protest.

Casey held up her hand. "It's frustrating, Victoria, but that's the way this Island's law enforcement is."

Victoria's face set. Casey sighed. "Do what you want, but you can't do it officially." She stood up. "I've got a meeting in Chilmark. Call if you need me." She held up her cell phone.

Victoria, too, got to her feet. "On your way, drop me off at the *Grackle* office, if you will, please."

Botts was at his desk working the keys of his old Underwood with two fingers when Victoria reached the loft.

Victoria studied him thoughtfully. "How many people on this Island still use typewriters?"

"A half-dozen. You, me, and a few others."

"Where do you get your typewriter repaired?"

"I don't," said Botts. "It never breaks down."

"What about ribbons?"

"I order them on the Internet."

Victoria sat. "Casey's fallen prey to bureaucracy," she said. "Therefore, it's up to us to investigate."

"What's this 'us' business?"

"You're publishing a newspaper, aren't you?"

Botts took off his glasses. "I want to publish a one-page broadsheet in my retirement. Not a newspaper. What are we investigating now, the death of Fieldstone?"

"What do you think?"

He put his glasses down beside his typewriter. "Where do you intend to start?"

"At the Oak Bluffs Harbor. With the two girls Fieldstone took out on his boat. What are you writing?" Victoria stepped over to his desk and looked over his shoulder. She read a few lines. "A romance? A bodice ripper?" She laughed.

"Pays the bills," said Botts.

"What name do you go by?"

Botts pulled the sheet of paper out of his typewriter. "Tara Waterstreet."

"I'll look for her in the library."

"You won't find her," said Botts. "Let's go."

Once down the rickety stairs, Victoria hoisted herself into the passenger seat of Botts's pickup truck and they headed for Oak Bluffs. On either side of the road new bright green beech leaves sparkled among the new pink oak leaves and dark pines.

In Vineyard Haven, storekeepers were painting the fronts of stores, cleaning windows, and arranging fresh displays. Window boxes were bright with geraniums, petunias, and ageratum. When they reached the shipyard they waited while two shipyard workers, a man and a woman, wheeled a boat on a trailer across the road. Everywhere there were signs of people getting ready for summer.

The drawbridge that spanned the cut into Lagoon Pond was open. Botts waited while a sailboat motored out of the pond into Vineyard Haven Harbor. He passed the entrance to the hospital and parked at the head of the Oak Bluffs Harbor. In another week, he would not be able to find a parking place. He set a milk crate on the ground for Victoria to use as a step and held his arm out for her.

They walked along the boardwalk that skirted the harbor to the harbormaster's shack, a small building that perched over the water on stilts. When they squeezed through the narrow door, Chuck looked up from the computer.

From the window that faced the harbor entrance, Victoria could see an osprey sitting on its nest. The nest was built on top of a telephone pole, and was a collection of sticks and fish bones that grew larger and more untidy every year.

A few minutes after they arrived, the harbormaster, Domingo, joined them. He was a short dark man with large dark eyes. Victoria introduced Botts and explained what she wanted. Domingo wet his thumb and shuffled through a sheaf of papers in a clear plastic box nailed to the wall, took one out, put on the glasses suspended from a cord around his neck, and studied the paper.

"Your granddaughter was on duty that afternoon. I was off Island. Chuck was here."

Chuck looked up. "Yessir. Curtis and me."

The harbormaster went to the door of the shack, put two fingers in his mouth, and whistled. A short, dark-haired high school boy appeared on the catwalk that led to the shack, hiking up his unbelted trousers.

"Both of you were here when Fieldstone took off, weren't you?"

"Yessir," said Curtis.

"Tell Mrs. Trumbull whatever she wants to know. She's doing some police work."

"Yeah?" Curtis's eyes were bright.

"Both of us handled his lines," Chuck said.

"Why did he need two of you?" Botts asked.

Chuck flushed. "It was pretty quiet. Mr. Fieldstone took a couple girls on board who didn't have experience."

Botts took his notebook out of his shirt pocket and his pencil from behind his ear.

"Do you know anything about the girls?" Victoria asked. "How old were they?"

Curtis said, "They're juniors at Hyannis Academy."

"Seniors next year," said Chuck.

"You didn't happen to get their names, did you?" Victoria asked with a smile.

The two looked at each other uncertainly.

"Answer Mrs. Trumbull's question." The harbormaster turned to Victoria. "Harbor staff are not permitted to fraternize with boaters."

"Yeah," said Curtis reluctantly. "Tiffany and Wendy."

"Phone numbers," the harbormaster demanded.

"*Did* you get their phone numbers?" Victoria asked.

"Well, yeah. We did," Curtis said. "We thought we might, like, go off Island for a game or something, you know." He brought a green Gore-Tex wallet out of his back pocket, opened it with the ripping sound of Velcro separating, riffled through dog-eared cards, and found a harbor receipt with the two names written illegibly across the front.

"Let me see that," said the harbormaster.

"But you said . . ." Curtis protested.

"Fraternizing I can overlook. Numbered harbor receipts I've got to account for."

"Do you have a receipt for Mr. Fieldstone?" Victoria asked.

The harbormaster jerked his head toward Chuck. "Look it up for Mrs. Trumbull." He held out his hand. "And give me that receipt you wrote all over."

Chuck leafed through the card file.

"Let's get back to the girls," Victoria said. "Were they friends or relatives of Mr. Fieldstone's?"

"They missed the ferry to Hyannis," said Curtis. "I seen them running up to the dock, but the ferry already cast off."

Chuck turned away from the card file. "They came to the shack. Asked could we help them."

The harbormaster rolled his eyes, stepped outside, leaned against the railing, and lit a cigarette.

Victoria said, "So you told them Mr. Fieldstone was about to take off to go fishing and suggested he might give them a ride?"

"Yeah," said Curtis. "He's okay. I mean, he was. He told them, like, Hyannis wasn't really out of his way."

"Here's Fieldstone's receipt, Mr. D.," said Chuck, handing it to the harbormaster.

Domingo pointed with his cigarette. "Show it to my friend here."

The receipt listed the boat's name, *S'Putter*, Fieldstone's name, and the time of departure as three-fifteen P.M. The estimated time of arrival back at Oak Bluffs and charges were left blank.

"Isn't that late to go fishing?" Victoria asked.

The boys looked at each other and shrugged.

"From what I understand, he was planning on staying out two or three days," said Domingo.

"Did he buy gas?" Victoria asked.

The harbormaster turned and faced the hotel at the head of the harbor and tossed his cigarette into the water below. The cigarette went out with a hiss.

"His boat had diesels," said Chuck. "He only fills up three or four times a season."

"Did he say where he was going?" Victoria asked.

"Just that dropping the girls off was no big deal."

Domingo turned, one elbow on the railing. "You knew, didn't you, that his boat washed up on Tuckernuck Island? Due south of Hyannis."

Both boys nodded.

Victoria turned to the harbormaster. "I need to find the girls."

Botts tore a piece of paper out of his notebook and the harbormaster copied the girls' names and phone numbers in an elegant script, his cigarette between his lips, and handed the paper to Victoria. Domingo faced the two dock stewards. "Get back to work."

"Can we have the phone numbers?" said Chuck.

The harbormaster handed him the receipt with the phone numbers written on it. "Make sure I get this back."

Botts tore another piece of paper out of his notebook.

"Thank you," Victoria said. "You've been most helpful."

That same afternoon, Phyllis and Tom Dwyer waited at the dock in Vineyard Haven for the three-thirty ferry from Woods Hole. Phyllis shaded her eyes from the glare of water reflecting off the sides of the approaching boat.

"There she is!" Phyllis waved. "She sees us."

As the ferry pulled into its slip, the dark-haired girl on the upper deck waved back. Phyllis saw her run to the stairway that led down to the gangplank, and reappear at the open door, among the throng of passengers waiting for the gangplank to be secured. She carried a red-and-blue backpack and towed a wheeled suitcase.

The ferry was crowded with early vacationers, college students arriving on the Island to work at summer jobs, and high school students like Lynn who'd been off Island at boarding school.

Adults described Lynn as "interesting looking." She had beautiful, shiny dark hair, and large, luminous brown eyes like her mother's. She was short and chunky, not fat, but straight-sided with an athletic field-hockey build. Phyllis, her mother, had the same brown eyes, but unlike her daughter, she was slender and had pale blond hair.

Phyllis looked from her daughter to Tom, whose face was shaded by his hat. His unlit pipe was clenched between his teeth.

A hundred, two hundred passengers debarked before Lynn finally came down the ramp, her wheeled bag clicking on the planks. Phyllis rushed forward and embraced her daughter. Tom removed his pipe from his mouth and hugged Lynn gently.

"It's great to be home," Lynn said. "What a gorgeous day. It's never like this in Hyannis."

Tom helped her with her backpack and carried her suitcase to the parking lot. "Did you take the shuttle from school?"

"The shuttle was full of freshmen." Lynn made a face. "Jamie's dad gave me a ride in their Lexus. She lives in Falmouth." Lynn took a deep breath, stretched her arms out, and looked up at the fishing rods on the racks on Tom's vehicle. "You've been fishing already. Awesome!"

"You heard Tom found a body?" her mother asked.

Lynn shuddered. "Everybody at school's been talking about nothing else all week. Not even finals. Gruesome."

"Hop in," said Tom. "We're having baked bluefish for supper tonight."

Lynn glanced quickly at him before she clambered into the back seat. "Do you think we could get a pizza instead? I mean . . ."

"Your call," Tom said. "First night home we'll serve whatever you'd like. Filet mignon, pizza." He grinned. "The bluefish will keep for tomorrow."

"Did you catch it the same time . . . ?"

Tom laughed. "Nope." He checked both ways and pulled out of the parking lot.

"It's hard to believe you're a senior now," Phyllis said. "Doesn't seem possible."

"Me either," said Lynn. "I barely squeaked through chemistry and precalculus."

They waited at Five Corners for the usual snarl of traffic. Tom removed his pipe from his mouth. "You may end up being a writer like your mother and me after all."

Lynn leaned over the front seat. "That's what I decided, Tom. Not fiction, like you, but journalism, like Mom. I'm going to apply for a summer intern job on the *Enquirer*."

Tom and Phyllis exchanged glances.

"I don't know, dear," said Phyllis. "Colley isn't someone I'd want to work for."

"But the *Enquirer* is one of the greatest papers in New England," said Lynn. "I can avoid Mr. Jameson. I mean, it's not like I'm a star reporter or anything. I wouldn't recognize him if I bumped into him. Please, Mom."

"We'll discuss it later," said Tom.

CHAPTER 10

This time it was a postcard, a photo of the Gay Head light taken around 1950 when the light still ran on kerosene and the lighthouse keeper had to wind the clock mechanism every night. The message was written in a tiny tight hand, and was addressed to "Editor, Social Notes."

Colley was talking on the phone when Faith came into his office with the Monday afternoon mail. She plopped a large stack of letters on his desk. "Nothing like a good recipe to bring out reader response." With that, she left his office and shut the door firmly behind her.

Colley was holding the phone between his shoulder and jaw, leaving both hands free to slit open the envelopes while he tried to talk. Ever since Tom Dwyer's recipe had appeared in the *Enquirer*, Colley's phone had been ringing constantly. His mail was running to two dozen or more letters a day, almost all of them critical of him, Colley, the editor, for printing the recipe.

The voice on the other end of the phone was high pitched and Colley tried unsuccessfully to invoke the paper's First Amendment rights in what he hoped was a tone of reason. While he halfway listened, he opened his mail.

That's when he came to the postcard.

The postcard was picture side up, and showed the lighthouse tinted a dark red, the grass colored a bilious green, the sky an unnatural blue. Next to the lighthouse was the lighthouse keeper's house, the way it had looked a half-century before.

Colley didn't realize what the card was at first. He turned it over, and when he saw the black border, he stood up and dropped the phone onto his desk with a clatter.

The high-pitched voice on the other end said, "Hello! Hello!" but Colley continued to stare at the card and the person on the other end of the phone hung up and a robotlike voice announced something Colley didn't hear.

The message side of the card read, "Colley Jameson, fifty-five, editor of the *Island Enquirer*, was found shot dead yesterday near the base of the Gay Head lighthouse. He was apparently climbing the fence and dropped his rifle, which must have discharged accidentally . . ."

Colley didn't read beyond that, but slapped the postcard onto his desk, hung up the phone, then thought better of it. He picked the phone up again and dialed Victoria Trumbull.

"Now what?" Victoria said when he identified himself.

"Get over here immediately. Take a cab."

"The bus is running." Victoria pronounced each word distinctly. "I can ride free because I'm elderly. Too old to work for the *Enquirer*."

"Come off it," Colley said. "I'll expect you within a half-hour."

"Don't count on it." As soon as she hung up, Victoria called William Botts.

"I'll pick you up in ten minutes," Botts said. "What's his problem now?"

"From the way he sounded, I'd guess he got another obituary. If so, it would be his third."

"Five minutes then," said Botts.

Victoria was waiting on the stone step by the kitchen door when Botts arrived. He sped down the Edgartown Road, swooping down into the glacial swales and up the other side in a way that made Victoria's stomach lurch. In less than twenty minutes he'd covered the nine miles into Edgartown and had dropped Victoria off in front of the *Enquirer*'s office.

Victoria strode up the brick walk leading to the front door, jauntily swinging her stick.

"Go right on up, Mrs. Trumbull. He's expecting you," said Faith.

Victoria went up the narrow steps slowly, holding the railing. This was no time to fall and break something. She marched down the aisle between the reporters' desks, nodding to her right and left.

Through the glass partition of the editor's office, she saw Colley hang up the phone and get up from his desk. He opened the door as she approached.

Victoria moved the chair at right angles to the window and sat. "I take it you received another obituary?"

Colley slid the postcard across to her.

Victoria examined the card, holding it by its edges in both hands to keep from smearing any fingerprints. "It's time you went to the police. You've got to take this seriously." She looked up at him. "This is from someone with a peculiar sense of humor, someone close to you, and someone close to the killings."

"Not 'killings,'" said Colley. "There's only been one death and the Coast Guard is calling that death a boating accident. No one was killed in the shooting."

"His death was no accident. You and I both know that. Why did you call me? I don't work for you."

Colley squirmed in his seat. "You made a crack about giving me your rate card."

"I was joking."

"You've had some lucky successes in solving little Island puzzles. I thought you might like the challenge of tracking down the obit writer. I'll pay you what I paid you for your column."

"Thirty-five dollars?" Victoria rose out of her chair. "No thank you. My rates are more competitive."

"How much?" said Colley.

Victoria headed for the door. "I'll mail you a proposal."

"Fax it to me."

"I don't have a fax machine."

"Oh, hell," said Colley. "How about seventy dollars? Twice what I paid you for your column."

"Seventy dollars an hour?" said Victoria. "That's still hardly competitive."

"Jee-sus Christ, Victoria. You know every goddamned person on this Island, their parents and grandparents, all their skeletons, the great-aunts in their attics. You're the only one I know who can figure this out without making a big scene about it. The shooting didn't kill anyone, and the Coast Guard is handling the boating accident. Who's writing these goddamned letters?"

"Eighty-five dollars an hour," said Victoria.

"Fine."

"Plus expenses."

"Fine."

"Plus an assistant at thirty-five dollars an hour."

"Anything."

"I want it in writing." Victoria returned to the chair and sat again. "Before I leave."

"Okay, okay."

"A retainer. In advance, of course."

"Jee-sus!"

Victoria motioned to the computer next to Colley's desk. His screen saver was flashing a series of pictures of Colley with various dignitaries. "I assume you can type that yourself?"

"Who's your assistant?"

"That's to be determined."

Colley's intercom buzzed. "Mr. Dwyer is here to see you, Mr. Jameson. He's on his way up."

"Oh, hell," said Colley. "The piping plover freak."

"I read his recipe in the latest *Enquirer*," said Victoria.

"Yeah," said Colley. "So has everybody else."

"It was actually quite funny," said Victoria.

"Glad you think so." Colley gestured to the pile of mail on one side of his otherwise tidy desk. "You're the only person on the Island who sees any humor in it." He picked up a few envelopes and riffled through them.

"They're blaming *me*, not Dwyer. That wasn't *my* idea to stew up piping plovers."

"The dish would probably be delicious made with chicken." From where she sat, Victoria could see the mystery writer striding down the aisle. She knew him slightly and knew he was one of the fishermen who'd found the lower half of what she thought of as *her* body. Tom was a young man, probably no more than fifty. He was well over six feet tall and was wearing the Australian bush hat she'd never seen him without. He was grinning as he burst into Colley's office, showing large white teeth. Colley ignored his outstretched hand and Victoria offered hers, which Tom shook instead.

He pulled up a chair in front of Colley's desk and sat down, his legs spread, still grinning. "Nothing like jerking the chains of the conservation types." He pointed at the stack of letters on Colley's desk. "Today's mail?"

Colley muttered something and swiveled in his chair.

Victoria said, "The piping plovers were there before your beach buggies. Why can't you walk to your fishing spots?"

"Hey," said Tom, turning to her. "Want to come fishing with me tonight? I've got an extra rod."

Colley scowled.

"I can't," said Victoria. "I've just accepted an assignment."

"I don't want to work for that self-centered creep," said Botts after they'd returned to his office and Victoria explained that he was now her paid assistant.

"You won't be working for him. You'll be working for me. I doubt if you're making thirty-five dollars an hour with your romance novels." Victoria leaned over and patted the black dog, who turned onto his back, his tongue out. "How does he get up and down those stairs?"

Botts indicated a trapdoor, originally used for dropping hay down to the horses. Over the open trapdoor was a tripod with a pulley and rope. "He rides up and down in a laundry basket," said Botts. "Assuming I agree to work for you, where do you intend to start?"

Victoria straightened up. "The two girls must have been the last people to see Fieldstone alive. We've got to talk to them."

The phone rang, and Botts answered. He listened and raised his shaggy eyebrows. "I'll probably be here another half hour," he said into the phone. He glanced up at Victoria, who was still standing. "I can't speak for Mrs. Trumbull," and he hung up.

"What can't you speak for me about?"

"That was Katie Bowen, the *Enquirer* reporter with the sexy voice."

"Oh?"

"She wants to tell you something and will be here in ten minutes."

"Did she say what she wants to tell me?"

Botts shook his head.

Victoria sat down in the armchair. The black dog turned back onto his stomach. "What's his name?" Victoria asked.

"Milton. As in John Milton."

Victoria leaned forward and patted John Milton, who thumped his tail on the floor.

In less than ten minutes, she heard the barn door open and Katie appeared at the top of the stairs.

Every time Victoria saw Katie, she had a queer sense of time standing still. Katie had the same dark eyes, dark hair, and husky voice as her great-grandmother, who'd gone to school with Victoria. Victoria didn't feel ninety-two, and whenever she greeted Katie, she was twenty again, sorting tissue-paper dress patterns with Katie's great-grandmother.

"I'm so relieved you're still here, Mrs. Trumbull." Katie burst into tears. John Milton looked up. Botts came out from behind his desk, moved a stack of papers off a wooden kitchen chair, and offered it to Katie, who sat down next to Victoria. "Colley fired me."

"Congratulations," said Botts.

Victoria offered her a paper napkin printed with green frogs from her cloth bag and Katie blew her nose.

"Why did he fire you?"

"I was unreliable, he said. I'm not, Mrs. Trumbull!" Katie hiccuped.

Botts leaned against his desk, his arms crossed over his chest. "Had he been making passes at you?"

Katie nodded. "He's older than my father. I told him I had a boyfriend."

"Well," said Victoria. "Another name for the *Grackle*'s masthead."

Botts stared at Victoria. "But . . ."

"We can give Katie a raise over what she was making on the *Enquirer*, can't we, now that we have money in our coffers." A statement, not a question.

Botts put both hands in the air, turned his back to Victoria, stepped over the dog, went to the back of the loft and stared out of the big hay window, returned to his desk, and sat down again. "*We*, eh?"

CHAPTER 11

"I tried to be polite. I didn't want to offend him," Katie said, blotting her eyes with the napkin. "When I started working on the *Enquirer*, he asked me to lunch and I went because I thought that was what bosses did, take their new employees to lunch. Then he asked me out for drinks one day and I said I couldn't. I've been dodging him ever since." She unfolded the napkin to a dryish section and blew her nose. "Every time I get within reach, he pats me or makes kissy sounds with those lips of his."

"Can't you file charges of harassment?" Victoria asked.

"With whom?"

"Good point," said Victoria.

"But you know, Mrs. Trumbull, it's more than just his hitting on me," Katie said, "I found something in the files I don't think he wanted anyone to know about."

Botts set his pencil on his desk. "What was this 'something' you found?"

"I was being really conscientious." Katie's voice caught. "That was my first big story, the body on the beach. A really big story even before we knew it was J. Ambler Fieldstone. When we found out . . ." she looked up at Botts. "You broke the story, didn't you?"

"Mrs. Trumbull did," said Botts.

"Well, when we knew it was Fieldstone," Katie went on, "I decided to look through the files to get some background on him. When I got to the *F* file I found this envelope addressed to Colley that had slipped down between the *F* and *G* folders." She paused. "It had already been opened."

Victoria listened. Botts was trying to balance his pencil on its eraser end.

"The return address was Fieldstone's development company. So I took the letter out, of course, thinking it was probably an ad order or something."

"But it wasn't," said Botts.

Katie shook her head. "It took me a while to figure out what the letter was about because it was written in a kind of code. When I first read it, the letter seemed to be a straightforward business deal, but then I realized everything had a double meaning, you know what I mean?"

"Was the letter from Fieldstone?" Victoria asked.

Katie nodded. "He seemed to be referring to Colley's wife, Calpurnia, although he didn't mention her by name. He talked about her as 'the merchandise,' and he seemed to be offering Colley a lot of money for the deal, and the deal seemed to include a percentage of ownership in the newspaper."

"Do you remember exactly what the letter said?" Victoria asked.

"I made a copy of it and put the original back in the files where I'd found it. Right about then, Colley came into the file room."

"Did he realize what you'd discovered?" asked Botts.

"I don't think so. I was closing the file drawer when he came in."

"What was his problem, then?" Botts asked.

Katie looked uncomfortable. "I'm on medication," she said, and blotted her eyes.

"You needn't tell us anything you don't want to," said Victoria.

"Yes, I do," said Katie. "I've got bipolar disorder, Mrs. Trumbull, and I take medication for it."

"What they used to call manic-depression," said Botts.

Katie nodded. "My doctor's been adjusting the dosage, and right after we found—you found, that is—Mr. Fieldstone's body, I had a sort of psychotic episode." Katie blew her nose.

"No wonder." Victoria found another napkin in her pocket and gave it to Katie. "This was on the day after the body was discovered?"

"I just freaked out and told Mr. Jameson off."

"Was he making passes at you?" Botts asked.

"Yes, and I just couldn't take it anymore."

"Doesn't sound psychotic to me," Botts said.

"Well I said a few things I shouldn't have." Katie blotted her eyes. "I used some pretty nasty words. Then when he saw me in the file room, he said he wanted to talk to me in his office. That's when he fired me." Katie sniffed. "That's when he said I was unreliable."

"You're 'well shet of him,' as your great-grandmother used to say," said Victoria. "What do you plan to do now?"

"Are you serious about my working for you, Mr. Botts?"

Botts started to say something, but Victoria interrupted. "We can only offer you a temporary job."

"I'd love to work for you. Even temporarily. Thanks, Mr. Botts!"

Five days after she'd been shot, Candy Keene was nicely recovered. The bullet had missed, by some miracle, every vital organ and major blood vessel in her body. She was ensconced in a comfortable bed she could raise or lower with the touch of a control button, in a private room in the Martha's Vineyard Hospital, with a window that looked out onto a rose garden, and an attractive young police officer who was stationed at her door to screen her flood of visitors.

She was dressed for visitors. She wore a fluffy hot-pink angora bed jacket over a matching pink satin negligee. A hairdresser—not her own Boston hairdresser but an Island person—had retouched her hair and arranged it in a sort of careless disarray. A manicurist had painted her nails a pink that exactly matched her nightie. She, herself, had applied her own makeup, subtly enhancing the invalid image.

Among her visitors, once she'd recovered enough to admit them to her presence, were Al Fox, her lawyer, who looked quite nice in his toupee; the female police chief from West Tisbury and her ancient sidekick; the gangly teenager and his father who'd been target-shooting the day she'd been shot—the father wasn't bad looking; Colley Jameson, her third ex-husband, although he thought he'd been her one and only; and that dreadful Mrs. Danvers from Town Hall, who'd brought Candy's mail and some things from her house that Candy had wanted.

Mrs. Danvers was still there, standing at the foot of the high-tech bed. Candy, with some effort, was trying to look weak for Mrs. Danvers's benefit.

"I told that female police chief—what's her name?"

Mrs. Danvers pursed her lips. "Chief Mary Kathleen O'Neill."

Candy sighed. "I told that woman I didn't want anyone shooting so close to me." She looked up mournfully. "You'll be getting a letter from my solicitor."

"Attorney," said Mrs. Danvers. "Solicitor is British."

"Well, the selectmen will be getting a letter from him. He brought a draft by this morning for me to approve."

"Whatever," said Mrs. Danvers.

Candy indicated the plastic Stop & Shop bag Mrs. Danvers was holding. "Is that my mail?"

"Mail and the items you wanted from your house," said Mrs. Danvers. "Do you think you're strong enough to take the bag, or shall I hand you one thing at a time?"

"Please. That would be so kind of you." Candy lay back on the satin and lace pillow that Al Fox had given her when he'd brought the letter for her approval.

Mrs. Danvers pulled items out of the bag. "A shoe catalog," she said. "Dress catalogs. An underwear catalog." She handed Candy a flyer from Victoria's Secret. "The *Enquirer*."

"Is there anything in the paper about me?" Candy asked, trying not to seem eager.

"Front page," said Mrs. Danvers. "With a picture that must have been taken at least twenty years ago."

Candy reached out for the newspaper. "One of my publicity stills. From my career as an artiste."

Mrs. Danvers continued to pull things out of the bag. "Letters, cards, bills, junk mail. A package from," she looked at the return address, "Frederick's of Hollywood. A box of candy that was on your hall table."

"That came before . . ." Candy's voice caught and she looked up at Mrs. Danvers. "Before I was gunned down . . ."

"Yes," said Mrs. Danvers.

"Divinity fudge. My favorite."

"Indeed."

"From one of my admirers." Candy looked up at Mrs. Danvers. "May I offer you a piece?"

"You may. However, I don't care for divinity fudge," said Mrs. Danvers. "Too sweet. I don't like nuts. I can't bear almond flavoring."

Candy set the fudge on her bedside table next to the latest Tom Dwyer mystery she'd been reading. "If you'll let me have my purse, I'll pay you for your time."

"That won't be necessary," said Mrs. Danvers, her mouth down, her nose lifted slightly. "I believe you have another visitor." She folded up the plastic bag, put it under the box of candy, and left, nodding, on her way out, to the police officer who was guarding the door.

"Harpy," Candy muttered. She was about to reach for the box of candy when an extremely good-looking man she had never seen before came into her room. He was wearing a blue blazer and pressed gray slacks, a pale blue shirt, and a tie with stripes that matched everything he had on. She lay back quickly and closed her eyes.

"Sorry to disturb you, ma'am," he said softly. "I'm Detective Horner from the State Police."

Candy opened her eyes. "What did you say your name was?"

"Horner. Detective Horner."

Candy smiled.

"I'd like to ask a few questions, if you're up to it."

Nice voice, too. "I'm up to it if you are," said Candy, half-closing her eyes and smiling. "Would you care for a piece of fudge?"

"No, thank you." He took a small notebook out of an inner pocket.

While Candy Keene was entertaining from her hospital bed, Botts, in his loft office, was sitting back in his chair with his hands clasped behind his head. Victoria was doing all the talking.

Victoria gave Katie the slip of paper on which the harbormaster had written the phone numbers of the two girls. "Your first assignment, Katie, is to contact these girls." Victoria had almost called Katie by her great-grandmother's name, Constance. "Set up a meeting with them here on the Vineyard, if possible. They may need to come over for a second interview with Colley."

Katie wrinkled her nose.

"You and William and I can meet with them at my house. At their convenience, but soon."

"Righto," said Katie.

"Has Colley paid you yet?" Botts asked Victoria.

"He gave me a retainer."

"A check?"

"I deposited it right away. We're working on his time now." She eased herself out of the overstuffed chair. "Did you know that the Coast Guard towed Ambler Fieldstone's boat from the shoals near Tuckernuck to the Coast Guard station in Menemsha?"

"Want to take a drive up there?" Botts asked.

"Certainly," said Victoria. "He's paying mileage."

After Detective Horner left, Candy picked up the copy of the *Enquirer* Mrs. Danvers had brought her and read the article about her shooting. Colley had written the article, carefully omitting the fact that he'd been married to her at one time. Well, she'd gotten even with him. Al Fox, her *solicitor*, had made sure of that.

Candy examined the photo, tilting her head first one way, then the other. It was a good photo, Candy thought. Certainly not twenty years old. But from her acting days. Colley must have found it in the files. The story was continued on an inside page and she read every word.

The same issue of the *Enquirer* had more about Fieldstone's death. She shuddered. She didn't care much for boats, herself, and she'd come awfully close to going with Ambler instead of flying to Nantucket that day. There she'd been, waiting for him, thinking the bastard had stood her up, getting madder and madder. And all that time, there he was, two halves of him floating in the ocean.

She turned the page. Colley had written a sappy editorial about Fieldstone and his golf course, and Candy read every word of that, too. The *Enquirer*, Colley had written, would continue to support the fine work J. Ambler Fieldstone had begun. Another golf course was badly needed on the Island. The *Enquirer*, wrote Colley, would work closely with Fieldstone's organization and would continue to run the informative advertising Fieldstone had scheduled.

"La-di-dah!" said Candy out loud, and tossed the paper onto the floor. She reached for the box of candy, opened it, and selected a large, fat piece from the middle.

She would love to be there when Mrs. Danvers read the letter from her solicitor. Al Fox was a *solicitor*, not a mere attorney, whatever that harpy said.

Candy bit daintily into the white fudge, licked her nicely manicured fingers, and bit again. She finished the first piece, blotted her mouth carefully so she wouldn't smear her lipstick, and took another, smaller, piece. Divinity fudge was so much more refined than chocolate. She preferred almond flavoring to vanilla, too. Imagine that woman not liking almond flavoring.

Who could have sent it to her? She didn't recall seeing a name on the note that came with the box, simply a typed message, "From a long-time admirer."

The hospital's food was delicious, so Candy didn't want to spoil her appetite for supper. But that was almost three hours away. One more little piece, she told herself, selecting just the right one.

CHAPTER 12

The drive from West Tisbury to Menemsha took Botts and Victoria through thick oak and beech woods that made a canopy of interlacing branches over their heads, then through open sheep pasture bounded by rough stone walls. Beyond the pasture to their left was the great sweep of the Atlantic, a brilliant blue this afternoon.

Botts turned on the scanner he kept in his truck.

Victoria snorted. "Worse than television and cell phones. Can't you do without that device for a half-hour?"

"We," said Botts, looking sideways at Victoria, "are newspaper people."

Victoria frowned and settled back in her seat.

Once they reached the center of Chilmark, which consisted of a store, a library, a school, a post office, a bank, a church, and an art gallery, they turned right at Beetlebung Corner.

"What do you expect to find on his boat?" Botts asked. "And how do you intend to justify this as an expense in connection with the obituary puzzle?"

"The deaths are related," Victoria said.

"One death," said Botts. "Miss Keene is recovering. And Fieldstone's boat? The Coast Guard has undoubtedly been all over it. What can we find that they couldn't?"

"I simply want to see it for myself," said Victoria.

"The boat's probably still in the water."

"I'm sure the Coast Guard hauled it out and set it up on a cradle. That's what they'd do."

Botts had started down the steep winding hill that led into

the fishing village and the Coast Guard station when the scanner cut in.

"Doc Jeffers, please call in to the communications center immediately."

"What's that all about?" Victoria asked.

"Shhh!" Botts pulled over to the entrance to Chowder Kettle Road and turned up the volume.

A second voice came over the scanner. "Do you need EMTs or an ambulance?"

"No, we need the medical examiner to report to the hospital," said the communications center voice.

"ME," said Botts. "That means somebody died under unusual circumstances."

"At the hospital?"

"Sounded like it, didn't it?"

"Candy Keene!" Victoria gasped. "Turn around."

Botts made a U-turn and started back up the hill. "Still on Colley's mileage?"

"Absolutely," said Victoria.

Botts followed North Road to the intersection with the great split tree, then drove fast enough so Victoria was uncomfortable in the swaying truck. Past the shipyard and the fuel tanks, over the bridge, up the hill to the emergency entrance. Botts parked next to a state police vehicle, an Oak Bluffs police vehicle, several pickup trucks with red lights over the cabs, and the West Tisbury police Bronco.

"Casey's here," said Victoria, hurt.

Botts comforted her. "You've been in the field. Out of touch."

Victoria led the way through the doors of the emergency room, where a group of uniformed police officers had gathered near the desk. Casey was standing with her back to the entrance and Victoria passed by her without speaking.

"What's going on?" Botts asked one of the officers.

"Sorry, sir," she responded. "We can't divulge any information at this point in time."

Casey turned at the sound of Botts's voice. Victoria ignored her. "Follow me," she said to Botts. She headed down the long hall behind the emergency room, turned right into another long hall with windows and benches on either side, and turned left into a wing marked ACUTE CARE.

A tall, slender, dark-haired nurse was standing at the desk filling out forms. She turned, and her face brightened. "Aunty Vic! What are you doing here?"

Victoria introduced Botts. "William, this is my great-niece, Hope."

They shook hands.

"William and I have come to pay another visit to Miss Keene," Victoria said.

Hope's face was suddenly sober. "You must not have heard."

"Heard what?"

"She died about an hour ago."

"But she was doing so well," Victoria said. "I was here just this morning. What happened?"

"Come with me, Aunty Vic, where no one can hear. If you don't mind, Mr. Botts, I need to talk to my aunt alone." Hope led Victoria partway down the long hall outside the Acute Care wing, and they sat on one of the benches by the window.

"Well?" said Victoria.

"She was doing okay," Hope said. "We were planning on discharging her tomorrow." Hope looked around as if to make sure no one was listening. "To tell you the truth, Aunty Vic, that woman was a real pain in the ass, excuse my language. 'Get me this, get me that,' as if we were her servants and this was a high-class hotel. And she wasn't really sick."

"She *was* recovering from being shot, though," said Victoria.

"*You'd* have been out two days after that shooting, Aunty Vic. She was here almost a week. Seemed like a month."

"What happened?"

"Don't quote me," said Hope. "You know Mrs. Danvers, don't you? The West Tisbury town secretary?"

"Yes, of course," said Victoria.

"Well, Mrs. Danvers brought Miss Keene her mail and some stuff from her house she'd asked for and no one thought anything of it. Mrs. Danvers greeted Andy, the policeman guarding the door, and went right in."

"Mrs. Danvers didn't throttle her, did she? Or stab her?"

"No, no," said Hope, shaking her head. "Mrs. Danvers gave her the mail and a couple of parcels from her house, one from Frederick's of Hollywood that the UPS guy delivered, and a white pasteboard box of candy. Miss Keene apparently knew about the candy. It had come to her house before she was shot. She offered a piece to Mrs. Danvers, who refused it, said she didn't like almond flavoring."

"Cyanide," said Victoria.

"Exactly," said Hope. "I went past the door while she was picking at the candy, nibbling it. I said hi to Andy, who was gathering up his stuff to go off duty. When I went past her door less than a minute later, I saw her thrashing around." Hope waved her hands in the air. "She'd turned a bright pink, and, excuse me, but my first reaction was to notice that she was the exact same color as that fluffy bed jacket she was wearing."

Victoria listened intently.

Hope continued. "I rushed into the room. There was that distinctive smell of bitter almonds. She'd knocked over the box of candy and it was all over the floor. I thought of cyanide right away."

"Cyanide acts quickly, doesn't it?" Victoria asked. "In a matter of seconds?"

"Depends on the dosage, Aunty Vic. Cyanide makes the cells in your body unable to use oxygen, so essentially you suffocate. When I first saw Miss Keene, she was breathing really fast, and was already that awful pink color."

"What causes the color?"

"Oxygen can't get to the body's cells, so it stays in the blood. That's what causes the patient, or victim, I guess, to look flushed like that. Almost a cherry red." Hope glanced at her great-aunt. "But you asked how quickly it acts. A pea-sized amount will kill a big man in less than a minute. Miss Keene must have gotten a pretty good dose."

"Is there no antidote?" Victoria asked.

"Sort of," Hope said. "If the dosage is small enough, you may have time to administer something like amyl nitrate. But between the time I saw her eating the candy and probably less than a minute later when I went by again and saw her thrashing around, it was too late. Cyanide poisoning is pretty rare, but I've had courses on poisons, and when I smelled that distinctive bitter almond smell, I immediately alerted Doc Erickson, who was on call. Believe me, he came in a big hurry."

"How horrible for you," said Victoria.

Hope shrugged. "I'm a nurse. I've seen worse, Aunty Vic, believe me."

"Now what?" Victoria asked.

"The state police are in charge, I guess. They have a detective named Horner or something who came by earlier to ask her about the shooting. She offered him a piece of her candy. Divinity fudge."

"I take it he didn't accept the offer."

"No, he didn't. Not every piece of candy was poisoned, though," said Hope. "They've already run preliminary tests."

"I suppose they'll want to question everyone who visited her at the hospital and also find out who sent her that candy," Victoria said.

Hope looked at her watch. "I've got to get back to work. It's been wild around here this afternoon."

"I can imagine," said Victoria. She stood and Hope hugged her.

As they rejoined Botts, who was waiting outside Acute Care, Hope said, "You know, Aunty Vic, I'm not supposed to be telling you all this stuff."

"I didn't hear a word," said Victoria.

Botts was scribbling something in his notebook. He put it in his pocket and stuck the pencil stub behind his ear. "Still working on Colley's dime, Madam Detective?"

Victoria nodded. "I told you, the killings are connected. How long do you guess it will be before Colley gets the next obituary?"

Al Fox didn't always wear his toupee. However, he was wearing it this afternoon, the day after Candy Keene's death. It was an expensive hairpiece, one of three that he usually wore only when conferring with female clients. He never wore a hairpiece when he was sailing or skiing or playing tennis.

He was conferring with a client now, Calpurnia Jameson. Calpurnia was in his office, pacing back and forth with long strides. Each time she came to the window that overlooked Pease's Point Way, she paused, then swiveled and paced to the opposite wall, which was covered with framed *New Yorker* cartoons having to do with lawyers. Each time she reached that leg of her pacing, she'd flick her shiny dark hair away from her face with a toss of her head.

"Where on earth did you get that hideous thing?" she asked, stopping in front of his desk long enough to read a cross-stitched motto surrounded by a border of cross stitched daisies in an enormous heavy silver frame embossed with rosebuds. "It takes up half of your desk."

The motto read, "The first thing we do, Let's kill all the lawyers."

"Shakespeare," Al Fox said. "King Henry the Sixth, part two." He stood. "I'll move it to where it doesn't block your view."

"As if I care," Calpurnia murmured.

He lifted the framed motto and set it on an end table next to the couch. "A client made it for me."

"Did she provide the frame, too?"

"The client was a he, and yes, he provided the frame."

"Some taste. Twenty pounds of silver?"

"Not quite. Anyway, it's silver plate," said Fox.

Calpurnia continued pacing, hands in the pockets of her custom-fitted jeans.

"You wanted to see me about Colley."

Calpurnia turned again. "I want to squeeze every last penny out of him, the self-absorbed bastard." She swiveled. "He makes ordinary self-centeredness seem positively philanthropic."

Al Fox nodded. "I know all about Colley Jameson."

"He's close-mouthed about what he's worth." She turned again. "What *is* he worth, by the way, Al?"

"Not much."

"His newspaper makes a fortune." She stopped at the window and looked out.

"As you know, he's got four ex-wives. You'll be number five, if you're saying what I think you are."

"He's down to three exes as of yesterday."

Al Fox said nothing.

Calpurnia paced.

Al Fox said, "You know, of course, that he doesn't own the newspaper."

Calpurnia stopped abruptly. "What?!"

"The *Island Enquirer* is owned by a trust."

"What about his father's money?"

"His father knew Colley. His widow will get a small pension. Of the remainder, one half of the trust fund goes to any issue, divided equally among them, and the other half goes to the *Enquirer*."

"He has no children. At least, none that I know about."

Al Fox smiled. "If it turns out there are no children, it's quite simple. One half of the trust fund goes to his widow, the other half to the newspaper. Upon her demise, her half reverts to the *Enquirer*. Otherwise, it's untouchable. Colley gets a small income from the fund. Period."

"You mean, in order to get the money from the trust fund I have to stay married to him?"

Al Fox nodded. "Until his death. Or," Al Fox looked at Calpurnia and smiled, "unless you can figure out some way to have him convicted of a crime. Almost any crime. According to the trust's conditions, Colley, in effect, would be dead, and his children would inherit accordingly. If he has no issue, their portion goes to his spouse."

"Ah!" said Calpurnia.

"Colley's going to get another obituary, William." Botts was dropping Victoria off at her house. "The question is, what form will this one take? So far he's been hanged, bitten in half by a shark, and shot with his own gun."

"Two for one with Miss Keene," said Botts.

"Come in for a moment. Do you have time?"

Botts checked his watch. "Enough."

Victoria brewed tea, and they seated themselves at the cookroom table.

"Whoever is writing those obituaries," Victoria said, "has what might pass as a sense of humor and knows how to write." She glanced at Botts. "We can rule you out, I suppose?"

"You suppose right." Botts tapped his fingers on the table.

"The first obituary was typed. You have a typewriter."

Botts said nothing.

"Tom Dwyer," Victoria said. "Tom invited me to go fishing with him. I believe I'll call him and accept."

Botts raised his eyebrows. "Surf casting?"

"Certainly."

Botts moved his mug in circles on the table. "Is it likely Dwyer wrote the obits?"

"Now that I think of it, it's entirely possible, though I can't imagine why." Victoria reached for the phone book and flipped the pages.

"Do you think it's wise to go off alone with him?" Botts continued to fiddle with his mug.

"The obituary writer and the killer are not the same person." Victoria found Tom Dwyer's number, picked up the phone, and dialed. "His answering machine," she said, after a pause. "I'll call later."

"Whoever killed Fieldstone had to know boats. Dwyer knows boats."

"He's not the killer," Victoria insisted. "The person who shot Candy Keene knew about the Thursday target practice. Candy never had a chance to tell us who lured her out that afternoon."

"He also had to know how to make divinity fudge and where to obtain cyanide."

"He may have bought the fudge," said Victoria. "We can put Katie to work tracking down candy shops that sell divinity."

Botts shook his head. "The killer wouldn't have risked that. It's an easy enough recipe."

"We need to eliminate the shops first." Victoria sipped her tea. "It's not difficult to obtain cyanide. New Zealanders use it to kill possums."

"Where did you get that information?"

"I have my sources," said Victoria. "By the way, the two girls are coming over tomorrow on the noon boat from Woods Hole. Katie's arranged to pick them up in Oak Bluffs at twelve forty-five and bring them here. Are you free around one o'clock?"

Botts stood up. "I'll clear my calendar, Madam Reporter."

Victoria suspected, when the phone rang, that it might be Colley and that Colley had received a fourth obituary. She was right.

"What does it say this time?" Victoria asked.

"How close are you to identifying this guy?"

"Close," said Victoria. "What does it say?"

"Jee-sus Christ, Victoria." She heard a rustling of papers. "This one says, 'Colley Jameson, fifty-five, was found dead in his hospital bed yesterday, apparently the victim of food poisoning. When found, Mr. Jameson, who was in the hospital for minor cosmetic surgery, had a partially eaten dish of Jello on a tray in front of him . . . ' "

"That's unkind," Victoria said. "The hospital's food is delicious."

"The hospital's food isn't the issue, Victoria. What are you doing about this?"

"I'll fax you a report the day after tomorrow from the office of the *West Tisbury Grackle*," said Victoria. "We have a fax machine there. I've got a meeting tomorrow."

Casey called Victoria at home that evening. "Victoria, I know you're mad at me, but I tried to reach you when the news came through about Candy Keene."

"Oh?" said Victoria.

"You weren't at home and you weren't at the *Grackle* office."

"I was in the field," said Victoria. "But I had a scanner."

"Well," said Casey. "I didn't know that. The state police have asked me to check for some stuff in Candy Keene's house tomorrow morning and I wondered if you'd like to come with me?"

"I'm going fishing," said Victoria.

There was a long silence from Casey.

"With Tom Dwyer," Victoria said. "The mystery writer. The one with the piping plover recipe."

"I know who he is. How come you're going fishing with him?"

"He invited me."

"I don't think that's real smart, Victoria. I mean, after all, you are . . ."

"Don't you start that too," said Victoria, and hung up.

Casey called back immediately. "Want me to take you to Edgartown tomorrow morning? For your fishing date?"

"No, thank you. He's picking me up," and Victoria hung up again.

CHAPTER 13

Victoria awoke at four-thirty to the dawn chorus, every bird in the universe, it seemed, announcing the new day. A robin led off. Then doves and cardinals, Carolina wrens, blue jays, chickadees, and flickers chimed in until their songs drowned out the occasional early morning car on the Edgartown Road and the ever-present sound of surf on the south shore. Victoria had known all the birds, once, but now she could identify only the most common ones.

The headlights of Tom's car turned in to her drive. She was waiting for him, a picnic basket next to her on the stone step.

He swung the passenger door open and helped her up into the high seat. "Morning, Victoria."

"It's going to be a lovely day," she said, once she had unzipped her sweater. "Where will we be fishing?"

In the dim light from the dashboard she could see Tom's profile, a smile around the pipestem clamped between his teeth. "You're not to tell anyone, Victoria. Promise?"

She smiled. "I promise."

"I've got a secret place on Chappy, around the corner from Wasque. There's an offshore eddy where the fish congregate."

"I suppose your secret place is in the midst of the piping plovers' nests?"

"We can walk there instead of driving, if you'd like."

"How far is it?"

Tom grinned. "From Katama? Not far. Four and a half, maybe five miles."

The road ahead was gradually becoming more visible in the

growing light. "I've brought breakfast," Victoria said, changing the subject. "Coffee, sandwiches, and some oranges."

"Great." Tom was still grinning.

"Does the Chappaquiddick ferry run this early?"

"We won't be going over on the ferry. We're driving along the beach."

"One of these days the ocean will cut through the bar. I remember that happening when I was a child," said Victoria. "Katama Bay poured into the ocean and swept the bar away and Chappaquiddick was cut off from the Vineyard."

"Almost time for it to happen again," said Tom.

They approached the outskirts of Edgartown and he turned onto Meetinghouse Way. "Avoiding traffic," he said, although there wasn't a car in sight.

He stopped at the South Beach parking area and got out of the car. "Letting air out of the tires so we can drive in soft sand," he told her.

As Victoria waited, the sun came up over the horizon. Golden light shone through thin crests of curling breakers. Not a footprint marred the beach as far as she could see in either direction.

"Ready?" Tom asked, getting back into the vehicle.

"Ready," said Victoria. "I've fastened my seat belt."

Tom drove east, dunes on their left, the ocean on their right. Victoria opened her window and sat up straight to see better. The car wallowed in the soft sand, making Victoria feel slightly seasick. The scenery passed by faster than she could ever hope to walk.

Within a half-mile the dunes petered out and Victoria and Tom were on the thin barrier bar with nothing but beach grass on either side between them and water. To their left, Katama Bay stretched out in a wide steel-blue sheet. To their right, the Atlantic Ocean gnawed away at the slender strip of sand that formed their road.

Victoria felt as though she were riding a circus car on a tightrope. Occasionally, a wave sent swash skimming across the bar, leaving a trail of foam that hissed as they drove through. The solid ground of Chappaquiddick seemed distant and it was. Safety was at least two miles ahead of them. Victoria felt a kick of adrenaline, excitement, or fear, she wasn't sure which. Tom drove slowly, ten miles an hour, then five miles an hour, then three, dodging places where the sand looked especially soft. Two miles would take, how long? Ten minutes? Fifteen? The minutes were more like hours. During those few minutes the ocean could break through and sweep the road out from under them, and sweep them with it.

When they reached Chappaquiddick at last, Victoria let out breath she hadn't realized she was holding. Tom hadn't spoken the entire time.

She broke the silence. "I've always come to Chappaquiddick by ferry. Never along the beach."

"The way the surf is washing over the bar, it won't be long before it cuts through. Then the only way over will be by ferry." The sand was firmer now, mixed with gray soil. Tom took his pipe out from between his teeth. "I brought a rod for you."

"I haven't held a surf-casting rod for a long time," said Victoria.

"You'll catch enough fish for supper, I guarantee."

Less than a mile farther, they reached Wasque, the southeastern corner of Chappaquiddick and of Martha's Vineyard. Victoria looked out at the tidal rip that angled out from the shore, a churning maelstrom as far as she could see. "Is that where you found your half of the body?" she asked.

Tom pointed with his pipe. "Right there."

"I'm glad we decided to drive, not walk," Victoria admitted.

"We're almost there. I don't think I ran over any plovers on the way."

"I suppose if you had, we could have tested your recipe. 'Four and twenty plovers baked in a pie.'"

Tom laughed. "It was stew, not pie."

He parked near the dunes, well away from the surf, helped

Victoria out of the car, and set up a folding aluminum chair for her near the water. He handed her an eight-foot-long surf-casting rod.

"You're serious about this, aren't you?" said Victoria.

"That's why we're here. To fish." When he finished attaching a lure to Victoria's line he cast it far out into the rip. "When you get a strike, start reeling in and call me." He set her rod into a holder he'd jammed into the sand. He laughed when he saw her expression. "You can do it, kid."

Victoria sat tensely, waiting for a bluefish to tear off with Tom's expensive gear. After a while she relaxed slightly. Neither Tom nor she had gotten a strike. Tom reeled in her line and cast again.

"I've read most of your mysteries and like them," Victoria said. "Especially the recipes."

"Thank you. That's a compliment coming from another writer. The *Enquirer* panned my last two."

Victoria unzipped her sweater. The sun was well above the horizon now and the day was getting warm. "Who wrote the reviews?"

"Colley."

Victoria frowned. "He doesn't usually write book reviews."

"He shouldn't," Tom said. "He has no idea how to critique. He thinks what he's writing is clever, but it's not. It's mean-spirited."

"As a writer himself, he should have some sensitivity for others."

"Colley? Sensitive to others?" Tom shook his head.

"Surely with your success those reviews of his don't affect you, do they?"

Tom took his pipe out of his mouth and tamped down the to-bacco with a wooden match. "I didn't think I'd be so bothered by his reviews, but I am. I've had writer's block since the last review came out six months ago."

"I can understand. We creative types are more sensitive than we want to admit." Victoria patted her hair. "Where do *your* ideas come from?"

Tom turned and swept his arm toward the Island behind them. "Need you ask?"

"People are always saying to me," she said, laughing, " 'It must be nice to live in such a quiet place.' And they're always asking, 'What do you do in the winter?' "

Tom laughed, reeled in his line, and flung it out again, then reeled in Victoria's and cast.

Victoria decided to bring up the subject that was on her mind. "You know about the obituaries Colley's received, don't you?"

Tom said, "Oh?"

"Four so far."

"Hey," Tom said. "I think you've got something on your line, Victoria." He reeled it in. "Nope." He detached a clump of seaweed and cast again. "I'd better check mine. When a blue hits you usually know, but they fool you sometimes. How about that breakfast of yours? I could do with a cup of coffee about now."

Victoria tried to catch his eye, but he wasn't looking at her. She opened the picnic basket and brought out the bacon and egg sandwiches she'd made so early this morning it had seemed like the middle of the night.

While they were eating, Victoria brought up the obituaries again, but Tom was as elusive as the blues.

It was almost an hour before Victoria got her first strike. Her rod arced and her line whizzed out. She called to Tom, who jabbed his own rod into its holder and rushed to her, and, by gosh, she'd hooked a bluefish. She reeled in the line until she was too tired to turn the small handle any more, then Tom did the rest.

"You'll eat tonight, Victoria. I'll fillet your fish for you."

While he was cleaning the fish, Victoria tried once again. "You knew, didn't you, that Colley fired that nice young reporter?"

"Katie? Yes. Damn shame. She's a good writer."

"Colley fired me, too."

"So I heard." Tom took his unlit pipe out of his mouth and re-lit it.

"I'm working with William Botts on the *Grackle*."

Tom nodded.

Victoria tried a more direct approach. "What's your feeling about Colley? Besides the fact that he's not a competent reviewer, that is."

"Tough job, being an editor." Tom turned away. "I'd better tend my own line if I hope to have any supper."

"Do your daughter and your wife like to fish?"

"Yes, they both do. They're both good cooks, too. Lynn is my wife's daughter from her first marriage, you know."

"Oh." Victoria felt unaccountably embarrassed.

"Sometimes they come fishing with me." Tom reeled in and cast again. "Not as often as I'd like. Lynn's sixteen now and has her own life. I usually fish with Simon Newkirk." Tom tinkered with his pipe.

Victoria shifted slightly in her chair. As she did, she saw her rod bend. "Another one!" she called out.

Tom reeled in her second fish. "Nice one. I may have to beg one of your blues for my own supper." Tom looked over at his rod, and his own line was streaming out. "They're running now."

For the next hour, Tom worked both of their lines. Victoria kept all five fish she'd caught. Tom had filleted them and stashed them in a plastic bag. The fillets would freeze nicely. But she hadn't been able to get a word out of him, one way or the other, about the obituaries. Tom had written them, she was sure. But why? What did he have against Colley that would make him play such an odd joke?

Victoria stared at the horizon line, where sea and sky met, puzzling. She was missing something, some piece that would explain things. Whoever had sent those notes to Colley had a peculiar sense of humor. Tom's piping plover recipe was that sort of humor. Was Tom hoping to jump-start his own blocked writing? Writer's block could be devastating. She shook her head.

Tom took his pipe out of his mouth. "Had enough, Victoria? The tide's about to change. The fish will stop running when it does."

"Are we going to return along the same way we came?" Victoria tried to keep the concern out of her voice as she thought of that fragile ribbon of sand road.

Tom checked his watch. "We'd better take the ferry. With the tide coming in, the bar can break through any time."

Victoria rose from her seat and carried her bag of fillets to the car. "Thank you for inviting me. And for doing all the work."

Tom took his pipe out of his mouth. "It's a pleasure to fish with a pro."

Victoria didn't believe in taking naps. When she got home, she settled into her mouse-colored wing chair with McCavity in her lap and a pad of notepaper and a pen. She intended to draft a poem about this morning's expedition. She had enough material for two or three poems. A sonnet and perhaps a sestina. She liked the challenge of formal poetry. Sestinas had a netlike quality that would work well with the motif of fishing.

But it had been a long and early morning.

She woke with a jerk when she heard a knock on the kitchen door, startling McCavity, who was dozing in her lap. Victoria ran a hand over her hair and eased herself out of her chair.

Botts had arrived a half-hour before Katie and the two girls were expected.

"Catch any fish?" he asked.

"Five."

"Surf casting? You caught five fish surf casting?"

"I don't know why you should be surprised. I used to fish quite often when I was a girl." Before they sat down she asked, "Have you had lunch yet?"

"I ate about an hour ago," Botts said. "I'm not sure I'd have the stamina you do."

"I had a bit of help casting and reeling the fish in. And Tom filleted them for me. How about some tea?"

"Please."

Victoria put the water on to boil, heated up some soup for herself, and when the tea had brewed, joined Botts in the cookroom with the tea, her soup, and a pilot cracker.

"Haven't seen pilot crackers for a while," said Botts. "We used to call them chowder crackers."

"Cronig's didn't stock pilot crackers for a few months, but there was such a furor from Islanders, we can now buy them again."

Botts waited until she'd poured tea. "Did you learn anything from Dwyer?"

"Nothing. He was evasive. I'm convinced he wrote those obituaries. Why, though, I can't imagine."

"And yet you don't think he's the killer?"

Victoria shook her head. "He's not the type."

"We all are, under the right circumstances."

Victoria broke the large cracker into small pieces and dropped them into her soup. "Did you know that Lynn is Tom's wife's daughter from a previous marriage?"

Botts looked up from his tea. "I had no idea his wife had been married before. Was her first husband from here?"

"I don't know. I didn't ask."

Botts checked his watch. "Katie's late."

"Did you talk to her this morning?"

"She was going to pick up the girls at the boat and bring them directly here. They have an interview with Colley this afternoon."

"I hope I did the right thing by taking them to the *Enquirer*. The *Grackle* could make better use of them."

"No, Victoria. Absolutely not. I've got more staff than I want."

"It's an idea." She glanced out of the window at the sound of a car in the drive.

Katie parked her sports car next to Botts's pickup and the three young women came into the house together.

"Good morning," Victoria greeted them. "Mugs are in the cupboard near the sink and the tea is brewed."

"It's afternoon," said Botts.

The two girls sat next to each other at the table.

"Are you finished with your lunch, Mrs. Trumbull?" Katie asked and when Victoria nodded, she took the tray into the kitchen and returned with mugs of tea. Both girls wrapped their hands around their mugs and gazed down silently at the table.

"Do you graduate this year, Tiffany? You are Tiffany, aren't you?" Victoria nodded to the blonde.

"No, ma'am. I'm Wendy. She's Tiffany," indicating the dark-haired girl. "We'll be seniors in September."

"We were wondering, Tiffany and me, how you ever found us?" Wendy asked.

"The dock attendants gave me your telephone numbers."

Wendy giggled. "They're cute."

Victoria smiled. "They are. I'm sorry they're not closer to my age."

The girls looked at each other and both giggled.

Katie, sitting at the end of the table, had her notebook out.

Botts said, "You two may have been the last people to see Mr. Fieldstone alive. You heard about his death, didn't you?"

"That was gruesome," said Tiffany. "He seemed, like, you know, a nice man."

"We heard a boat ran over him," said Wendy.

"Really horrible," said Tiffany, and shook her head.

"Before he dropped you off at the Hyannis dock, did Mr. Fieldstone say where he planned to go?" Victoria asked.

Tiffany looked up from her tea. "He was, like, meeting someone on Nantucket."

"Could you tell from anything Mr. Fieldstone said whether or not the friend had a boat of his own?" Botts asked.

"I don't know. I mean, Mr. Fieldstone didn't mention anything about another boat. When we told him thank you, he said it wasn't out of his way. He was meeting someone on Nantucket."

"His boat was awesome," said Wendy. "He let us look around the cabin downstairs."

"Did anyone call him on his radio when you were on board?" Botts asked.

The girls looked at each other. "No," Tiffany said. "He turned on the weather channel and we, like, listened to that. It was supposed to be nice, the radio said. Then he turned to Channel sixteen, the emergency channel, and we listened to the Coast Guard talking to someone whose engine had quit."

"They ran out of gas," said Wendy.

"Did Mr. Fieldstone have a cell phone?" Victoria asked. "Did he make any calls, or did anyone call him while you were on board?"

"He did, didn't he?" Wendy said, turning to Tiffany.

"Someone called, but we couldn't tell who it was. He said something about fishing. It might have been his wife. I wasn't really listening, you know?"

Victoria looked from one girl to the other. "Did he tell the person on the phone where he was going?"

Wendy piped up. "He said fish were running in Muskegut Channel."

"From what he said, did it sound as though the person Fieldstone was meeting lived on Nantucket?" Botts asked.

Wendy shook her head. "I wasn't really listening. It was like he was just telling her he was going fishing. I'm not sure it was a 'her' on the phone. Could of been a guy, I guess. He didn't mention Nantucket on the phone."

"Did he talk to anyone on the dock when he let you off?" Victoria asked.

"When we tied up in Hyannis, they seemed to know him,"

said Tiffany. "Said 'hi' and 'how you doing' and 'what brings you here.' That kind of stuff."

"Did any of them ask where he was going?"

"I guess. Like, 'Where you going?' and he said, 'Cruising around Nantucket,' and they all laughed. That was about it. Almost what he said to us." Tiffany looked around. "Does anyone have the time? We're supposed to meet Mr. Jameson at two o'clock."

Katie looked at her watch. "It's twenty of now."

"Mr. Botts and I are going that way," said Victoria. "We can give you a ride."

"So we're going that way, eh?" said Botts, when the girls were out of hearing.

"I need to report to Colley about my progress on the obituary writer."

"Are you telling him that Tom Dwyer wrote the obits?"

"Of course not," said Victoria.

CHAPTER 14

Katie drove straight to Edgartown after her meeting with Victoria, William Botts, and the two girls from Hyannis Academy. She had met Ed Prada twice over beers at the Waterfront Pub since the day Fieldstone's half-body had washed up on Wasque, and she was meeting him again today for a late lunch. She'd felt guilty for not offering to drive Wendy and Tiffany to the *Enquirer* for their second interview, since she'd be going within a block of the paper, but then Victoria and William Botts had volunteered.

Ed, looking both handsome and non-Island in his summer uniform, was sitting at a table by the window when Katie arrived at the pub. She made her way through the late-lunch crowd and greeted him in her husky voice.

Ed stood up and held a chair for her. "Matt Pease may stop by to show you some photos." He looked at his watch. "We'd better order right away. I have only a half-hour."

Katie glanced at the menu and set it aside. "Tuna salad sandwich and iced tea, I guess. I wonder what Matt's photos are of?"

"He didn't say. I assume they have something to do with Colley."

"He's more upset with Colley than I am, and I'm pretty angry. Matt's been with the paper longer than Colley has."

"Here he is now." Ed signaled to Matt, who was standing in the doorway, looking around. He made his way to their table, carrying a large manila envelope.

"Pull up a chair," said Ed. "How about lunch?"

"I've already eaten, but I could use a cup of coffee." He laid the envelope on the table.

The waitress came to their table and smiled when she saw Matt. "I've been meaning to call you, Matt. Jared and I are getting married. We want you to be our photographer."

"Congratulations," said Katie. "When?"

"In September."

"I'd be delighted." Matt took a business card out of his wallet and handed it to her. "Give me a call when you get off work."

"Thanks, Matt." She noted down their orders and left.

"Looks like you don't need to worry about your career," Ed said.

Katie indicated the envelope. "Are those the photos Colley wants so badly? The ones taken at the funeral?"

"I've got several photos of his wife and Audrey before and after the funeral." Matt opened the envelope, removed a sheaf of eight-by-ten glossy prints, and spread them out on the table. "Here the two women are, scowling at each other, but that's hardly a big deal. Everybody on the Island knows Calpurnia and Audrey's husband had a thing going." Matt shuffled the photos, putting them in some kind of order. "I don't know why Colley is so eager to get the pictures. He wants the negatives, too."

"Has he seen the prints?" Ed asked.

"Not these. I gave him—rather, I sold him—a shot of him and Audrey after the funeral where Colley's looking suitably sympathetic and Audrey seems to be grieving." He slid the photo out from the stack. "And I sold him a real arty photo of the crowd in front of the church, umbrellas adding to the atmosphere of gloom. Front-page news photos, both of them."

In a short time, the waitress returned with sandwiches and Matt's coffee. "I know you're in a hurry, Ed. I'll take your money now, if you want."

"Thanks." Ed handed her a bill.

Katie stirred sugar into her iced tea. "Why did you want me to see the pictures? I was there, as you know, and heard what

Audrey said about Calpurnia, right to her face. No love lost between them."

"Those weren't the photos that I wanted to show you." Matt shuffled the prints. "I have others from the beginning of the roll of film." He slid several glossy prints in front of Katie, avoiding her tuna sandwich. "The funeral photos were at the end of the roll. I'd taken a couple of dozen shots around town for about a week before. Local color. Merchants getting ready for summer, that sort of thing." He slipped the funeral prints back into the envelope and spread the others out on the table. "I wanted to get your reaction to these, this one in particular."

Katie wiped her hands on her napkin and picked up a photo of the Edgartown harbor. In the background, she could see the Chappaquiddick shoreline. Several boats were in the channel—the ferry, two small sailboats, an inflatable dinghy with a man at the tiller, and an old runabout. Sunlight glinted off the varnished brightwork of the runabout. Two people were in the boat, one at the helm, the other reaching for something in the stern.

Katie glanced up. "What am I supposed to be seeing?"

Matt pointed at the runabout with his pen. "I'm interested in antique wooden Chris-Crafts, so I enlarged this portion of the photo. I hadn't seen this one around the harbor before. It dates from around nineteen-thirty, and only about five hundred of this model were built." He smoothed the photo. "It could make better than thirty miles an hour. Probably still can." He sighed. "Someone takes good care of her." He moved the harbor photo to one side and slid out the enlargement of the boat. "Notice anything?" he asked.

Ed leaned over to examine the photo.

"Looks like a woman at the controls," he said.

"What's wrong with that?" asked Katie.

"The passenger seems to be a woman, too," Ed said.

Matt took a small hand lens out of his shirt pocket. "Look

closely at the woman at the wheel." He handed the magnifying lens to Katie.

The images of the two people in the grainy enlargement were fuzzy. The woman at the controls was wearing sunglasses and a dark anorak with the hood pulled over her hair. The ends of a scarf she had tied around the neck of the anorak had blown in front of her face, partly obscuring her mouth and chin.

"It's hard to tell who she is." Katie looked up at Matt. "She looks a little bit like Audrey Fieldstone."

"Look at the other woman," said Matt.

The other woman was even more difficult to make out. She was reaching into the backseat of the boat. Her dark hair was blowing in front of her face.

"Calpurnia wears her hair something like that," said Katie. "But there's no way it can be Audrey and Calpurnia. When did you take the picture?"

"Early afternoon, about five days before the funeral."

Ed, eating quickly, was halfway through his sandwich. "Had Fieldstone's body been found by then?"

Matt shrugged. "I'm not sure."

"His body—half of his body—washed up on Friday, almost two weeks ago," said Katie. "I covered the story."

"The boat belongs to Audrey Fieldstone. She keeps it in Lagoon Pond, at Maciel Marine."

"*Is* that Calpurnia with her?"

"Here's another photo taken the day before the funeral." Matt shuffled the prints again and picked out one taken on Main Street not far from the Whaling Church. In the picture were two women, one with dark hair walking away from the photographer, her back to the camera. The other was clearly Audrey, frowning, a hand partially raised as if to ward off something. She was wearing a dark anorak.

Katie took a deep breath. "Audrey and Calpurnia."

"What do you make of that?" Matt asked. "Four or five days before the funeral they're in Audrey's boat. They must have been on speaking terms. Was Fieldstone already dead? And did they know?" He shuffled the photos back to the one of Audrey with her hand raised. "Yet look at this. Audrey is not exactly friendly, but she's acknowledging Calpurnia. At the funeral she's really hostile."

Ed looked at his watch and wadded up his napkin. "I hate to leave, but I have to get back to the station house. I'll give you a call, Katie."

After Ed left, Katie asked Matt, "What's going on?"

"I don't have a clue. They have every reason to hate each other. But why are they together in Audrey's boat?"

"Is it possible that Audrey didn't know about her husband and Calpurnia? And found out before the funeral?"

Matt shook his head. "I doubt it. Everybody on the Island knew about the affair. And everybody knew how the two women felt about each other."

"Sometimes wives can be in deep denial."

"I don't know," said Matt. "Doesn't make sense, their going out in that boat together."

"You've got to show these photos to Victoria Trumbull. If anyone can make sense out of them, she can."

"I'll be at the historical society museum, Victoria." Botts said as he dropped Victoria and the two girls off at the *Enquirer* for their interview with Colley. Victoria went into the newspaper office with them.

They stopped at the reception desk and Victoria introduced the girls to Faith. "These two young ladies are here for their appointment with Colley."

Faith looked at her calendar. "Mr. Jameson must have forgotten. He's with his attorney right now."

Victoria's face flushed. "The girls have come from off Island at Colley's request. They made a special trip."

"I'm so sorry, Mrs. Trumbull." Faith rose out of her seat. "I don't know what to say. Would you care to wait?"

Victoria tapped her fingers on the reception desk. "When do you expect him back?"

"It's okay, Mrs. Trumbull," said Tiffany. "We don't, like, want to be a bother."

"He probably won't be more than an hour," Faith said.

Victoria turned to Tiffany. "Mr. Jameson made an appointment with you. You set aside your entire day to meet with him for a half-hour. It's not much to ask of him that he remember the appointment that *he* made."

Tiffany and Wendy looked at each other. "Really, Mrs. Trumbull. We can come back another day," said Tiffany.

Victoria turned to Faith. "Is Alfred Fox his lawyer?"

"Yes. At Pease's Point Way."

"I know where it is. Come along, girls," said Victoria. "That's only two blocks from here."

"Perhaps I'd better call Mr. Fox's office?" Faith said. "To let him know you're on your way?"

"That won't be necessary," Victoria said, and marched out, the two girls trailing after her.

Al Fox had hung his toupee on the coat rack by the door, where it looked like a dead raccoon. It was a fine hairpiece, but it itched, and he preferred to wear it only occasionally.

He was sitting behind his kidney-shaped desk, made from a slice of maple burl. The sun reflected off his head and his polished desk and into Colley's eyes. Colley moved his chair to one side, thinking about Victoria as he did.

"Isn't there some way I can get at the principal of the trust fund?" he asked Al Fox.

Al fiddled with his letter opener, a dagger he'd picked up in Majorca. "Your father tied that trust fund up every which way. He made sure you would receive a regular allowance, but the principal will go, upon your death, half divided among your issue, half to the newspaper trust, and an allowance to your surviving wife."

Colley got up from the chair, walked over toward the wall and studied the framed *New Yorker* cartoons of lawyers. "There are no children."

"If it is proven that there is no issue, your surviving wife will have the use of one half of the fund until her death, at which time the money goes to the newspaper."

"Can't I borrow against the fund?" Colley stopped at the framed embroidered quotation that was now taking up most of the space on the end table beside the couch.

"No way."

" 'Let's kill all the lawyers,' " Colley read.

Al shrugged. "Right or wrong, your father didn't want you to have control of that trust fund. He and his Boston lawyers worked out the wording. I didn't."

Colley's face was getting pink. "Part of my problem is that you're representing a bunch of my ex-wives, and you and they are squeezing me dry."

"Come now, that's not fair," said Al, running his hand over his smooth head. "I represented only two of the four, and one of those is dead now. You made your own deal with college sweetheart number one, I didn't. Granted, number two took you to the cleaners . . ."

"With your help."

"Shall we say she stripped you clean? Ha, ha!" said Al, with no trace of mirth.

Colley didn't laugh.

"She was my client. You weren't. Ecdysiast. Ha, ha!" Al took off his glasses and wiped them on a tissue. "Number three— where is she, by the way?"

"She remarried."

"Number three didn't want a penny from you—'dirty money,' according to her. I tried to convince her she was entitled to a sizable alimony."

"Thanks a lot," said Colley.

"Not at all. Number four's checks go to Majorca."

127

"Understand you're hand delivering my checks to her."

"I'd say you got off easy," Al said, ignoring the remark. He played with the letter opener, twisting it around and around in his hands. "You should stop shedding wives, Colley. You can't afford the luxury."

"The fact remains," said Colley, seating himself again, "that trust fund has better than eight million dollars in it, and all it's doing is growing."

"Not these days, it isn't."

The intercom on Fox's desk buzzed and he pressed the switch. His assistant Martha Jo was on the line. "Mr. Fox, Victoria Trumbull and two girls are here to see Mr. Jameson. Shall I send them in?"

Al raised his hairless eyebrows. "What have you done now, Colley?"

At the Waterfront Pub, Matt and Katie got up from the table and Matt left a tip under the napkin holder.

"Ed already tipped her," Katie said. "You'd better save your money."

"The waitstaff doesn't get paid enough. By the way, after I leave here I'm going over to the *Enquirer* to pick up my paycheck. Did you get your severance pay yet?"

"No. I didn't want to chance running into Colley."

"Let's go over there now, together."

They walked down North Water Street with the harbor on their left, the white-painted captains' houses on their right, each house angled to face the harbor. On the way to the *Enquirer*, people said hello, nodded, lifted a hand in greeting, stopped to talk.

A stocky man in white painter's overalls approached them. "Hi Matt, Katie. Nice day."

"Seth. How you doing?"

"Not bad. You?"

"Great."

"Hear you've got a new job working for the competition, Katie. That right?"

"Kind of," said Katie.

"Well, good luck."

In another week, in another couple of days, the streets and brick sidewalks of Edgartown would be filled with strangers wearing slacks and shirts printed with whales and seagulls and bluefish. A week from now, neighbors would be too busy to chat.

"How *is* the new job?" Matt asked Katie.

"Interesting," Katie answered cautiously. "Mr. Botts had always dreamed of writing and publishing a nice newsy one-page newsletter in his quiet retirement. Now he's got a staff of three, he's embroiled in a murder investigation, and the *Grackle* has gone to four pages. His wife is demanding that he buy an answering machine to handle subscriptions that are pouring in. Mrs. Trumbull keeps adding staff. He's not at all happy."

"Does he need photos?"

"Ask Mrs. Trumbull. She's orchestrating everything."

They turned the corner onto Main Street.

"And there she is," said Matt.

Victoria Trumbull and Colley Jameson were striding, side by side, along Main Street. Behind them, looking uncomfortable, were Tiffany and Wendy.

"I wonder what happened?" said Katie. "Mrs. Trumbull has that look she gets."

Victoria's large chin jutted out. Her nose lifted. Her deep-set eyes were hooded. Her back was straight. She held her lilac stick by its middle like a baton, horizontally, as if she might use it to emphasize some point. However, she was not talking.

Colley was.

"Wouldn't you love to hear what he's saying?" said Katie.

What Colley was saying was, "You didn't need to show up at my attorney's office with those girls in tow, Victoria."

"You made an appointment with those two girls."

"I'd have gotten back to the newspaper sooner or later. I had to discuss something with my attorney."

"You made an appointment with them and you forgot it."

"You didn't need to show up at his office."

The two girls lagged behind, taking small, slow steps. One of them ran her hand along the picket fence, avoiding the rose canes that were trained along the top.

Colley went on the offensive. "Have you found out who's writing those phony obits yet? I've been signing a lot of checks made out to one Victoria Trumbull."

Victoria stared ahead. "I've identified the writer."

Colley stopped. The two girls behind him also stopped. The blonde fingered a rose that was hanging over the fence. Pale yellow petals dropped to the brick sidewalk.

"Who is he?" Colley demanded.

"I haven't completed my investigation," said Victoria. "I'll let you know when I do."

"For Christ's sake, Victoria. I don't want to see another one of those damned things."

"Unlikely unless someone else is killed. I know who's writing them and I'll take care of the writer."

"I suppose you'll continue to bill me?" Colley started to walk again and the two girls moved away from the fence.

"We have a written agreement," said Victoria. "Until I take care of the matter, I will continue to bill you."

They had reached Summer Street, where the *Enquirer* had its offices.

"Hi, Mrs. Trumbull."

Victoria looked up and smiled. "Katie. And Matt Pease. Nice to see you again."

Colley scowled.

"Are you heading our way?" Victoria asked. "To the newspaper?"

"To pick up our final checks," Matt said.

Colley's scowl deepened. "I don't suppose you've changed your mind about those photographs, Matt?"

Matt clutched the envelope he was carrying. "No, sir," he said. "They're not for sale."

"That remains to be seen," said Colley.

CHAPTER 15

It was late that same afternoon when Martha Jo left work. She took her beige sweater from a hanger in the closet and went to the door of Al Fox's office. "Is there anything else you'd like me to do before I go, Mr. Fox?"

"No, thanks, Martha Jo. I'll close up."

"I wish you'd *lock* up, Mr. Fox. You really should pay more attention to security."

Al looked over his glasses and grinned. "This is the Vineyard, not the mainland."

"This is an *attorney's* office, Mr. Fox."

He dismissed her with a wave of his hand. "I don't keep sensitive material in the office."

"Nevertheless . . ."

Al took off his glasses and asked politely, "Do you have big plans for tonight?"

"I'm going to work in my garden until dark, do my laundry, wash my hair, and finish my book."

"What are you reading?"

"Tom Dwyer's latest mystery."

"The one Jameson wrote such a scathing review about?"

"I can't imagine why. I think it's his best so far." Martha Jo slung her sweater over her shoulders. "If there's nothing further you need, Mr. Fox, I'll be leaving. You won't stay late, will you?"

"I shouldn't be here much longer than nine-thirty or so. A client is coming by after supper." He looked at his watch. "I'll grab a sandwich at the deli." He stood up. "Enjoy your evening with Tom Dwyer."

"Good night, then, Mr. Fox."

A half-hour later, after Al had finished his sandwich and tossed the wrappers into his wastepaper basket, he heard footsteps on the stairs up to his office. His client was earlier than he'd expected. He hurriedly adjusted his toupee, brushed crumbs off his desk, and busied himself with the papers he'd been working on when Martha Jo left.

When he heard a knock on the outer door he called out, "The door's not locked." He straightened the collar of his shirt and looked up. The visitor was Colley Jameson.

"Not you again," Al grumbled.

"I thought you might still be here." The newspaper editor waved at the toupee. "Expecting someone else?"

"As a matter of fact, yes. I have an appointment with a client in," Al checked his watch, "a little over an hour. What brings you here tonight?"

"We didn't finish what we were discussing earlier," Colley said, settling himself in one of Al's leather chairs and straightening the crease in his trousers.

"I already gave you the answer when Mrs. Trumbull, er, arrived."

"I didn't get around to asking you about obtaining some photos Matt Pease took."

"I understand he's no longer working for you."

"Not full time," said Colley.

"Did he take the photos with your camera?"

"No."

"Develop them on your time on your premises with your equipment?"

"No."

"If he doesn't want to sell them to you, you don't have a leg to stand on. What's in the photos that you want so badly?"

Colley shifted in his seat. "My wife and Audrey Fieldstone."

"Together?" said Al.

"I believe so."

"Have you seen the photos?"

"No." Colley shook his head. "But I have reason to believe one of them may shed light on Ambler Fieldstone's so-called accident."

"I suppose you could get the Coast Guard to subpoena the photos."

"I'd rather not involve the Coast Guard."

Al Fox laughed. "Thinking of a touch of blackmail, are we?"

Colley adjusted his tie. "I didn't get a chance to explain my financial situation to you this afternoon."

"Seems to me you did," said Fox.

"I've got to get hold of four hundred fifty thousand, Al, and soon."

"Are the photos worth that much?" Al stared at Colley for several seconds. "A half million?"

"This has nothing to do with the photos. I've changed the subject." Colley examined his fingernails. "Four hundred and fifty thousand is what I need, not a half million."

"What in God's name do you need that much money for, Jameson?"

"I've made a financial commitment I'd rather not talk about, and I've got to borrow against the trust fund."

"We've been through that," said Al, scowling. "The discussion's closed."

"When Victoria Trumbull showed up with those girls I hadn't been here more than ten minutes."

"The discussion's closed," Al repeated. "Sorry."

"You know how to slither around technicalities, Al. I've seen you do it. Shaking loose a few hundred thousand out of eight million shouldn't be much of a problem."

Al leaned back in his chair. "See here, Colley, the lawyers who wrote the trust up for your father knew what they were doing. You know how it's to be distributed. Half to your issue, half to the newspaper trust, and a nice pension to whatever wife is," Al smirked, "still married to you at the time of your death."

"I have no children."

Fox smiled. "Really?"

"Jee-sus, Al, you're insufferable," said Colley, shifting uncomfortably in the soft seat. "You know my situation. My expenses are going up and the worth of that damned stock is dropping every day."

"Ex-wife number two's timely demise has certainly eased your cash flow."

"Not enough," said Colley. "Al, I've got to have that money. I'm desperate, or I wouldn't be coming to you."

"You get a handsome allowance. Plus the income from the *Enquirer*. What are you doing with it all?" Al asked. "As far as I know, you were paying alimony to only two of your four ex-wives, and now it's down to only one." He picked up his letter opener and toyed with it.

Colley gestured at the dagger. "From Majorca? Hand delivering my check to my ex-wife, all expenses paid. By me. Did I pay for that piece of junk, too?"

Al ignored him. "You're not into drugs, are you?"

"No way," said Colley.

"Gambling?"

Colley shook his head.

"What, then?" Al looked at his watch again.

Colley shrugged, then straightened his tie again. "I sold some shares in the *Enquirer* to Fieldstone."

"What! You can't do that!"

Colley sat back in the chair and folded his arms over his chest. "That's what I found out."

"How much did you sell?"

"Thirty percent. Nine hundred thousand dollars."

Al stared at his client. "Fieldstone gave you close to a million dollars?"

"He gave me half of the amount. Four hundred fifty thousand."

"What kind of paper did you give him?"

"A notarized receipt for four hundred fifty thousand as half payment for thirty percent of the ownership of the newspaper."

"Why didn't you check with me first? That's what lawyers are for, for God's sake. You don't own the *Island Enquirer*. The trust does."

Colley said nothing.

Al Fox slid the point of his letter opener under the corner of his blotter. "I suppose the executors for his estate want their money back?"

Colley nodded.

Al leaned back in his chair again, his elbows on the armrests, his fingertips steepled under his chin. "You know, don't you, that Fieldstone had mob connections?"

Colley smiled. "I know. A couple of their minions have been to see me."

"Threatened to break both legs, I suppose?"

"They were more subtle."

"So what did you spend the money on?"

"I can't say."

"Can't, Colley? Or won't?"

"Same thing."

Al stood up. "What an ass you are, Colley. I can't help you. That trust fund is airtight, watertight, and monkey-proof."

Colley looked up. "How about a personal loan?"

"Surely you're joking." Al came from behind his desk. "I don't have that kind of money. If I did, I sure as hell wouldn't give it to you." He looked at his watch again. "You'll have to excuse me. I need to get some things together before my client arrives."

Colley stood, his feet apart, his blazer jacket open, his hands thrust into his trouser pockets. "Look, Al, I know a lot about your legal shenanigans."

Al smiled.

"The board of bar overseers would be interested in knowing about your overlapping clients. Conflicts of interest is putting it mildly."

Al's smile widened. "I don't think you want to do that, Jameson."

"We'll see," said Colley, and stalked out of the office.

"Shut the door behind you," Al called out, and the door slammed. He sat again, still smiling, toying again with his letter opener.

Fifteen minutes later he had finished most of the paperwork for his client when he again heard footsteps on the stairs. He patted his toupee, picked up the papers on his desk, and when there was a knock on the door, said, "Come in, my dear." He stood, and the door opened.

Al grunted. "I was expecting someone else. Matt Pease, isn't it? I don't think we've met." He held out his hand and Matt shook it. "How can I help you?" Al sat down again.

"I'll get right to the point," said Matt. "Colley Jameson . . ."

"Ha, ha!" said Al.

Matt paused briefly, then went on. "I used to work for the *Enquirer*."

Al nodded. "I've seen your photos in the paper. Nice."

"Thanks. Well Colley Jameson fired me."

"So I understand. Have a seat."

Matt looked around and sat on the edge of one of the leather chairs. "He cut back my hours to a point where I had to get another source of income, so I started my own business."

"Good move," said Al. "Photography, I assume?"

"Weddings, baby pictures, postcards."

"You should do well."

Matt made a face. "Colley's now claiming that the photos I've taken on my own time are his property, and he's threatening to sue me."

Al smiled. "I take it you're not using his film? His darkroom? His equipment?"

"No." Matt leaned forward and clasped his hands.

Al leaned back in his chair. "Does he claim all of your photos or only specific ones?"

"I took some pictures of his wife that he wants."

Al's smile broadened. "Sell them to him, then. Bill him."

"I want to keep the photos for my own use."

Al laughed. "Blackmail?"

Matt's face reddened. "Of course not. Not at all."

"Do you have any idea why Colley wants the photos so badly? What do they show?"

"His wife and Mrs. Fieldstone in Mrs. Fieldstone's boat."

"When did you take them?"

"About two weeks ago."

Al Fox whistled. "I see." He looked at his watch. "If you're not planning blackmail, then you don't need to worry about a thing. I won't even bill you for this consultation." He stood. "I'm expecting a client any minute."

"Mr. Fox," said Matt, still sitting, "Colley Jameson said he's planning to sue me for those photos. I can't afford to defend myself against even a frivolous lawsuit."

"Don't worry," said Al. "He won't sue you. If he does, call me."

"But . . ." said Matt.

"Understand you expect a new addition to your family any minute?"

"Yes sir, but . . ."

"Congratulations." Al held out his hand. "Don't worry about a thing. I'll see you to the door."

Matt got up, shook Al's hand, and walked slowly out of the office. Al closed the door behind him and looked at his watch again.

Less than five minutes later, he heard heavy footsteps on the stairs. He went to the door and opened it. Tom Dwyer was almost on the top step.

"To what do I owe this pleasure?" Al said, looking up at the tall writer. "I'm expecting a client any minute."

"Won't take me long." Tom followed Al into the office and shut the door. He sat in the armchair Matt had vacated, crossed one leg over the other, and put his hand on his ankle. Al sat in the chair across from him.

Tom pushed his bush hat back from his forehead and said, "Can you get that bastard to submit to a DNA test?"

"Which bastard?"

"Jameson."

"Jameson," Al repeated. "Ha, ha!" He added, almost to himself, "Naturally."

"DNA," said Tom.

Al was silent for several moments. "Possibly."

"What do we need to do, get a sample of his blood or whatever?"

"We?"

"You—you're the lawyer."

"Ummmm," said Al.

Tom uncrossed his legs. "You know Jameson is Lynn's father, don't you?"

Al said nothing.

"Lynn. My stepdaughter," Tom said. "The bastard has never paid a cent for her support. She's sixteen now."

"Ummmm," said Al.

"He claims she's not his child." Tom sat forward. "All you have to do is look at her."

"Want me to research the legal procedures for DNA testing, do you?"

"She starts college a year from September. I can't swing it alone. It's time he helped out."

Al thought for a few moments more. "You may not need to go the DNA route. A letter from an attorney should do the trick."

"Will you write that letter?"

"Let me get back to you," Al said. "Colley's hard up for cash at the moment."

"Tough," said Tom. "Aren't we all." He got to his feet. "I'll expect a call from you tomorrow, then."

Al, too, got up and held out his hand. "I enjoyed your last book. Great setting, great characters."

"Thanks," said Tom. "I suppose you've read *his* review?"

Al shrugged. "No one pays any attention to Colley."

"I do," said Tom. He wheeled around, jammed his hat down on his forehead, opened the door, and pounded down the stairs.

In a few minutes Al heard light footsteps coming up the stairs. He got up, opened the door, and was startled when he saw the slim form of Calpurnia.

"This is a pleasure," said Al, recovering quickly. "I expected someone else."

"I tried the downstairs door and it was open," said Calpurnia. "I need to talk to you."

"This is not a good time. I'm expecting a client. How about first thing tomorrow morning?"

As he was saying "morning," he heard another set of light footsteps coming up the stairs.

"Your client?" asked Calpurnia, smiling.

"Have a seat," said Al. He went to the door and opened it, partially blocking the view into his office. "Good evening, my dear. I have an unexpected client. An emergency. Would you mind waiting in the reception area?"

"No way," said Audrey.

Al continued to block the door. "Have a seat out there and let me fix you a drink."

"Forget it," said Audrey, brushing past him into his office, where she stopped abruptly. "What the hell are *you* doing here?"

Calpurnia, seated in the far chair, swished her hair away from her face and smiled.

Al looked from one to the other. "Let me fix you both drinks. Scotch for you, Audrey?"

"Make it a double."

"And you, Calpurnia, bourbon, isn't it?"

"No, thank you."

Al went into the reception area where there was a small kitchen and bar. There was no sound of voices from his office. He returned with two drinks, scotch for Audrey, vodka for himself. Audrey was sitting in the armchair across from Calpurnia. Al handed her the scotch and sat on the couch. He set his vodka on the end table next to the framed motto.

"Which one of you wants to go first? Sure you won't change your mind about a drink, Calpurnia?"

"No, thank you." Calpurnia settled back in the chair and crossed her legs.

"As the attorney for both of you, I must remind you that each of you has a right to privacy."

"I suspect we're both here on the same business," said Calpurnia, swinging a sandal-clad foot.

Audrey raised her eyebrows. "I believe I am the one paying Mr. Fox for this appointment."

"He'll double bill us," said Calpurnia.

Al looked from one to the other. Audrey, chewing gum, was wearing black slacks and a bright silk blouse the exact shade of her hair. The top two buttons were open, showing a chunky gold chain necklace and an edge of black lace bra. Calpurnia wore no makeup. Her dark hair set off her pale face. Her eyes were half-closed. She wore beige slacks with a matching short-sleeve sweater, no jewelry. Al had dealt with each of the two women individually, never together.

"I want my husband's estate settled right away, Al," said Audrey. "I don't need to tell you, he's left bills I can't pay until it *is* settled."

"Of course," said Al. "These things take time, Audrey, especially when one is dealing with a sizable estate." He smirked. "And, of course, my dear, there may be one or two technicalities that have to be worked out, you understand. A man named Buddy has contacted me."

Audrey stopped chewing. "I'll need to talk with you privately about Buddy." She started chewing again. "I'm here because Colley Jameson owes my husband's estate almost a million dollars."

Calpurnia took a deep breath and let it out audibly.

"Oh?" said Al. "A million, is it? For what, may I ask?"

"Colley sold shares in the *Enquirer* to Ambler, and now we learn that Colley doesn't own—and never has owned—the newspaper. I want that money back. Nine hundred thousand," Audrey added.

Calpurnia unbuckled her leather purse and removed a business-size envelope with *Island Enquirer* and an Edgartown address printed in the upper left corner. "It's four hundred and fifty thousand, not nine hundred thousand." She handed the envelope to Al, who put on his reading glasses.

After he'd studied the papers for a few minutes he looked over his glasses at Calpurnia. "I'm not sure I understand your role in this. Seems to me this is something Colley has to work out."

"I'd like to know what my husband did with the four hundred and fifty thousand dollars."

"Nine hundred thousand," said Audrey.

Al held the paper up. "Calpurnia is right, according to this. It's a notarized copy of a dated receipt from Colley Jameson to J. Ambler Fieldstone for four hundred fifty thousand, one half of nine hundred thousand, with the remaining four hundred fifty thousand to be paid by Ambler when the stock is handed over." Al looked from Calpurnia to Audrey and back. "There was another consideration that we won't go into."

Calpurnia's pale face flushed.

Al continued. "The stock has not changed hands, of course."

"I haven't been able to find a trace of that money," Calpurnia said.

Al put the paper back in its envelope and handed it to Calpurnia. "Colley didn't consult me on selling stock he didn't own, nor did he take me into his confidence about how he disposed of the money. He claims he's not into drugs."

"He's not," said Calpurnia.

"Nor gambling?"

Calpurnia shook her head. "Not that I'm aware of."

"Women?"

"He has his pick of summer interns and he pays them with bylines." Calpurnia folded her arms across her chest. "Now that he's getting a bit shopworn, he's having to give them bigger bylines."

Al took off his glasses and ran his hand over his toupee. "Damned if I know what he's done with that kind of money."

Audrey sipped her drink. "Four hundred fifty thousand, then. I want that money and I want it now."

"What could he have done with it?" Al murmured. "He tried to borrow money from the trust fund. Tried to borrow money from *me*." He started to say something about blackmail, but stopped.

"What do you plan to do about all this, Al?" Audrey took a last swallow of her drink and set the glass next to the silver-framed motto. "That thing is grotesque."

"A client stitched it. Expensive frame," said Al.

"Hang it in your closet behind your toupees."

Calpurnia got up from her chair. "It sounds as though I need to hire myself a more competent attorney." She turned to Audrey. "Does *my* husband need police protection from *your* husband's goons?"

Audrey snapped her gum before she replied. "I think *your* husband needs protection from himself."

Calpurnia tossed her hair away from her face and stalked out. Al listened to her footsteps on the stairs, across the downstairs hall, and the sharp click of the outer door.

Audrey rattled the ice in her glass.

"May I refresh your drink?" Al asked.

Audrey handed him the glass. "I think I'm going to need it. What about Buddy?"

"Buddy came to see me a couple of days ago. Nice chap." Al returned with the refilled glass.

Audrey took a swallow.

Al went to his desk, opened a drawer, took out a lined yellow legal pad with notes scribbled on it, and returned to the couch. "According to Buddy, you and he were married fourteen years ago in a civil ceremony in Jersey City, New Jersey. Is that right?"

"Sounds about right," said Audrey.

"That was fourteen years ago." Al looked up from the notes. "How long were you married before you divorced Buddy?"

"None of your business," said Audrey.

"But, my dear, it's very much my business. I'm your attorney. Buddy is claiming you and he are still married, that there never was a divorce. Surely he's mistaken?"

"We're not married," said Audrey.

Al sat forward. "Where were you divorced? Do you have any papers proving the divorce? Better think this over, Audrey. You know as well as I do what the consequences are if you're still married to Buddy. Bigamy is the least of your worries. There's a small matter of a very large estate."

Audrey took a gulp of her drink. "Fix it, then, Al."

Al laughed. "A post-dated divorce? Maybe a Mexican divorce?"

"Pay him off."

"He claims he likes the idea of being married to you. Says he's making a good salary as a mechanic and can support you just fine. Nice guy. Doesn't want any part of Fieldstone's millions. Billions, I should say."

"He's playing cutesy. He can be bought." Audrey finished her drink in one long swallow and stood. "Take care of it, will you? And do something about the money Colley owes me."

"Mechanics make good money," said Al. "You won't have to work. I don't think Buddy wants you to work. You're still young enough to start a family."

"Bugger off," said Audrey, and strode out.

Al put the yellow pad back in his top drawer, took the empty glasses to the kitchen behind the reception area, went back to his office, and turned off his desk light.

He was about to turn off the overhead light when he heard footsteps on the stairs again. He looked at his watch, sighed, and opened the door.

CHAPTER 16

The next morning, Martha Jo Amarel found the body. When she arrived early in the morning to finish up some letters, the front door was unlocked. This didn't surprise her, since Mr. Fox was notoriously lax about security and few Islanders even owned keys to their houses. However, ever since she had started working for him, Martha Jo had been attempting to train him in the need for security. This was an attorney's office, after all. She was positive he hadn't arrived at the office yet. That would have been completely out of character.

She hung her sweater on a coat hanger and stowed it in the closet, turned on her computer, and opened the window that faced onto Pease's Point Way. The office seemed stuffier than usual.

The morning breeze wafted the smell of the sea and the scent of roses into her office and Martha Jo set to work happily. She could always get a lot done before Mr. Fox arrived and the telephone started to ring.

After she'd finished typing both letters, addressed the envelopes, stuck on stamps, and tucked the letters under the envelope flaps for Mr. Fox's signature, she looked at her watch. After ten o'clock. She pursed her lips in mild disapproval. A client was scheduled for ten. Fortunately, he—Martha Jo looked at her calendar and corrected herself—*she* hadn't shown up yet. Martha Jo carried the letters to Mr. Fox's office, knocked on his door by habit, opened the door, paused for an instant to absorb what she was seeing, and then screamed.

The client, Mrs. Jameson—Calpurnia Jameson—came into the reception area at that moment.

"What is it?" she said. "What's the matter? What happened?"

Martha Jo stumbled out of Mr. Fox's office and leaned on the doorframe. Her face was paler than usual.

"Are you all right?" Calpurnia seized Martha Jo's arm and shook her. "What is it?"

Martha Jo's eyes rolled up so only the whites showed. She slid down the white-painted doorframe, and collapsed on the floor.

"Oh for God's sake," Calpurnia muttered. She went to the water cooler, removed a paper cup from the dispenser, held it under the spigot, and pressed the button. Bubbles gurgled to the top of the water jug. Calpurnia carried the full cup of water back to Martha Jo and splashed a few drops in her ghastly face.

Martha Jo opened her eyes. "Police," she murmured. "Call the police."

Calpurnia helped Martha Jo to her feet and handed her the cup of water. She then went to the open door of Al Fox's office.

"Good Lord! I might have known," she said, loud enough for Martha Jo to hear, and backed away from the room.

Martha Jo had recovered enough to dial 911. She and Calpurnia waited for the police, Martha Jo behind her desk, Calpurnia in one of the two visitor's chairs. Both had their arms crossed tightly. Neither spoke.

The Edgartown police arrived within a few minutes and the ambulance and EMTs came shortly after.

The officer in charge, a sturdy black woman whose name tag read BARBARA DEMPSEY, came out of Al Fox's office and turned to Ed Prada, who was on duty that morning. "We need the hearse. Call Toby. And call the state police. Better use your cell phone."

"Yes, ma'am," said Ed.

Al Fox's body was lying on its back on his mocha-cream leather couch. The cross-stitched Shakespearean quote in its heavy silver frame was lying on the floor, the glass smashed, the frame bent. Only part of the saying was visible, the part that read, ". . . kill all the lawyers."

Al Fox's head was bare, shiny except where it was cut. The resulting flow of blood had bypassed most of his scalp and run down onto the soft leather of the couch. What had not soaked in had congealed in a sticky-looking puddle.

His face was partially covered by his hairpiece and it became apparent, even before anyone touched the body, that the hairpiece had been stuffed into Al Fox's mouth.

The state police declared the law office a crime scene and ushered Martha Jo and Calpurnia out of the building and into the fresh June morning, where they seated themselves on a park bench in the grassy triangle out front.

"We'll need to ask you a few questions, Martha Jo," the state trooper said. "I guess, Mrs. Jameson, we'll need to talk to you, too."

Calpurnia nodded. "Of course."

Martha Jo said, "Do you suppose I could go back upstairs and get my sweater? I feel a little chilly."

"I'll get it for you, ma'am," the trooper said. "Wait right here, if you don't mind."

While they waited for him to return with Martha Jo's sweater, Calpurnia muttered, "Wonder what the obituary will say this time."

"I beg your pardon?" said Martha Jo, her arms wrapped tightly around her sturdy body.

"Nothing," said Calpurnia.

Before Victoria got the call from Casey reporting Al Fox's apparent murder, she heard from Colley, who sounded almost self-satisfied.

"You said you know who's writing those goddamned obits, Victoria. He's done it again. I've got another goddamned one. Obituary number five. Get here right away, will you?"

Victoria hung up and was about to call Casey to ask for a ride into Edgartown when the phone rang and it was Casey, telling her about Al Fox.

Victoria explained about the latest obituary.

"I'll be right there," Casey said.

Five minutes later, they were on their way to Edgartown, siren wailing. Victoria pulled down the visor so she could see in the mirror how her blue baseball cap looked; when she was satisfied, she moved the visor back up and settled into her seat.

"Five obituaries," said Casey. "There were only two deaths. Three, now. Not five."

"The first was Colley's tie getting caught in the press," said Victoria, counting on her knobby fingers. "Hardly a death, but that was the start of the obituaries. The first had him hanged. The second was Ambler Fieldstone's boating death, and the obituary had Colley attacked by a shark. Candy's death accounted for two obituaries." Victoria stopped talking while Casey passed a slow-moving tractor. Then she continued. "The obituary for her nonfatal shooting said Colley had shot himself. Candy's divinity fudge death was the fourth and the obituary said he'd been poisoned by hospital food."

"Wonder what the killer has come up with this time."

"The killer can't possibly be the obituary writer," Victoria insisted.

"He has to be pretty close to the murder for Colley to get the obit this soon. I heard about Al Fox's murder less than," Casey looked at her watch, "less than fifteen minutes ago."

Traffic was light, but the few cars they overtook had pulled off to the side at the sound of the siren. They were in Edgartown by the time Casey pulled her jacket cuff back over her wristwatch. She slowed at the school zone and turned right at the jail, which had the most beautiful roses on Main Street, tended by inmates.

"I'll drop you off at the paper, then I'm going over to Al Fox's. Don't do anything rash, you hear?" When Casey saw Victoria's expression she added, "They won't let you anywhere near the crime scene. You'd have to wait in the Bronco. You might just as well talk to Colley."

Once inside the building, Victoria nodded to Faith, went through the back door, and climbed the stairs that led to the editorial offices. Only a couple of reporters were at their computers.

Victoria stopped at the door to the morgue. "Where is everyone? It's awfully quiet."

Charity looked up from the files she was sorting. "They're covering Mr. Fox's murder. But Mr. Jameson is waiting for you in his office."

Victoria continued down the aisle between the reporters' desks and stepped into Colley's office.

"What took you so long?" he grumbled. "This guy," he slapped a paper in front of him, "This guy got the obit to me before Fox's body was discovered. He's the killer. And you say you know who he is."

Victoria shifted the chair at right angles to the window and sat down. "I know who wrote the obituaries. He has a serious something against you, and I need to hear from you what that is."

Colley toyed with his beach stone paperweight. "I suppose it's time I went to the police. Save myself some money." He glanced up at Victoria without lifting his head. "You and your so-called assistant are costing me as much as my ex-wives."

"That's your problem, not mine." Victoria settled into her chair. "As you know, I urged you, right from the beginning, to go to the police. However, I've changed my mind. It's not a police matter after all. It's the writer's idea of a joke. What you thought from the beginning." She held out her gnarled hand. "Let's see what he's said this time."

Colley slid an eight-and-a-half-by-eleven-inch sheet folded in thirds across his desk. Victoria picked it up and unfolded it. The message this time was in calligraphy, elegant thick and thin lines and swirls of India ink artistically centered on the page with a border of hand-colored daffodils.

Victoria examined the border and looked up at Colley. "Narcissus," she said. Before she read the message, she turned the letter over, examined the back, then held it up to the light. "You know what kind of paper this is, don't you?"

"Twenty-four-pound white bond," said Colley. "High rag content. I suppose you think you've found a clue."

"The writer is out-and-out telling you who he is."

Colley folded his arms over his chest and gazed out of his window.

"This is different from the others," Victoria said. "When did it arrive?"

Colley continued to stare out of the window. "In this morning's mail."

"Was there a postmark?"

"Buzzards Bay."

"That's where all our letters go if we forget to put them in the 'Island only' mailboxes."

"For God's sake, Victoria. Everyone knows that."

Victoria continued. "From Edgartown, letters go to the steamship dock in Vineyard Haven. From Vineyard Haven they go by ferry to the mainland, where a truck carries them to Buzzards Bay to get postmarked."

Colley sighed.

Victoria continued. "Once they get stamped with 'Buzzards Bay' another truck carries them back to the ferry, the mail returns to the Island, and a mail carrier takes them right back to the same post office in Edgartown—the only post office in Edgartown—where they were mailed in the first place and where the recipient has a post office box."

"Thanks for telling me, Victoria. I've only lived on this Island for five years."

"In other words," Victoria tapped the letter with a knobby finger, "this was mailed at least two days ago."

"Okay, then. Before Al Fox was killed. Which proves conclusively that the killer and obit writer are one and the same."

Victoria read from the letter, which was centered like a formal wedding announcement. "Viewing hours for the late Colley Jameson, editor and publisher of the *Island Enquirer*, who drowned in Uncle Seth's Pond, are from ten o'clock AM until two o'clock PM . . ."

"You don't need to read it out loud," said Colley.

". . . and from seven o'clock PM until nine o'clock PM at the Rose Haven Funeral Parlor on Friday and Saturday."

Colley sighed again.

Victoria continued. "In lieu of gifts to charity, viewers may bring a daffodil bulb to plant at the edge of the pond as a memorial." Victoria laughed and handed the letter back to Colley.

Colley thumped the beach stone on his papers. "It's not the least bit funny. It's not clever. It's stupid."

"You do know the myth about Echo and Narcissus?"

"What's that supposed to mean?"

"No matter," said Victoria. "Tell me about your wives."

Colley sat up straight. "Where did that come from? What do my wives have to do with anything?"

"From what I understand, your first wife was your college sweetheart. Where is she now?"

"You're wasting my time, Victoria."

"Bear with me."

Colley fiddled with the stone. "She married a petroleum geologist six or seven years ago. She and her husband live in Bartlesville, Oklahoma."

"Do they ever come to the Island?"

Colley shook his head. "Not that I'm aware of."

"You're not paying her alimony, are you? Or child support?"

"Where's this leading? Of course, I'm not paying her alimony or child support. We didn't have children."

"Candy Keene was your second wife, right?"

Colley nodded. "Silly woman."

"I assume you're no longer making payments. To an heir? Child support?"

Colley turned his back to the desk.

"Are you?"

"Certainly not."

"What about your third and fourth wives? I know Calpurnia is your fifth. I don't know anything about the other two."

"My fourth ex lives in Majorca on a handsome monthly stipend Al Fox extorted from me, and that he delivers to her. In person."

"Delivered," said Victoria. She glanced up from the notes she had been writing. "I should think you might have learned after two or three wives that you're not cut out for marriage."

Colley looked offended. "*They* left *me*. I didn't leave them. Except for the first one. I should never have divorced her." He swiveled his chair. "That second marriage was a mistake. Stripper. Artiste. What a phony. Sat around all day in her negligee popping candy into her fat face."

"You won't need to worry about her any longer. Any children with the third and fourth wives?"

Colley stood up and looked out of the window. "This is getting nowhere, Victoria. If you know the obit writer, come out with it."

"I have to be sure, Colley. I don't want to give you the wrong name and have you riding off in all directions."

"Just give me the name and I'll handle it."

"That's what I'm afraid of. We can go to the police, if you want, but if we do, you'll be sorry."

Colley sat down again.

Victoria looked at her notes. "You skipped your third wife. Where does she live? And you'll need to answer me. Any children?"

Colley sighed. "The third ex is from the Vineyard. She married a guy she went to high school with. They live here in Edgartown with her daughter."

"*Her* daughter, Colley? Or hers and yours?"

Colley said nothing.

"We may be able to deal with this quietly, but not if you're going to keep things from me."

"Not my daughter," Colley said finally. "She was pregnant when she left me. The baby wasn't mine. I never wanted a kid. The kid was some other guy's." He picked up a letter opener and shifted it from one hand to the other. "She swore she'd never slept with another man while we were married."

"So you had an argument. She claimed she'd been faithful, you claimed she hadn't been. And she packed up and left?"

Colley said nothing.

Victoria sat for a long while. She looked down at her knobby fingers. She smoothed her worn corduroy trousers. She finally looked up at Colley.

"She's now Tom Dwyer's wife, isn't she?"

Colley said nothing.

"The girl *is* your daughter. You must know that every time you pass her in the street and see her eyes and her build and the way she walks."

Colley turned his chair away from Victoria.

"How do you deal with your daughter, Colley, pretend she doesn't exist? Ignore her when you see her? Cross to the other side of the street?" Victoria's voice was getting lower and firmer. "How can you look at yourself in the mirror?"

Colley still said nothing.

"I suppose you never paid child support, did you? Even when you must have become convinced you were wrong. Or are you never wrong?"

"Now they're trying to extort college tuition out of me," Colley muttered, turning back to face Victoria. "When she left me, I offered her child support, even though the kid wasn't mine."

"She *was* yours. *Is* yours."

"Al Fox wrote up an agreement," said Colley, "but the ex refused to sign it."

"I can imagine what sort of humiliating caveats you and Al

Fox cooked up between you." Victoria got to her feet. "I'll send you my final bill."

Colley tossed the letter opener onto his desk and stood too. "Who wrote the obits?"

"That's the last letter or obituary you'll get from him." Victoria pointed to the letter. "That paper is not only twenty-four-pound white bond with a high rag content, but if you'll look at the watermark it says 'Plover Bond.'"

Colley sat again. "Cute. Real cute. I should have guessed. That hack writer Dwyer and his vendetta against me. Goddamned fishermen, all of them. Wrecking the Island for the rest of us."

"I went fishing with Mr. Dwyer," Victoria said stiffly. "I caught five blues, and his books are excellent."

Chapter 17

Casey had parked in front of the *Enquirer* and was doing paperwork when Victoria came out of the newspaper office.

"That was the final obituary," Victoria said with assurance as she got into the Bronco.

"I hope you're right." Casey turned onto Cooke Street. Every white-painted, black-trimmed house had a neatly maintained picket fence in front, and every picket fence was still swathed in roses.

Victoria took a deep breath and let it out slowly. When she was a girl, the houses in Edgartown were shabby, except for the captains' houses on North Water Street. The streets had been paved with crushed scallop shells. She could remember the sound of the crushed shells beneath horses' hooves as they trotted down to the wharf with a wagon rumbling along behind. Chicory and bouncing bet had lined the streets, not roses. Except for the wild beach roses and the pink ramblers, which tumbled in profusion over her grandfather's barn, only wealthy people grew roses. Not many wealthy people lived in Edgartown then.

"Who wrote the obits, Victoria? Have you told Colley yet?"

Victoria inhaled the sweet-scented air and let her breath out again. "It was an unfunny practical joke, and the joker knows it now."

"Most practical jokes are not funny. Who was it?"

"Tom Dwyer."

"The mystery writer? Your fishing buddy? You're not serious, are you?"

Victoria nodded.

"His piping plover recipe sure got tongues wagging. Why the obits?"

"Ever since Colley wrote those reviews of Tom's latest two books, Tom has had writer's block. I think the obituaries were a way for Tom to get over the block and get even at the same time."

"Creative types are weird." Casey shook her head.

"But I think there's a stronger reason. You know who Tom Dwyer's wife is, don't you?"

"Phyl something. I don't know her."

"Phyllis Jameson."

"Oh yeah? Any relation to Colley?"

"Phyllis Dwyer is Colley's third ex-wife." Victoria braced herself against the console.

Casey pulled back onto the blacktop. "No kidding!"

"Tom Dwyer and Phyllis were high school classmates here on the Vineyard. They both went off Island to college and after she graduated from Columbia Journalism School, she met Colley, who was wifeless at the time."

"Oh yeah? Go on."

"A year into the marriage Phyllis became pregnant."

"Didn't think Colley had it in him."

"Colley didn't think so either. I understand they had a scene in which he accused her of infidelity."

"He should talk."

Victoria nodded. "Phyllis got a divorce, moved back to the Island, and after the baby was born, married Tom."

A hay truck turned onto the road and Casey slowed. Bits of hay flew up into the air, swirled in the truck's wake, and patted against the Bronco's windshield.

"Wonderful smell," said Victoria, sniffing the air.

Casey sneezed. "Apparently that wasn't the end of the story?" She sneezed again. "I gotta pass this guy."

"Phyllis asked for child support, but Colley attached so many strings, she refused to sign the papers Al Fox had drawn up."

The stripe in the middle of the road went from solid to dashed and Casey pulled around the hay truck. Victoria waved.

"Who's that?" asked Casey.

"Ira Bodman. He lives in West Tisbury." She looked thoughtfully at Casey. "He's single. His wife left him. He has a daughter about the same age as your son."

"No thanks, Victoria." Casey eased back into the right lane in front of the truck. "Keep talking."

"Colley's daughter Lynn, Tom Dwyer's stepdaughter, will be a senior at Hyannis Academy this fall. Tom approached Colley for help with college tuition and Colley refused."

"Doesn't Colley's family have money?"

"Colley himself doesn't. His father set up a trust fund, but Colley can't touch the principal. After Colley's death, the newspaper gets half of the money and his children split up the other half."

"What about his wife?"

"The surviving wife gets half if there are no children. Otherwise, she gets a nice enough allowance."

"How much is in the fund?"

"Around eight or nine million dollars."

Casey whistled. "Not bad. Colley's daughter gets four million. Does Calpurnia know about the daughter?"

"I have no idea. I don't imagine so. Colley never has admitted he has a daughter."

They had reached the eastern edge of the State Forest. Acres of tall red pine snags stood out against the sky, skeletal branches contrasting with the new growth of scrub oak and jack pine below.

"Pretty, those silvery trunks," said Victoria, looking out at the dead red pines.

"They're a fire hazard," said Casey. "One of these dry summers we're going to have a big problem."

Sunday was the Fourth of July. The West Tisbury Fire Department held a cookout at the New Ag Hall in the afternoon. Anthony Rebello, the tall, bulky, black-bearded fire chief, seated Victoria at a round table under an umbrella, where she held court.

Villagers milled around the smoky grills. Volunteer firefighters served up hot dogs and hamburgers and, paper plates in hand, the villagers moved on to tables piled with lobsters and ears of corn and roasted potatoes and salads and coleslaw. A knot of people hung around the beer keg, waiting until the pressure was pumped up enough to tease out more beer and less foam. Children and dogs ran around, getting underfoot, getting lost, getting into fights, crying or barking.

Grandchildren and great-grandchildren of Victoria's schoolmates brought her plates of coleslaw and salad, ears of corn, oysters on the half-shell, bowls of steamed clams and mussels, a lobster, a slice of watermelon, chocolate cake, Toll House cookies, brownies. Victoria ate all she could and surreptitiously fed what she couldn't eat to John Milton, who had come to the picnic with William Botts and settled himself at Victoria's feet.

Victoria held out until after the fireworks and then her eyes started to close. She awoke with a start and a small snort. Anthony offered her his arm and escorted her to Elizabeth's battered convertible, which was parked in front of the hall. Elizabeth drove home with the top down and Victoria watched distant fireworks over Edgartown to the east and Oak Bluffs to the north.

"I won't need to eat for a week," said Elizabeth, once she'd parked under the Norway maple and put the duct-tape-mended top back up. She patted her stomach.

Victoria sighed. "Another grand Fourth. I hope Colley's all right."

Victoria slept late the next morning and awakened to the smell of coffee and rum-raisin muffins. She dressed hurriedly in her gray corduroy trousers and a turtleneck shirt printed with small rosebuds.

"Morning, Gram. It's supposed to be hot today. You'll be too warm in that outfit."

"I don't pay attention to weather reports." Victoria helped herself to her usual shredded wheat with sliced banana, then looked up at her granddaughter. "You may need a sweater later."

Elizabeth laughed. "Want me to drop you off at the *Grackle* on my way to work? The harbor's crazy busy this whole week."

"Thank you."

After they'd washed the dishes and cleaned the kitchen, Elizabeth drove her grandmother to the *Grackle* office. Victoria waved good-bye and climbed the stairs to the loft. Botts was hunched over his Underwood. He looked up, the bags underneath his eyes more pronounced than ever.

"One hundred and fifty-two subscriptions now. My wife hasn't been able to use the phone for her own calls."

"I thought you got an answering machine."

"Yes, but no sooner does one person hang up than another would-be subscriber gets on the line."

Victoria patted John Milton, who wagged his tail and looked up with eyes less baggy than Botts's. "Wonderful!"

"I don't *want* to publish a big city daily, Victoria. I keep telling you I don't *want* to compete with the *Enquirer*. I liked what I had before. One page of West Tisbury news. Printed on the library copier. Subscribers I knew. Nice small-town stuff."

Victoria shook out the bright serape that covered the easy chair's bare spring, put it back on the chair, and sat down. "You can't halt progress."

"I don't call this progress. Now I have a hundred and fifty-two subscribers and a staff of four to worry about."

"Four?"

Botts nodded. "Matt Pease joined us."

"Good."

"He's a photographer, not a writer. That means we have to run pictures. We're going from four pages to eight this week." Botts sighed and tapped his pencil on his desk. "This is not what I want out of life, Victoria."

"That reminds me, Matt has some photographs he wants me to see."

"Photographs? Of what?"

"He didn't say." Victoria made a note to herself. "The subscriptions will cover staff salaries, now that I'm no longer on retainer to Colley."

"That's another thing. With Colley's money dried up, subscriptions won't cover our costs. I'll have to accept ads. Which means I have to get someone to sell ads."

"Good."

"Not good, Victoria. Where am I going to put all these staff people?" Botts gestured around the loft. His desk was in the middle of the floor. The trap door through which he raised and lowered John Milton's basket was immediately behind his desk. On either side of his desk, the roof sloped down toward the floor, meeting it at a sharp angle. Light streamed through the big, open hay window at the back of the loft. In the one small space where another desk conceivably could be squeezed, a black area on the roof boards and a matching area on the floor beneath indicated a serious leak.

"The library copier can't handle the new eight-page format, nor can it handle the volume I now have to print, so I've had to work out a deal with Tisbury Printer."

"They'll advertise."

"They've already agreed. Their ad is running this week." Botts flipped his pencil onto a pile of papers on his desk. "I don't have a spare moment to write."

"You need a business manager."

Botts groaned. John Milton looked up and thumped his tail. The telephone rang and Botts answered. His entire end of the conversation was a series of grunts.

He hung up the phone with a decisive slap. "According to my wife, we're now up to two hundred and three subscribers."

Victoria scribbled something else. "You'll need to raise subscription rates. We'll do more promotion. Perhaps an ad in the *Enquirer*. That would show Colley."

"No," said Botts. "No, no."

The phone rang again. After a conversation that Victoria didn't try to follow, Botts told the caller how to get to the *Grackle* office. "I'll be here all afternoon, I'm afraid." He hung up and folded his arms on his desk.

"Who was that?" Victoria asked.

"Two more job applicants. The high school kids."

"Tiffany and Wendy?"

Botts nodded.

"So they decided not to work for the *Enquirer* after all."

Botts tugged off his glasses, polished them, and put them back on. "I'm too old for this, Victoria."

"I think Wendy, the blond-haired girl, is interested in advertising. I'm sure Tiffany would like experience in the business end."

"High school kids?"

Victoria looked up from her notebook. "You know, don't you, that age discrimination applies to everyone?"

"How do you expect me to pay them, Madam Reporter?"

"The girls will work for room and board. They want the experience. Colley was foolish not to hire them."

"And just where are you going to find a place for them to live on Martha's Vineyard in the height of the season?"

"They can stay at my house," said Victoria. "I've got plenty of room."

Botts leaned back in his chair, his hands behind his head, and looked up at the slanted boards of the roof. "And what will we use for office space? There's no room here."

"I'll think of something," said Victoria. "If you need a break, why don't we drive up to Menemsha now and examine Fieldstone's boat?"

"I have to wait for my new staff members."

John Milton got unsteadily to his feet and put a large black paw on Botts's knee.

Botts patted the dog and stood. "Come on, boy."

John Milton climbed into his basket, which Botts then lowered to the barn's ground floor, where the stalls still smelled of hay and horses.

"Of course!" said Victoria.

"'Of course' what?"

"The horse stalls would make ideal office space."

"You're talking money we don't have." Botts stopped. "Money *I* don't have."

"Nonsense. All we need is a broom and dustpan. The barn has great character. Wendy and Tiffany can clean the stalls, and we can find furniture at the dump."

"When can we start?" Tiffany said.

"Six staff members," Botts muttered. "Six."

The girls were sitting on the loft floor with their backs angled to accommodate the slope of the roof.

Wendy said, "You know, I bet, like, Lynn would love to work here. I mean, this place is awesome."

"Lynn?" said Botts.

"She lives on the Island," said Tiffany. "She's in our class at Hyannis Academy."

"Lynn?" said Victoria.

"Lynn Dwyer. You must know her, Mrs. Trumbull. Her dad, like, writes mysteries."

"Lynn Dwyer." Victoria repeated.

Wendy nodded. "She says everybody knows her dad. He's a fisherman *and* a mystery writer."

"Well," said Botts. "Well, well."

"Seven is a lucky number," said Victoria.

Chapter 18

Victoria and Botts left the girls to clean the horse stalls with push brooms, trash can, window cleaner, and a heap of rags, and headed to Menemsha.

They passed Chowder Kettle Lane and continued on to the small fishing village.

"Have you eaten yet?" Botts asked.

Victoria shook her head.

"Neither have I. After lunch I'll go up to the Coast Guard Station while you check Fieldstone's boat."

They stopped at the small shack, newly opened for the season, that advertised the best quahog chowder on the Island and Botts went in to order. Victoria sat outside at a picnic table.

The air smelled of honeysuckle, wild roses, and the ocean. A slight sea must have been running because Victoria heard the bell buoy on the other side of the jetty. Bees worked the honeysuckle on the fence behind her. She unzipped her sweater.

Botts came out of the restaurant with two containers of chowder and packets of oyster crackers. They ate while the bees hummed, gulls mewed, and the buoy chimed.

Botts finished his chowder first. He folded the cardboard soup container in on itself and tossed it into the trash receptacle. "I'll get a copy of the accident report, Victoria. I'm not sure what you'll be able to tell from looking at the boat."

"I'm not either," Victoria admitted. After she'd scraped out the last morsels of clams and potatoes from her own container they drove over to the boat launching ramp, a short distance from the galley shack. *S'Putter* was high off the ground on wooden cradles.

"I shouldn't be more than three-quarters of an hour," Botts said when he dropped Victoria off.

"I don't mind waiting."

Victoria leaned on her stick and watched until the truck was out of sight. Then she walked around the boat, watching where she put her feet on the uneven ground. The bow faced in, pointing up toward the red-roofed Coast Guard Station on the hill overlooking Menemsha Basin.

The air was full of seagulls, swooping at fish in the tidal waters that raced through the inlet into Menemsha Pond. Victoria stopped, shaded her eyes with a hand, and looked up. A steep ladder leaned against the port side of the boat. She stepped back to get a better overall view and still had to crane her neck to see the top of the boat's tuna tower, where the lookout could watch for fish. The view of the water from there must have been spectacular. She was no great judge of height, but the tower must have been at least twenty feet above the waterline.

Victoria had sudden misgivings. Who was she to think she could find something on or around the boat that the Coast Guard had missed? The Coast Guard was trained to do this sort of work. She wasn't.

But the Coast Guard investigators had seemed so young. The lieutenant in charge was no older than Elizabeth, her granddaughter, and his helpers seemed like high school children playing dress-up in their trim uniforms.

She might, after all, have an edge of experience they lacked. Victoria turned back to the boat.

She examined the ladder that leaned against the side of *S'Putter*. The rungs seemed far apart. She held the sides, put one foot on the bottom rung, and looked up. The ladder was shaky. She set her foot back on the ground.

She walked slowly to the boat's stern. The blades of the twin propellers were twisted, as she'd heard they were, and the starboard shaft was bent slightly. What had she expected to see?

Beach grass rustled against the hull of an overturned dinghy that lay in the sand next to the cradled boat. Behind the dinghy Victoria saw a beach plum bush with a great quantity of small green plums. She must remember to return in October, when the plums ripened, and pick them for jelly. She brushed dried seaweed from the hull of the dinghy and sat down to think.

The Coast Guard had concluded that Fieldstone had fallen off the bow, had been swept under the boat, and been sliced by the propellers. The Coast Guard was forever warning boaters against bow riding for this very reason.

Victoria drew circles in the sand with her stick while she thought. The boat's engines must have been engaged and the boat moving forward. Why would Fieldstone leave the wheel with the boat moving like that? He was an experienced boater and would probably have disengaged the engines before he went forward. Victoria shook her head. There was no way he could have fallen accidentally. Certainly not over the bow. Had someone pushed him?

Victoria rose from her seat on the overturned dinghy and continued to study Fieldstone's boat. She could see faint marks along the smooth finish on the starboard side. Possibly marks from another boat's fender?

She moved toward the bow and looked up again, half-closing her eyes. She could imagine Fieldstone facing someone, perhaps arguing with him. She could picture that person shoving Fieldstone and Fieldstone toppling over the bow pulpit.

She made a sketch in her notebook. In the seconds after Fieldstone went overboard, he'd have tried to twist to avoid the propellers. Instead of hitting his head, the props cut across his spine. Victoria shuddered. He must have died quickly. Even the most hardened killer would have been appalled at the slaughter that resulted.

She was still thinking when Botts returned and parked his pickup next to the *S'Putter*.

"I've got a copy of the accident report," he said. "We can go over it on the way back to West Tisbury. Did you learn anything?"

Victoria showed him her sketch of the stick man toppling into the water. "You can see how his backbone must have met the propellers."

Botts studied Victoria's sketch. "Not pretty."

Victoria put her notebook back into her cloth bag. "Someone killed him. No question about it."

"The Coast Guard is calling his death an accident."

"The Coast Guard is wrong," said Victoria. "He would never have gone up to the bow with the engines engaged. Unless, of course, there was someone else running the boat."

Botts folded his arms over his chest. "That's a grisly way to kill someone."

"The killer may not have planned to kill him that way. Once Fieldstone went overboard, his chances of swimming to either Nantucket or the Vineyard were slim. The water in June is still too cold for long immersion."

Botts nodded. "Do you want to check anything topside?"

Victoria gazed up at the deck and the steep ladder.

"If you tell me what you're looking for, I'll climb up," Botts said.

Victoria hesitated. "I think I know enough. Did the Coast Guard check for fingerprints?"

"I doubt it," said Botts.

"Then I'll ask Casey to check."

"She won't like that. Menemsha is not her town, and murder belongs to the state cops."

"We'll see." Victoria got back into the truck. "Now we have to figure out how the murderer got onto Fieldstone's boat and how he enticed him up to the bow."

When Victoria and Botts returned to the *Grackle*'s barn, John Milton was lying in the warm sun in front of the open barn door and the transformation from stable to office was almost complete. The windows, swung open and cleared of cobwebs, let in a flood of light and sweet air. The rough wood sidings of the stalls had been brushed. The concrete floors were swept and scrubbed. Wendy was on her knees with a bucket of brick-red paint and a sponge.

"What the hell are you doing?" said Botts, scowling.

Wendy looked up and grinned. "I'm painting the floor." She held up the sponge. "See? I'm, like, making it look like bricks. Watch." She dipped the sponge lightly in the paint bucket, then carefully stamped another brick on the concrete.

"Matt Pease is picking up school desks and chairs in the old airport buildings. The dumpmaster said we can have them if we haul them away."

Botts growled and turned away from the workers.

Wendy paused in her brick-printing. "I just remembered, Mrs. Trumbull. Matt's got pictures he wants you to see."

Botts stomped off toward the stairs that led to the loft. John Milton got to his feet, scratched behind an ear with a back paw, looked up mournfully as the boss disappeared into the loft, and hobbled over to the back of the barn. Victoria heard the squeal of the pulley that raised his basket.

"Mr. Botts isn't mad, is he?" Tiffany asked. "We didn't spend any money."

"He's just being a typical man," said Victoria.

Tiffany rolled her eyes. "We know all about that."

Victoria looked around at the tidy stalls. "You're doing a better job than I could have imagined. There's enough working room for Mr. Botts and all six of his staff members."

"Six?" said Wendy. "He hired Lynn?"

"I'm sure he will," said Victoria.

"Awesome!" said Tiffany.

When Matt returned from the dump, Victoria watched him set up the desks and chairs he'd scrounged. When he finished, she asked about the pictures.

"You knew that Katie Bowen covered the story of the half-body washing up at Wasque?" Matt saw Victoria's expression and added quickly, "You, of course, found the half that could be identified."

Victoria nodded.

"Katie thought I ought to show you these photos." He laid the pictures of the two women in the Chris-Craft on one of the new-old desks and Victoria pulled up a chair and sat down. Matt handed his magnifying lens to her.

Victoria studied the photos. "When did you take these?"

Matt pointed to the picture of the two women in the runabout. "That one was taken about two weeks ago, about five days before the funeral."

"Several days before we found Fieldstone's body."

"The Chris-Craft photos were on the beginning of the roll." Matt scratched behind his ear. "After I saw the boat—an antique, incredibly beautiful—I wanted to know more about her, maybe do a story on who owned her, where they got her, maintenance, that sort of thing."

Victoria continued to study the photos while Matt talked.

"Domingo, the Oak Bluffs harbormaster?"

Victoria smiled.

"Domingo said he'd seen the boat around. He thought the owner was a woman and that the boat was kept in Vineyard Haven. The Vineyard Haven harbormaster told me the Chris belongs to Mrs. Fieldstone, who keeps the boat at Maciel Marine."

"And you talked to Maciel?"

"Bob Maciel takes care of the Chris, treats it like his own boat. Tunes up the engine, polishes the copper tubing. Goes over the brightwork with a chamois after Mrs. Fieldstone takes it out."

Victoria leaned forward, elbows on the desk. "Does she use the boat much?"

"A couple of time a week during the summer, according to Bob. Takes out houseguests. Wants to show off the boat, you know. She's a pretty good skipper, he says, not afraid of anything." Matt slipped the photo to the bottom of the pile. "And this one," he said, pulling out the photo of Audrey raising her hand to Calpurnia, "was taken the day before the funeral. Not exactly a friendly greeting."

Victoria drummed her fingers on the desktop, pursed her lips, looked off into the distance, then got to her feet, bracing her hands on the desk. "Do you know if the *Enquirer* is open today?"

"It's closed. Colley's given everyone the day off because the Fourth was on a Sunday."

"I've got to talk to him."

"I'll take you first thing tomorrow, if you want."

Victoria picked up her stick. "I'd better ask William to take me. But thank you."

"Sure thing," said Matt.

Oddly enough, no one in town seemed to have picked up on the resemblance between Lynn Dwyer and Colley Jameson. But then, she'd been away at boarding school since seventh grade, home only on weekends when no one was around, and summers when the Island was crowded with summer people.

Both her mother and Tom had discouraged her from applying for a job at the *Enquirer,* so when Tiffany and Wendy, her classmates, told her the *Grackle* was looking for summer interns, she decided to apply for a writing job there. She took the bus to West Tisbury and walked from Alley's, where the bus left her off, to the *Grackle* office.

Wendy bounced out to greet her. "What do you think?"

Lynn grinned and sunlight glinted off her braces. "Awesome!"

"Come up to the loft and meet Mr. Botts. He's, like, editor and publisher. He's dying to meet you," said Wendy.

"Do you think he'd let me, you know, write?"

"Ask him. We told him you're a dynamite writer, just like your dad. He'll hire you. He needs a writer."

Lynn followed Wendy up the steps to the loft and there, facing her, was a gnomelike man with white tufts of eyebrows, a pencil behind his ear, and a serious scowl on his leathery face, hunched over an antique typewriter exactly like the one her father used.

"Mr. Botts," said Wendy, "this is Lynn."

Botts snatched off his glasses. "You're Dwyer's girl?"

"Yes, sir," said Lynn.

"Can you write?"

"Yes, sir," said Lynn.

The dog on the floor next to Botts opened his eyes and thumped his tail.

"I can't pay you."

"That's okay, Mr. Botts."

"Have you published anything?"

"Yes, sir." Lynn handed him her scrapbook of clippings from the *Hyannis Academy Scroll*.

Botts put his glasses on and turned back to his typewriter. "You'll have to talk to the personnel department," he muttered. "Mrs. Trumbull."

CHAPTER 19

The next morning was the sort of rare day Islanders call "typical Vineyard weather." The sky was a brilliant clear blue with puffy summer clouds. The humidity was low, the temperature in the high sixties. Victoria, wearing a clean pair of corduroy trousers and a worn-thin sweatshirt with ALICE ROCK emblazoned in faded letters, was waiting on the steps when Botts pulled up.

"I gather you saw something in Matt's photos," he said, helping her into the passenger seat.

"I'm not sure what I saw. I know I need to talk to Colley." She was quiet until they passed the youth hostel. "I can think of one theory that fits all three killings," she said.

"Oh?" said Botts.

Victoria rolled her window down partway. "Calpurnia expected Ambler Fieldstone to leave his wife for her. When she learned that Colley had set her up with Ambler as if she were a call girl, Calpurnia was humiliated and outraged." She glanced at Botts who was watching a slow-moving car ahead of them. "Enough to kill, I think."

Botts said nothing.

They were almost at Willow Tree Hollow before Victoria spoke again. "Have you seen the photos?"

Botts shook his head. "I heard Colley is desperate to get hold of them."

"The photos show Audrey and Calpurnia together on Audrey's boat, possibly the day Ambler Fieldstone was run over. Colley wants the pictures for blackmail. I'm convinced of that."

"Against his own wife?"

"Against Calpurnia *and* Audrey. All Colley needs to do is show those pictures to the authorities to reopen the investigation. We know Colley needs money for some reason. Quite a large amount."

"And you think he'll get that by exposing his wife as the killer and getting Audrey to pay? I don't think so, Victoria."

Victoria was quiet again until they reached the airport entrance. "What about this: With Fieldstone dead, Audrey inherits a fortune and Calpurnia gets her revenge. They both benefit. Suppose they got together to kill him. Both women know how to run power boats."

Botts shook his head. "That might explain the women together in Audrey's boat, but the photo is no secret. Matt's showed it to several people. Colley can hardly say, 'Give me two- or three-hundred thousand dollars, and I'll give you the photo.' "

The car ahead of them signaled for a left turn onto Airport Road and they were able to speed up.

"Furthermore," Botts continued, "I don't think the deaths of Candy and Al Fox fit your theory."

"But they do," said Victoria. "You knew, didn't you, that Candy flew to Nantucket to meet with Ambler the day he was killed? She may have learned, or guessed, that Calpurnia and Audrey met up with him . . ." She stopped.

"Go on," said Botts.

"It's an awfully gruesome way to kill someone," said Victoria. "Even someone you loathe."

"How do you figure the Candy and Al Fox killings?" he asked when he was back up to speed. "Who lured Candy into the field and shot her? Was it Calpurnia or Audrey? Surely not both of them. Which one sent her the cyanide divinity fudge?" Botts laughed. "And why would either of them kill their lawyer?"

Victoria turned toward him. "What's so amusing?"

"The murder weapon. The framed Shakespeare quote about killing all the lawyers."

Victoria drummed her fingers on the arm rest. "Every lawyer in the world has that quote hanging in his or her office. Candy undoubtedly told Al Fox she was suspicious of one or both of the women. One of them convinced Candy that she should be out in that field the day the boy and his father were shooting. Candy complained to Casey about the shooting practice so close to her."

They swooped into Quampache, one of the glacial drainage channels that marked the halfway point between West Tisbury and Edgartown. Victoria's grandfather had always pronounced the valley's name "Quam'-pa-chee." But Leonard Vanderhoop, a Wampanoag from Gay Head, told Victoria at the senior center that the Indian pronounciation accented the second syllable, so Victoria adopted the new, to her, pronounciation.

"You think Calpurnia shot Candy?"

"It seems likely. Calpurnia knows enough about guns to aim and pull the trigger. Since the shots didn't kill her, her aim wasn't great. Candy would never have suspected Calpurnia."

"Tell me this, Victoria. What does Calpurnia say when she calls Candy—'I want to meet you in the field behind your house where the boy and his father are shooting to show you a new dress I just bought'?"

"You needn't be sarcastic."

"I suppose the poisoned divinity was easy enough. 'From an admirer.' That would be enough for Candy, I'm sure. Anyone might have sent that to her."

A flock of wild turkeys started across the road and Botts stopped until they reached the other side.

"You're going to ask me why Calpurnia would have killed Al Fox, aren't you?"

Botts smiled.

"Candy probably told Al Fox that she believed the two women had killed Fieldstone. Knowing Al Fox, he probably told Calpurnia."

"You think all this leads up to Colley being the next victim. He hasn't been threatened, as far as we know."

"Calpurnia wouldn't threaten, she would act. Once she's killed three people, Ambler Fieldstone, Candy, and Al Fox, she has nothing to lose. By killing Colley, she'll have completed her revenge and will inherit, she thinks, close to four million dollars."

"Does Calpurnia know about Colley's daughter?"

Victoria sat up straight. "We need to warn Colley, and we need to warn Lynn's mother and stepfather."

"The whole scenario sounds far-fetched to me."

"Can you think of another explanation?"

"Not at the moment. If you're convinced that Calpurnia is the killer, you need to talk to the state police. I'll take you there, if you'd like."

"They'll need proof, and I don't have proof. I'll have to talk to Colley first."

They didn't talk about the murders after that. Botts turned right onto Main Street, right again onto South Summer Street, and dropped Victoria off in front of the *Enquirer*.

A few roses still bloomed along the picket fence, but rose season had passed and now the small garden in front of the newspaper office was filled with newly planted bright annuals, blue ageratum, red salvia, yellow marigolds.

Down the aisle between the reporters' desks, in the editor's office, Colley was on the phone with his back to the door, his feet on the windowsill. He swiveled around, scowled, and put his hand over the mouthpiece. "I'm on the phone, Victoria." Turning back to the window, he continued his conversation.

Victoria knew he expected her to leave. Instead, she sat in her usual chair and heard him say, ". . . I'll have the balance when I arrive."

"Colley, I must talk to you. Right now."

Colley looked up at her again and his scowl faded slightly. He said into the phone, "I'll call you back. Give me your number again." He jotted the number on a notepad and hung up.

Victoria moved the visitor's chair and sat down.

"What the hell is bugging you now, Victoria?"

"I've changed my mind about the murders."

"Bravo," said Colley. "A first."

Victoria leaned forward. "I told you I thought the killings were over. I believe, now, that they've been leading up to at least one more death, possibly two."

Colley laughed. "Let me guess. You think I'm the target. You're here to warn me."

"It's not amusing, Colley."

"Come, now, Victoria. You're being ridiculous. Tom Dwyer doesn't have the guts to kill me."

"I've told you repeatedly, he's not the killer."

"You're not getting senile, are you, Victoria?"

Victoria flushed. "You're the common element in all three murders." She tapped her gnarled forefinger on his desk. "You've got to listen to me."

"I certainly *don't* have to listen to you." Colley leaned back in his chair. "Fieldstone's death has been declared an accident. No question."

Victoria shook her head.

"Granted, both Candy and Al Fox were killed. But I'm the logical suspect in both of those, don't you agree?" He patted his chest, straightened his tie, and smiled. "One less alimony payment to make and a new and better lawyer."

"This is not a joking matter, Colley. You've made a number of enemies."

Colley waved his hand dismissively. "You did what I asked you to do, Victoria, and at a usurious price. You identified Dwyer as the sick character who was writing those obits. Thank you. Leave the murders alone, will you?" He sat forward again. "The police don't need some interfering old lady bothering them." He stood. "I have to get back to that phone call. I appreciate your concern. I'll accompany you to the door."

"Don't bother." Victoria stood up, went out of the office, and strode between the rows of reporter's desks, looking straight ahead, eyes glittering. As she went down the stairs, she held the rail firmly. She stopped at the reception desk.

Faith looked up. "Do you need something, Mrs. Trumbull?"

"You keep Colley's schedule, don't you?"

"When he remembers to tell me his appointments, yes."

Victoria leaned on her stick. "Do you know if he's planning an off Island trip sometime soon?"

Faith paged through her desk calendar. "He's going on vacation at the end of September. Three weeks. Things slow down then."

Victoria acted casual. "I suppose he's going to Vermont to view the leaves?"

"He's going to miss the New England fall colors. He's heading for Arizona."

"That's a lovely state," said Victoria. "One of my grandnephews goes to school in Phoenix. Will Colley be near there?"

Faith shook her head. "He gave me a phone number, but I don't know where he's staying."

"My grandnephew would love to meet him, if Colley's nearby."

"Would you like the phone number?" Faith riffled through some papers on her desk.

"May I?"

"I don't know why not, Mrs. Trumbull." Faith wrote the number on a slip of paper and handed it to Victoria, who thanked her and went out to Botts's truck, which was still parked in front of the building. He opened the passenger door for her.

"Did you get anywhere with Colley?"

Victoria shook her head. "Stubborn, opinionated, obstinate . . ."

"That pretty well describes our Colley Jameson."

"Would you mind taking me to Al Fox's office?"

"Some loose ends, Madam Reporter?"

Victoria nodded. "Colley's going on a three-week vacation at the end of September."

"That seems reasonable," said Botts.

"I heard Colley say on the phone that he'd pay the balance when he got somewhere," Victoria said.

"Hotel accommodations, probably."

Victoria glanced at him. "Is that how you take care of hotel bills? Don't you pay with a credit card once you arrive?"

Botts shrugged.

The law office was only a few blocks from the *Enquirer*, but a long way by car down narrow one-way streets that went the wrong direction. Victoria wound down the window and took a deep breath. "What do you suppose he did with the four hundred and fifty thousand dollars he got from Ambler Fieldstone? I have a feeling his vacation and the money are related."

"A four-hundred-and-fifty-thousand-dollar vacation?"

"He's spent the money already. He needs to repay the Fieldstone estate and he was trying to pry some of the trust funds loose from Al Fox."

Botts eased over to the far-left side of the narrow road to pass a couple on bicycles. They were wearing matching blue-and-yellow skintight pants that showed off their thigh muscles.

Victoria watched the bicyclists until Botts had passed them, then continued, almost to herself. "According to his wife he's not a gambler and he's not involved with drugs. He's a womanizer, but doesn't need money for that."

"Ugh," said Botts.

The one-way street made a sharp turn to the left into another street and Botts stopped at the stop sign.

"Those are the only expensive habits I can think of," Victoria said. "Gambling and drugs. What could he be doing with that kind of money? Paying the balance when he arrives?" She thought. "Real estate? Would he be buying property in Arizona?"

Botts said nothing. They'd reached the corner where the law office was located, and he turned into the small parking area.

"Want me to go up with you, Victoria?"

"No, thank you. This shouldn't take long."

"I have to do an errand for my wife. She's having another telephone installed." He glanced sideways at Victoria. "I'll meet you back here."

When Victoria reached the upstairs office, Martha Jo was standing over her desk, sorting a pile of papers into stacks. She smiled when she saw Victoria. Her face, usually pale, was pink and blotchy and her eyes were red-rimmed.

"Can I help you, Mrs. Trumbull? I'm afraid I'm not myself today."

"I'm so sorry. You were the one who found Mr. Fox, weren't you?"

"Yes." Martha Jo looked down at the papers she was sorting. "I really miss him. A lot of people didn't like Mr. Fox. But he was a good boss." She looked away.

"Have the police finished up?"

Martha Jo nodded. "The cleaning people will be here tomorrow morning. The police left powder all over everything. His couch . . . his beautiful leather couch . . ."

"Do you mind if I look around?"

"Not at all, Mrs. Trumbull. I'll be out here, if you need me. I can't face going in there."

Victoria walked across the soft carpet of the reception area and entered Al Fox's office. Every surface that someone might have touched was dusty. Victoria stood inside the doorway and looked around.

She took in the leather couch, the two leather easy chairs, the coffee table, and the two end tables that made up a relaxed setting for clients. A dark reddish-brown stain had soaked into the leather of the end of the couch nearest her. The stain covered part of the arm and one of the cushions. It had dripped down the front of the couch onto the oriental rug beneath. The office smelled of rust.

Victoria moved into the room. The big desk, usually brightly polished, was filmed with the police dust. There was nothing on the desk but a telephone and a pencil and a couple of ballpoint pens. No desk calendar, no diary, no papers of any kind. Victoria supposed the police had taken those things as evidence. No letter opener. She recalled how Al Fox had toyed with that Majorcan dagger every time she'd been in his office. The police had probably taken that, too.

The framed embroidered Shakespeare quote was missing, of course. She'd heard that that was the murder implement. Somehow, it seemed unlikely that someone could be killed with a framed picture. She supposed that if you hit him just right . . . But why all the blood? She'd also heard that his hairpiece had been stuffed into his mouth. The killer's warped sense of humor? Al Fox, the mouthpiece? Victoria shook her head. None of it made sense. She stood in the center of the office for a long time, ten minutes or more, leaning on her stick with both hands, studying the couch, the desk, the framed cartoons on the wall, the carpet, the bloodstain. Finally she returned to the reception room.

Martha Jo was seated at her desk, labeling file folders.

Victoria pulled up the visitor's chair next to her desk. "I suppose the police took his desk calendar and diary?"

"Yes."

"And that letter opener as well?"

Martha Jo looked up, surprised. "I don't think so. I haven't seen it since . . ."

"Did the police say anything about going through his files?"

"They said they might send someone over later to go through them. Mr. Fox was terribly secretive about his cases. I tried to organize his files, but he didn't want me to touch some of them." She shook her head. "All I handled was wills and real-estate transactions, that sort of thing. But nothing personal. Mrs. Jameson and Mrs. Fieldstone and Mr. Jameson and Mr. Fieldstone were always in here, always separately, and I have no idea what they talked about."

"You didn't type any letters for them?"

"Mr. Fox had his own computer, and he typed out the private things he didn't want anyone, not even me, to see."

"I didn't notice his computer," Victoria said. "I suppose the police took that away?"

"Yes." Martha Jo blew her nose on a tissue she'd been holding.

Victoria indicated the file folders on Martha Jo's desk. "What are those?"

"Papers from Mr. Fox's file cabinet. I'm trying to organize them for the police. I don't honestly know what is supposed to be done with these. Most lawyers have associates who take over in case of death. Mr. Fox worked alone." She sighed.

"It must be difficult to decide what to do with those scribbled notes." Victoria indicated one of the piles Martha Jo had sorted out.

"He looked so tidy on the surface, but he was actually a mess. These were stuffed into his top drawer." She riffled through a stack of crumpled sheets torn from a yellow legal pad. "There's no way of knowing whether they're important or not. I guess it won't hurt to show you, Mrs. Trumbull. Look at these." She handed Victoria a dozen of the yellow sheets.

The papers were covered with doodles, cartoon sketches of people, clients, perhaps? Intersecting circles inked in darkly, swirls and curlicues, stars, three-dimensional boxes, elaborate flowers.

"He was quite an artist, wasn't he," Victoria said, leafing through the papers. Occasionally she stopped and read what she could of the scrawled notes. She saw a notation, "$450,000—$900,000?" underlined five or six times, with the zeros inked in, and next to that a comment printed in capital letters, "WHAT FOR?" And "Dwyer's girl." On another page, surrounded with sketches of daisy chains she saw, "Buddy" with a phone number. And on the same page, "annulment? Mexican divorce?? pay-off???"

Victoria looked up from the papers. "Who's Buddy?" she asked Martha Jo.

"I'm not sure. He was connected in some way with Mrs.

Fieldstone, I think. The first time I saw him was right after Mr. Fieldstone's death. He talked with Mr. Fox for at least an hour."

"Did Mr. Fox bill Buddy for the hour?"

Martha Jo shook her head.

Victoria continued to page through the scribbled notes from Al's desk drawer. She saw "DNA" circled with rays extending from the circle, and leaves and flowers and vines drawn all around.

"What are you going to do with these?" Victoria asked.

"I was going to shred them. I didn't see anything on them that could be of any use."

"Let the police examine them before you do that." Victoria held up one of the elaborate sketches of vines and flowers, bunches of grapes and tendrils. "This is wonderful. Do you suppose I might have copies of a few of these?"

"Certainly, Mrs. Trumbull," said Martha Jo. "Something to remember Mr. Fox by. I'll copy them for you, if you'd like." She took the papers from Victoria and switched on the copying machine. While Martha Jo waited for the machine to warm up, she held up the doodle of grapes and vines. "I'm glad you suggested that, Mrs. Trumbull. I'm going to make a copy of this one for myself. He was always doodling." She wiped her nose and put the tissue back in her pocket. "I think he could have been a fine artist, if he'd wanted."

Chapter 20

A soft rain had fallen during the night. The wind veered around to the west, carrying the clear, bright sound of the town clock across Doane's pasture and the brook.

Victoria was kneeling on her flat padded bench, weeding the flower border. Her hands were muddy from the wet ground. She probably should wait until it dried a bit but the morning was too beautiful to waste. Elizabeth had not yet gotten up. McCavity was lying on his back next to her in a heap of pulled-up weeds, soft belly fur exposed, paws in the air, the pupils of his eyes tiny slits.

The police Bronco pulled into the driveway and Casey leaned out of the window. "You're up early, Victoria. What's with McCavity?"

"Catnip," said Victoria. "I've been pulling it out of the iris bed."

"I haven't seen you for several days. Do you have time for a cup of coffee?"

Victoria eased herself up with the handles of the kneeler and straightened her back. She clapped her hands together, knocking off clods of wet earth. "I've been involved with the murders. No one else seems to be concerned about them."

"That's not true, Victoria. The state police are working on both murders."

"Three murders." Victoria picked up her kneeler and started toward the house.

"I hate to interrupt your gardening."

"I've done enough for this morning."

"I'll carry that in for you."

Victoria handed her kneeler to the police chief. "I keep it in the entry with the gardening tools."

"I know," said Casey.

Casey took cups and saucers from the cupboard over the sink while Victoria put on a fresh pot of coffee.

"I went to Al Fox's office yesterday," Victoria said, when they were seated at the table. "I don't see how a framed picture, even a heavy one, could have killed him."

Casey started to interrupt, but Victoria hadn't finished. "Furthermore, I don't understand how there could have been so much blood. Head wounds bleed profusely, I know, but even so, there was a great deal of blood. And I don't understand how blood from a head wound could have spilled down the cushions the way it did. The cushions were not under his head."

"The picture didn't kill him," Casey said, once Victoria had come to a stopping place. "Doc Jeffers says Fox was probably stunned with the picture. His head was cut by slivers of broken glass, then, apparently when he was still alive, his toupee was stuffed into his mouth and he was stabbed. That's what killed him. The stab wound. Brutal. The police are looking for the murder weapon now."

Victoria set her cup firmly in its saucer. "Why didn't you tell me this right away? I might have helped."

"I keep telling you, Victoria, I'm not on the case. I got to work earlier than usual this morning and the state police had left a message for me to call. I found out about the stabbing only a couple of minutes ago and came right over. What do you know that the state cops don't?"

"Al Fox's letter opener is missing, a souvenir dagger from Majorca."

"Sharp enough to kill?"

"A souvenir, but yes, pointed and sharp."

"Let me use your phone, Victoria. I'll call the state guys back, let you talk to them."

After Victoria described the missing letter opener to the state police, Casey dropped her off at the *Grackle* office and promised to pick her up later. It was still early, a little after eight o'clock. Victoria walked to the back of the stables and found Matt working at a table, pasting photos onto large sheets of layout paper. Botts watched, hands in his pockets, shoulders hunched.

"I thought newspaper layout was all done by computer these days," Victoria said.

"Gimme a break." Botts turned his back on her and stomped out through the wide barn doors in the direction of his house.

"Now what's his problem?" Victoria asked.

Matt grinned. "Subscriptions are up to three hundred and twelve."

"What are you working on?"

Matt held up a sheet of photos and large type. "Trustees of Reservations took out a full-page ad. They're having a field day this weekend on Chappaquiddick."

"Field day?"

"Free kayak and canoe rides, a trip along the beach in a four-wheel-drive vehicle. Bird walks. Several boat owners have volunteered to take people for rides on Cape Poge Bay. Including—guess who?"

"I can't imagine."

"Audrey Fieldstone."

"In her Chris-Craft? The antique boat?"

Matt pointed to one of the photos on the layout page. Here's a picture of the Chris. Beautiful, isn't she."

Victoria craned her neck to look. "That's different from the picture Colley wants."

"The ones he wants all show Calpurnia and Audrey together."

"What do you plan to do with them?" Victoria asked.

Matt shrugged. "I was so pissed off at him—excuse me, Victoria—that I wouldn't sell them to him for any price. I don't have any plans for them."

"I hope you have them in a safe place."

Matt stacked the pasted-up pages to one side and started on a fresh sheet. "Mrs. Fieldstone plans to take her boat to Chappy a couple of days early." He reached for another photo, moved it around on his layout, then cropped it to fit. "Trustees has set up a temporary floating dock next to Dike Bridge."

"Why does she want to go so early? She'll have to stay on her boat, won't she?"

"I guess," said Matt. "Her boat doesn't have a cabin, but she can stretch out on the banquette in a sleeping bag. There'll be four or five other boats tied up at the dock, I guess. The ferry from Edgartown doesn't run after eleven, so no one from the Vineyard will bother her."

"They can drive along the barrier bar," Victoria said with assurance. "I've been that way myself recently."

"They've closed the beach road now. The police and the Trustees put up signs, warning people to stay off. The ocean's going to break through the bar any minute."

Victoria sat down at one of the desks next to Matt's layout table. "How is the advertising coming along?"

"Good. Enough to cover costs, salaries for eight staff members, and a bit left over."

"Eight? Who's the eighth?"

"Mrs. Botts."

"Do I get a salary now?"

"Yup."

"Well." Victoria patted her hair. "How many pages in this issue?"

"Sixteen," said Matt. "Lots of ads, lots of photos, lots of good stories. Katie is a real pro, you know, and Lynn's writing is okay. Straightforward. Mrs. Botts has decided the newspaper is great fun, after all, now that we're making money."

"It's too bad William can't accept his success."

"Mr. Botts hates the whole idea. He's talking about starting up another one-page newsletter."

"What will he name that one?"

"*Chanticleer.*"

Victoria laughed. "A medieval rooster fits William's image."

Matt cropped another photo with a pair of long scissors and, tilting his head first to one side, then another, added it to the layout. "Colley's feeling the competition, I hear."

Victoria coughed softly. "I wanted to talk to you about Colley."

"Yeah?" said Matt, looking up from his work.

"I have an idea he may be the next victim."

"Serve him right," said Matt.

Victoria smoothed her trousers over her still handsome legs and picked a stem of dried grass off one of the worn knees. "When's your baby due?"

"Momentarily. Suitcase is all packed and I carry my cell phone with me." He held up the small instrument. "What did you want me to do about Colley?"

"You live fairly close to him, don't you?"

"Too close."

"Would you keep an eye on him? Call me if you see anything unusual?"

"Why not ask his wife? She's lucky enough to live with the guy."

Victoria traced the deeply carved initials on the desktop that made it too uneven to use as a writing surface. "I'm not sure about Calpurnia."

Matt laughed. "You think she might do him in? I wouldn't blame her. She's got good reason, I hear. If she can get away with murdering him, she stands to inherit a chunk of money from that trust fund."

Victoria looked up from the graffiti on the desk. "Why do you suppose Colley needs so much money?"

"You mean the four hundred fifty thousand he got from Fieldstone?" Matt laughed again, harder. "To get a facelift, maybe? He's showing his age. Every time he looks in a mirror . . ."

The Bronco pulled up in front of the barn and Victoria got to her feet.

Matt said quickly, "I'll watch him when I can, Victoria. Can't promise to do a real stakeout, but if I happen to notice something fishy, I'll call you."

CHAPTER 21

It was after nine that night when Matt called. Victoria had been dozing in the wing chair with McCavity in her lap and a book she thought she ought to read.

"You wanted me to call if Colley left the house. He just did."

"Now?" Victoria wiped the sleep out of her eyes with the back of her hand. "Where are you calling from?"

"I'm following him in my truck. He's heading south out of town on Katama Road toward South Beach."

"At this time of night?"

"It's a beautiful night. Full moon and heavy surf. He might be going fishing."

"Not Colley," said Victoria. "I know where he's going. Call Tom Dwyer, would you please? Tell him to meet us at the parking lot."

"Want me to come to West Tisbury to pick you up?"

"There's not time. I'll get Casey to take me in the police car. Give me your cell phone number in case I need to reach you."

She wrote down the number, then called the police station. When she got the answering machine, she left a message telling Casey she was going to Chappaquiddick along the beach and then called William Botts.

Victoria could hear voices in the background. "I'm watching the game on television," Botts grumbled.

"What game?" asked Victoria.

"*Jeopardy.*"

"I need you here right away," said Victoria. "I'll explain when you get here."

When Botts's pickup truck rattled into the South Beach parking lot twenty minutes later, Tom Dwyer was talking to Matt, pipe between his teeth. The tires on his SUV were almost flat.

Tom saluted Victoria. "Okay, boss. Give us our orders."

"Where's Colley?" Victoria asked.

"He took off down the beach toward Chappy," Matt said. "Stupid thing to do."

"What is he driving?"

"The newspaper's Jeep."

Victoria turned to Tom. "Can you catch up with him?"

"I got a speeding ticket last summer for going more than five miles an hour along that stretch of beach. You willing to pay the ticket if I get caught?"

"We've got to hurry," Victoria said.

Botts hesitated. "Are we all expected to go on this trek?"

"Hurry," said Victoria. "Get in, all of you."

Tom put the car into four-wheel drive and eased onto the beach. "This is a lousy night to be driving along that barrier bar, you know that, don't you, Victoria?"

"With the moon, we can see things," Victoria said.

"A full moon means higher than normal tides and the surf is heavy. The bay is going to break through the bar any time now. The ocean was already washing over in places the other day."

"The Trustees have posted 'Danger' signs telling people not to drive on the beach," Matt said.

"We have to reach Colley before he gets to that narrow place, then," said Victoria. "The killer has laid a trap for him at Dike Bridge."

Botts was sitting next to Matt in the back. "I thought Dike Bridge connected Chappaquiddick with the Vineyard."

Matt shook his head. "Nope. It crosses a creek on the far east side of Chappy. Saves a long drive, if you're trying to get to the beach."

"And avoids piping plover nests," said Tom, with a grin Victoria could see in the moonlight.

"Hurry," said Victoria.

The moon was high above the ocean ahead of them. A path of dazzling moonlight led from the horizon across the confused sea. Moonlight highlighted the crests of breakers, and flooded the beach with white light. Every small shrub, every bunch of tall beach grass, every footprint left over from the day, showed up clearly, dense black against the moonlit sand.

Tom switched off his headlights. The SUV wallowed in the soft sand, swaying in a way that made Victoria queasy. She took a deep breath to settle her stomach. "Can you see the Jeep yet?"

"I'm following his tracks," said Tom. "And I'm driving a hell of a lot faster than I like." He glanced at Matt in the rear view mirror. "How much head start did he have?"

Matt, behind Victoria, leaned forward, swaying with the motion of the careening vehicle. "Twenty-five minutes."

"To think I could still be watching *Jeopardy*," Botts muttered thickly.

"Hurry," said Victoria.

Tom glanced at the speedometer. "Fasten your seat belt, Victoria."

"I'm feeling a bit of mal de mer," Botts mumbled.

"Open the window," said Tom.

Matt peered ahead between Tom's seat and Victoria's. "I think I see him."

"Hurry," said Victoria.

"If we capsize," said Tom, "we'll never catch him."

The gap between Tom's SUV and the Jeep closed slowly.

"Has he spotted us?" Victoria asked.

"I doubt it." Tom held the steering wheel tightly in both hands and the muscles in his forearm stood out. "He's not expecting you to follow him, is he?"

In the back seat, Botts groaned. "How much farther?"

"Katama Bay is on our left now. Norton Point is up ahead. The bar narrows from here on. The break is likely to occur just ahead of Colley, beyond Norton Point."

Victoria could see the Jeep clearly now, a few hundred feet ahead of them.

Tom took a hand off the wheel long enough to remove his pipe from his mouth. "Colley may not realize there's quicksand ahead of him, right about where he is now."

"Quicksand?" said Botts.

"The sand gets saturated with water just before the bar breaks through."

"Maybe the quicksand will suck him down, and then we can go home," said Botts.

"The quicksand probably is only a couple of feet deep," said Tom. "Enough to stop a vehicle dead, though."

Matt was still peering ahead. "Uh, oh!" he said. "The Jeep's stuck."

Tom was studying the sand ahead of him. He stopped the vehicle, pulled on the hand brake, and left the engine running. The SUV was well back from the Jeep, which was axle-deep in sand and tilted to one side. Colley was standing on the front seat, holding the roll bar and waving to them.

"About time!" Colley shouted above the roar of surf. "You got a rope?"

A large breaker sent a thin sheet of water racing up the beach toward the Jeep. The water stopped before it got to the Jeep and receded. Some sank into the already soupy sand.

"Some timing Colley's got," Tom muttered. "According to him, Nature will hold back earthquakes and volcanoes just for his convenience." He flung his pipe onto the dashboard, and the three men scrambled out of the SUV. Tom hauled an enormous coil of rope out of the back, fastened one end around his front bumper with a quick hitch, and hurled the free end across the stretch of quicksand to Colley.

The end of the rope went over the top of the Jeep, and Colley grabbed for it. And missed.

Colley screamed, "You've got to do better than that!"

Another breaker sent another sheet of water toward the stuck Jeep and again, the water stopped before it reached Colley. The Jeep settled several inches more.

Tom hauled in the line and flung it again.

"Don't let it tangle," he shouted to Botts, who was standing next to the rope coil on the beach.

Botts fed the line through his hands. "I'm getting blisters."

Again, the line went over Colley, and again Colley failed to catch it.

"Gloves in the car, Matt," Tom called over his shoulder.

Matt ran to the SUV. Victoria, still sitting in her seat, handed the gloves to him, and Matt took them to Botts, who put them on.

Victoria had just opened the door on the passenger side when Matt shouted, "The ocean's breaking through!"

A sheet of water had pooled briefly around the Jeep and then washed all the way across the bar.

Tom dashed back to the SUV. "Shut the door, Victoria. I've got to get the car out of here. All hell is going to break loose in seconds."

He looked over his shoulder, his arm thrown over the back of Victoria's seat, and backed away a hundred feet or so. The rope he had attached to his front bumper uncoiled from the bottom of the heap on the beach. Botts was feeding line to Matt, who had thrown a third time to Colley, who missed a third time.

Victoria leaned forward. "Is the rope long enough?"

"Let's hope so. I don't want to back up much farther because of the rope."

"Shit! Shit!" Colley screamed. He was holding the roll bar so tightly, Victoria could see his white knuckles in the pale light. The Jeep tilted still more into the soft sand.

Tom pulled on the hand brake again. "Rising tide," he mumbled to Victoria, who understood what that meant. As the tide rose, more and more ocean water would pour across the bar, finally cutting a channel through the bar. When that happened, water from the bay, which had a two-foot head, would tear into the beach, washing sand and cobbles and driftwood and anything else in its path out to sea. Colley's Jeep would be tumbled like driftwood along with tons of sand.

"Colley! You gotta grab it!" Matt shouted, and he hurled the line once again. "Grab it!"

Victoria watched with horror. Sheets of water were washing across the bar continuously now. The foaming edges glistened in the moonlight.

Colley stretched out his hand for the line. Just then the Jeep lurched and sank another foot into the sand and Colley missed a fourth time.

"The Jeep's in too deep to pull out," Tom shouted. "Gotta save Colley."

Back at the SUV, Victoria opened the passenger door and stood carefully on the frame, holding the top of the open door with one hand. She reached with the other hand for one of Tom's surf-casting rods on the roof and when she felt it, let go of the door so she could use both hands to unhook the shock cord that held the rod in place. Her hands shook so badly, it took several attempts. Finally she worked the rod off the roof. She stepped carefully from the car down onto the sand, holding the rod like a tightrope walker's balance pole. She slogged through the sand as quickly as she could to where Tom, Matt, and Botts were trying to reach Colley with the rope.

She jammed the butt end of the rod into the sand and leaned on it, catching her breath.

"Colley, jump!" shouted Tom. "Get out of the Jeep! Jump! Now!"

Colley shook his head and hung on. The Jeep was now tipped at almost a forty-five-degree angle, and looked as though it might roll over any second. The rising tide poured water across the bar.

"It's broken through!" Matt shouted.

Victoria, holding the fishing rod for support, saw the channel form, first snaking slowly, then, in an instant, deepening. Ocean water swept into the bay. A tongue of bay water licked against the incoming ocean water, forcing the ocean water back. And then, abruptly, with the sound of a waterfall, bay water began to pour out to sea, cutting and tearing through the sand, swirling, frothing, foaming. Victoria could see clearly. Fish and seaweed and rocks tumbled over and over through the rush of water. The channel grew wider and deeper in seconds, making a vertical cut through the beach. Victoria could see strata of black-and-white sand in the cut. Within seconds the cut had become almost six feet deep. Rushing water carved under the steep banks. Sand slumped into the channel with a hiss and swirled out to sea.

She could hear Colley scream, but she could no longer hear his words above the noise. As the channel widened and deepened, water undercut the soft sand around the Jeep. The Jeep lurched, slowly turned over, and slipped sideways into the channel, where it tumbled end over end out through the channel into the surf.

"Colley?" Victoria gasped.

"He got out in time, but he's in trouble." Tom pointed. Victoria could see Colley's head emerge from the curl of a breaker. He was moving rapidly out to sea.

Victoria pulled the surf rod out of the sand and handed it to Tom. "Can you use this?"

"Good girl!"

Tom checked the end of the line, raced to the edge of the channel and leaned back to cast.

Matt pointed. "There he is!"

Victoria looked toward where they'd last seen Colley's head in the line of breakers. A wave broke and Colley's dark head surfaced. She could see him gasp for breath before another breaker engulfed him.

Tom cast. The weight on the end of his line went over Colley's shoulder and dropped into the water immediately beyond him.

"Nice cast," said Matt. "Right across his shoulder."

"Colley can't hear. Hope he feels the line. It's his only chance."

Colley's head surfaced again. He reached over his shoulder.

"Don't pull too hard, Colley," Matt murmured. "What weight line, Tom?"

"Twenty-pound test," said Tom. "Gently, Colley." He played the line as if Colley were a large fish on a much too light line.

Matt had retrieved the end of the rope Colley had failed to grab. "Sould I attach the rope to the line?"

"You know knots?" said Tom.

"Yup."

"Quick, then. Hope to hell Colley has some sense of self-preservation."

They could see Colley struggle to keep his head above water.

"He's weakening," said Botts.

Colley had been pitched out of the Jeep, tossed about in the channel, and tumbled in the surf. The current had carried him off to one side, but he was moving away from shore.

"Pull, Colley, pull!" Tom shouted.

The rope attached to the light line spun out with Colley as he was carried out. He seemed to understand what he had to do because he pulled, hand over hand, on the filament line that now had the rope attached. The surf dunked him again and again. He emerged each time, gasping and tugging on the light line.

"Atta boy!" shouted Tom, as though Colley could hear. "Pull, Colley! Pull!"

Hand over hand as his head dipped under a breaker and emerged again, Colley pulled the rope toward him. Victoria saw him reach the rope, then struggle to wrap it around himself.

Tom dropped the rod onto the sand, and he, Matt, and Botts, hauled in.

"Smooth rhythm," Tom shouted. "Don't jerk it, or we'll lose him."

Colley had been swept to the far side of the channel. The three maneuvered him back through the rip at the mouth of the cut. When Colley was close to shore, seaward of the line of breakers, Tom tossed off his hat, kicked off his shoes, and waded into the surf. The breakers lifted Colley high on their crests, then rolled him down and under and slammed him onto the sand and pebble floor. Botts and Matt still held the rope that was wrapped around Colley. Tom was waist deep in water, but each breaking wave lifted him off his feet and dropped him again. He landed on his feet, but Colley was as limp as the half-body Tom and Simon Newkirk had fished out of the surf, was it three weeks ago?

Colley rose to the crest of a breaking wave and Tom seized the front of his windbreaker, now torn and ragged, and struggled to the beach. Botts and Matt kept tension on the rope until they, too, waded into the surf and brought Colley onto the beach and dropped him onto the sand.

Victoria was waiting just above the swash line. "Is he alive?"

Tom shook his head. "I can't tell."

"He must have swallowed a great deal of seawater," Victoria said. "We've got to get it out of him, quickly." She knelt by his head. "Can you hear me, Colley?"

He lay on his stomach, arms over his head. The rope was still wrapped around his shoulders and waist. Coils and snarls of rope lay in a tangled heap on the sand where it had been dropped.

Colley's eyelids fluttered and his mouth moved.

"He's alive." Victoria looked up with relief. "He's going to throw up. Can you elevate his feet?"

All three men were soaking wet. Tom was barefoot and shivering. Botts breathed gently on his hands. Matt untangled the coils of rope that Colley had wrapped around himself. They hauled him away from the water by his feet, and Colley vomited up what seemed like gallons of seawater.

"Thank God," said Tom. "I was afraid I was pulling another body out of the surf."

"We've got to get him back to civilization," Victoria said.

"I've got beach towels in the car," Tom said, teeth chattering. "Bundle him up."

They stood Colley up, and, one man on either side, dragged him, on legs that didn't work, to the SUV. Victoria toweled him as dry as she could, then wrapped the towels around him. They lifted him into the backseat, where he slumped with Botts on one side. Matt gathered up the tangle of rope, dumped it into the back, then sat on the other side of Colley.

Tom started up the SUV, turned on the heater full blast, and retraced the route along the beach back to Katama.

"There's a vehicle coming this way," Matt said.

"Who in hell . . . ?" said Tom.

"It's the police Bronco," said Victoria. "Casey got my message."

Casey and Junior Norton pulled alongside. Casey ignored Tom and glared at Victoria. "What do you think you're doing, Victoria? Are you out of your mind? The cops have signs all over the place telling idiots like you guys to keep off the beach." She waved her arm behind her. "Can't you ever do what you're supposed to do? The bar's going to break through, like tonight."

"It did," said Victoria.

Casey took a deep breath. "Lord, Victoria. Who's with you. Are you okay?"

"We need to take Colley to the hospital," Victoria said softly.

"What happened?" Casey asked, anger gone.

Tom looked in the rear-view mirror at the men in the back seat. "Colley would be dead, Chief, if it weren't for your deputy here. Drowned."

"How can I help? Escort you to the hospital?"

Tom said, "He may be better off in his own bed with some hot chocolate."

Colley murmured something.

"What did he say?" Victoria turned around to look.

Botts grinned. "He said 'whiskey.'"

CHAPTER 22

They carried Colley home to South Water Street. The light beside the front door was still on; otherwise, the house was dark. Tom knocked with the whale-shaped doorknocker and when there was no response, pounded with his fists. Finally, an upstairs light went on, then a downstairs light, and Calpurnia opened the door a crack.

Her hair was tousled and a terry-cloth robe was thrown over her shoulders. "What is it? What's the matter?"

"Colley's had an accident," Tom said. "He's okay," he added quickly.

"What time is it?"

"Almost two."

Calpurnia opened the door wider. "What happened? Where is he?"

"He's in the car. We'll bring him in."

"What's he done now?"

"He was driving to Chappy and the bay broke through. He's wet and exhausted and he needs a drink."

"Naturally." Calpurnia smiled faintly. "Who else is in the car with him?"

"Victoria Trumbull, William Botts, and Matt Pease."

"The photographer?" she said. "Well. That's ironic." She opened the door all the way. "Better bring Colley inside."

Colley's legs almost worked. Matt and Botts supported him up the front steps and into the front parlor and sat him in one of the wing chairs that flanked the fireplace. Victoria followed.

Calpurnia lighted the fire, which was already laid, then turned to Colley, hands on her hips.

"What were you thinking of? What on earth were you doing there?"

Colley shook his head.

The fire crackled and blazed up.

"He's had a difficult time," Victoria said. "He needs dry clothes and a blanket, not a scolding."

"It was Mrs. Trumbull who saved him," Botts said from the back of the room, where he'd located the bar.

"I'm not sure he's worth saving." Calpurnia's hands were still on her hips. "You left the house before nine. Why were you driving the beach route? The ferry runs until eleven, as you well know."

Colley shook his head slowly.

Botts said, "He takes scotch, doesn't he?"

"Anything alcoholic," said Calpurnia. "Give me a straight bourbon, while you're at it. And whatever the rest of you want."

Victoria sat in the wing chair across from Colley. Botts handed Colley a tumbler of scotch, which he took and gulped.

Calpurnia left the room and returned several minutes later with her hair combed, wearing a purple-and-blue dressing gown. She carried a flannel shirt and a blanket, and wrapped them, none too tenderly, around Colley.

Colley said nothing.

Calpurnia perched on the arm of the couch at right angles to Colley's chair and crossed her legs and her arms. "You must be out of your mind. What a weird coincidence that you were at that spot just at that moment."

Tom was coming out of the kitchen with a bottle of Sam Adams for himself and a glass of cranberry juice for Victoria. "Actually, he triggered the break when he drove onto that unstable sand. All it needed was a catalyst and Colley was it."

The color was returning to Colley's face. He pulled the blanket around himself.

The fire snapped. A log settled. Sparks flew up.

Victoria half-closed her eyes. "Were you supposed to meet someone on Chappaquiddick tonight, Colley?"

Colley muttered something Victoria didn't understand.

"At Dike Bridge?" Victoria persisted.

"Dike Bridge," said Calpurnia. "*That* figures."

Colley had been staring into his drink glass. He said nothing.

"It's fortunate you got stopped by the break and even more fortunate that we were there."

Colley murmured, "On the spot."

Tom said, "You're still alive, Colley, thanks to Victoria."

Colley turned his head.

"Who asked you to meet them at the bridge?" Victoria persisted.

Colley moved his head from side to side.

Tom yawned. "He needs to get some rest, Victoria. So do we all."

"I don't think we should leave Colley alone," said Victoria.

Calpurnia smiled.

Victoria said, "I think someone should stay with him tonight."

"Calpurnia's here," said Tom.

Hours later, Calpurnia was alone in the kitchen, pouring herself a glass of iced tea. Colley was still upstairs. Calpurnia was about to take the tea and her book into the back garden when the phone rang. When she heard Audrey Fieldstone's voice, Calpurnia almost slammed the phone down.

"Don't hang up," Audrey said loudly. "We've got to talk."

Calpurnia sat down at the kitchen table with the phone against her ear. "If it's about the money, you'll have to talk to Colley, not me. Your goons are welcome to go after him."

Audrey laughed. "You'd like that, wouldn't you, darling? Once I set my 'goons' on your husband, your worries are over, aren't they?"

Calpurnia could hear a slight clicking sound. She could picture Audrey tapping her long red fingernails against the mouthpiece of the phone.

"How much do you inherit from the trust? Four million? Five? You won't even miss the four hundred fifty thousand."

"I've got to go," said Calpurnia, pushing her chair away from the table and standing up.

"Don't you dare hang up on me!"

"Oh?" said Calpurnia.

"If you do, you'll regret it."

"I regret everything I've ever had to do with you, *Mrs.* Fieldstone."

"I'm going to the police."

Calpurnia sat down again. "You wouldn't."

"Wouldn't I? What makes you think I wouldn't, darling?" The clicking continued.

"You know why."

Audrey laughed. "You have more to lose than I do."

"I think not, *Mrs.* Fieldstone," said Calpurnia.

"You don't need to use that snotty tone of voice."

Calpurnia smiled into the phone. "Come now, Audrey. Someone named Butch, or Buddy, or something, has been making teensy weensy ripples."

The clicking stopped. "Where did you hear that?"

Calpurnia laughed. "On the defensive, are we? We *do* live on an island, you know." She held the phone away from her ear. "This connection is awful. Where are you calling from, overseas?"

"What about Buddy?"

"Buddy, is it? Where *are* you calling from?"

"Chappaquiddick. I'm on my cell phone."

"I suppose that's overseas. You're there early, aren't you?"

"What did you hear about Buddy?"

"You're not supposed to be there until tomorrow," said Calpurnia. "Maybe we should talk, after all."

"I have some information on your husband's latest sweetie."

Calpurnia sighed. "I know all about his college girls."

"This one is a lot older than me. Almost your age. Meet me at Dike Bridge."

Calpurnia couldn't help asking, "Who is she?"

"Got your attention, didn't I darling? He met her on the Internet."

"What are you talking about?" Calpurnia asked.

"You can give me a ride back to Edgartown and I'll tell you all about her."

"Why on earth would I want to do that? Get yourself back somehow and we can meet on the porch of the Harbor View. In plain sight."

"Oh for God's sake," said Audrey. "*You're* not afraid of *me?*" She laughed. "It should be the other way around." She paused. "Calpurnia, you and I are in deep, deep doo-doo. The sooner we talk, the better. Meet me at the bridge."

Calpurnia set her tea glass on a paper napkin on the counter. "I was in Al Fox's office when his secretary discovered the body."

"Congratulations."

"Nice touch, Audrey. His toupee."

"What do you mean?"

"I suppose you want me to meet you at the bridge at midnight?"

Audrey laughed. "The Chappy ferry doesn't run after eleven. Come over now. Since I need a ride back to my car, I'm not likely to murder you until I'm back in Edgartown, am I? Besides, don't you want to hear all about the Internet romance?"

"Colley's still upstairs. He came home this morning around two, soaking wet."

"Really? Out for a moonlight swim?"

"He had a rough night. You wouldn't happen to know anything about it, would you?"

"Moi? He's not my type. Besides, he doesn't have two cents to rub together."

"Butch the mechanic *is* your type, I gather."

"Buddy, darling. Buddy doesn't owe me four hundred fifty grand." She laughed. "Besides, I've taken care of Buddy."

"Really? Permanently, I suppose?"

"I rather hope so. Will you have to feed Colley breakfast and lunch before you leave?"

"What have you done about Buddy?"

"That's my little secret, isn't it? What about Colley?"

"I'll leave him a note."

"I haven't had lunch yet myself," said Audrey. "I'll buy, once we get safely back to Edgartown."

Calpurnia looked at her watch. "I'll be there in a half-hour."

"Make it an hour," said Audrey. "I have to secure my boat," and she hung up.

Calpurnia took her time getting ready. She found Colley's car keys on top of the refrigerator, thought about leaving him a note, then didn't.

She put down the top of his MG, backed out of the driveway onto South Water Street, drove around several blocks of one-way streets to get onto North Water Street, and turned onto the road that ended at the ferry dock. A car and an empty hay truck were ahead of her in the ferry line. She could see the small open ferry in the middle of the channel, crabbing its way across from Chappaquiddick to Edgartown. The current seemed unusually strong. Then she realized that now, with the bar breached, the tidal pattern would be different. Water from Nantucket Sound would pour through Edgartown Harbor and into Katama Bay, as it always did on a rising tide, but now the flow, or much of it, would continue into the Atlantic instead of returning to the sound.

The ferry swung into its slip. Captain Brad unhooked the chain and slipped the chocks out from under the tires of the first car, an SUV.

"Have a good day, Mr. Updike," he said, slapping the hood of the SUV.

"Same to you, Cap'n."

The captain beckoned the car, the hay truck, and the MG onto the ferry and headed for the Chappaquiddick side. He leaned out of the wheelhouse. "How're you doing, Mrs. Jameson? A real classic you got there." He blew the two-seater a kiss. "Wicked current today."

Before Calpurnia had time to comment on the break in the bar, the ferry was nudging the wooden pilings of the slip on the Chappy side and she drove off.

She passed a couple on bicycles on the road. Two and a half miles farther on, the paved road made a sharp right turn and she continued straight ahead onto the unpaved road that led to Dike Bridge, another mile and a half.

As she passed the Japanese garden, she could see a few scattered rhododendrons in bloom, past their prime but still a splash of pink, white, and red showing through the pines.

The road ended at the bridge, which spanned a narrow, deep creek and led across to the barrier beach. She pulled off onto a sandy parking area to the left of the bridge. Ahead of her where the creek widened, the Trustees had erected a temporary floating dock. The only boat tied up at the floating dock was Audrey's Chris-Craft. Two immaculate white fenders protected the varnished wood hull from chafing against the metal dock.

She looked around. The place was desolate even when people were around. Now it seemed deserted.

Where was Audrey?

A gull dived into the swift current that flowed under the bridge and lifted again on strong wings with a wriggling fish in its bill. Five or six other gulls attacked the first gull, screaming, and the gull dropped the fish.

On the other side of the bridge was a small shack, where, during the season, someone from the Trustees checked beach stickers. The door was closed now, and the window shuttered. Beyond the shack, low dunes hid the ocean from her view. Surf on the other side of the dunes rumbled. Wind blew her hair into her face and flattened the shiny beach grass that covered the dunes.

Where was Audrey? No one seemed to be around.

Calpurnia suddenly felt chilled. She reached into the back of the MG for her sweater. She had decided this was not a place she wanted to be all by herself and was about to get back into the car and leave when she heard Audrey's voice. She started.

"You certainly took your time."

Audrey was sitting in the shade of the bridge. She got to her feet and came toward Calpurnia.

"Where is everyone?" Calpurnia asked. "I thought there'd be several boats and lots of people."

Audrey shrugged. "Change your mind about driving me back to Edgartown?" She held out her arms. "No weapons, see? Cute car."

"Get in," said Calpurnia. "What about Colley's Internet affair?"

"I knew that would interest you," Audrey said. "I'll tell you when we have a private place to talk."

They drove to the main road in silence. The sand road was overhung by trees and shadows and light flickered across the women's faces.

When they reached the paved road, the light was suddenly glaring, reflected from the waters of Nantucket Sound to their right. Audrey put on sunglasses.

Calpurnia broke the silence. "Did you stay on your boat last night?"

"Never again," said Audrey. "I tried to sleep on the backseat in a sleeping bag. It was colder than hell and everything I own got soaked by dew. The moon was like a searchlight, the wind howled, and the surf was so loud I couldn't think straight. I was afraid my boat would get banged up on that cheesy metal dock."

"Why on earth did you bring your boat over so far ahead of

time?" Calpurnia asked. "It's not exactly a room at the Harbor View." Calpurnia pulled into the ferry line on the left side of the road behind one other car. "And where are all the people you said would be around?"

Audrey smirked, and took a package of chewing gum out of her pocket. "I knew you wouldn't come over if you thought I was alone." She took out a stick, unwrapped it, and put it in her mouth, without offering a piece to Calpurnia.

"Why get there so early?" said Calpurnia again. "It's only a couple of hours, three at most, from Maciel Marine."

Audrey chewed without answering.

The ferry arrived and Captain Brad waved them aboard. He looked from one woman to the other, not hiding his surprise at seeing them together.

"I hear you're taking people out in your Chris this weekend, Mrs. Fieldstone. Getting things ready at the bridge?"

Audrey smiled. "It seemed like a good thing to do."

CHAPTER 23

Calpurnia parked in front of the Harbor View Hotel at the end of North Water Street. She and Audrey politely discussed the best place for a private yet visible talk and decided on the beach next to the harbor lighthouse. They trudged down the sand path between the wild beach roses, now covered with marble-size green rose hips and a few blossoms, some pink and some white.

The high tide of several hours ago had washed away footprints from the day before and left a line of tangled seaweed and shells that paralleled the water's edge. They sat back from the tide line on clean sand, several feet apart.

Audrey peeled the silver wrapper from another stick of gum, added it to the piece already in her mouth, and said, "What shall we start with, Colley's new fling or the reason I called you?"

"I know all about Colley's 'flings,'" said Calpurnia.

"But this chick has money. Lots and lots of money."

"Where did you get this?"

"I told you, my goons are observing your husband. They've been asked to get my money from Colley."

"The Internet, I suppose?"

Audrey shrugged. "You can find anything you want on the Internet."

"Who is she?"

"I thought that would get your attention. She's a computer software developer, a nerd, who invented some gizmo that blocks spam. Now she's got more money than God."

"Why on earth should she be interested in Colley?"

"She doesn't care whether he has money or not. He can be quite charming when he wants to be."

Calpurnia smiled wryly. "I suppose Colley figures she'll be so charmed, she'll give him the half million?"

"I don't care where he gets the money," said Audrey. "The name she uses on the Internet is Joy. Cute, huh? She lives in California someplace. That's all I know about her."

Calpurnia slipped off her sandals and dug her feet into the sand. "Why are we meeting, besides my being conned into chauffeuring you?"

Audrey chewed her gum slowly, then spoke in a low voice. "I'm going to the police. I haven't had a decent night's sleep since Ambler was killed."

"I don't want to hear about it, Audrey."

"We've got to talk."

"I don't know why," said Calpurnia.

Audrey picked up a scallop shell and dusted off the sand. "He didn't make a sound."

"It's convenient to have him dead, though, isn't it? How many millions will you inherit?" Calpurnia looked out at the harbor. A sailboat was tacking into the narrow channel between Chappaquiddick and Edgartown. "That is, if things go according to plan, right? Did he know about Buddy?"

"I keep seeing the blood." Audrey tossed the shell toward the water.

"Don't forget whose idea it was to play a little trick on Ambler."

"I never intended it to end that way."

"No?" Calpurnia stretched her legs out in front of her, crossed them, put her arms behind her and leaned back. "You were going to let him swim to shore, right? Five miles to Nantucket, ten miles to the Vineyard, in fifty-degree water?"

"We were going to circle around and pick him up."

"Right," said Calpurnia. "Is that what you're planning to tell the police?"

"He'd still be alive if you hadn't put the boat in gear."

Calpurnia sat up straight and brushed the sand off her hands. "You're blaming me, are you? You shoved him overboard, or would you rather forget that part?"

"Am I the only one who's having trouble with this? Can you sleep after what happened?"

"The whole thing was your idea, remember? First Ambler and Colley cook up that scheme with me as a cheap call girl . . ."

"You weren't cheap, darling, as I recall." Audrey, too, stared out at the sailboat.

"Then you call me to play a little trick on Ambler because, in your words, he was two-timing both of us. Meeting Candy Keene on Nantucket." Calpurnia drew up her legs and put her arms around her knees.

Audrey muttered, "That cheap stripper."

"Really? 'Cheap stripper'? He marries the daughter of an alcoholic pig farmer from Secaucus? Who's still married to a garage mechanic? Not that there's anything wrong with garage mechanics. Or pig farmers." Calpurnia laughed. "Candy Keene flies over to Nantucket, intending to tell Ambler about Buddy, who had tracked his wife Audrey to Martha's Vineyard after a fellow mechanic pointed out his wife's picture in a year-old copy of *People* magazine." Calpurnia took a breath. "Only his wife was not identified as Mrs. Buddy whatever, she was identified as the elegant Mrs. J. Ambler Fieldstone. Okay?"

Audrey got to her knees and slapped Calpurnia.

Calpurnia's head flew back and her eyes watered. She laughed again. "Finally getting through to you, am I? You still want to go to the police?"

"I wasn't the one who killed Ambler, darling."

"Let me guess what your rationale is. If you tell the police you ran over your alleged husband by accident . . ."

"I wasn't at the controls."

"... the police will think, such a nice conscience-stricken widow would never, ever shoot and then poison her rival, nor would she ever, ever clobber her shyster lawyer, who—this is an editorial aside—knew about Buddy and was probably threatening to blackmail her."

Audrey put both hands over her ears. "Stop it!"

"You're getting sand in your hair," Calpurnia said.

Audrey stood up. "Calpurnia, we've got to stop fighting. We have to come to some kind of truce."

"We tried that once before, and look what happened."

"I can't sleep." Audrey chewed. "Whenever I close my eyes I see blood foaming up behind the boat, then his body . . ."

"You think telling the police will cure all that? You go to the police and I'll tell them the whole story." Calpurnia leaned back on her hands again, and Audrey sat down.

"Let's look at it from the viewpoint of the police. Suppose I tell them the rest of the story. Ambler wasn't your husband. Buddy was. When the police learn about Buddy, that's all they need for motive."

"I've taken care of Buddy."

"So you said. Are you going to tell the police that you have? Where have you hidden *his* body?"

"Don't be ridiculous."

"Are you going to tell the police that you made some nice divinity fudge for Candy Keene because you knew she'd enjoy it and how could you possibly know it was laced with cyanide? Is that what you're going to tell the police?"

"*I* didn't kill Candy."

"The identity of the killer will seem damned obvious to the police. Then, of course, when you learned that Candy had told Al Fox about Buddy, you had to take care of him, too. Are you going to tell the police all that? That all three deaths were accidents? And now you've taken care of Buddy?"

Audrey's face had paled. "I didn't *kill* Buddy."

"Your words. You took care of Buddy 'permanently.' My interpretation of 'permanent' is 'permanent.'"

"I *paid* Buddy off. Buddy loves money."

"More than being married to you?"

"More than anything. He found a lawyer who's getting us a retroactive Mexican divorce. As long as Buddy doesn't make waves, he knows I'll pay." Audrey sifted sand through her long fingers with their red-tipped nails and continued to chew. "I didn't kill either Candy or Al Fox. I didn't need to."

"Who did, then? You're going to wreck your manicure doing that."

Audrey stopped playing with the sand and brushed her hands together. "I assumed you were the killer, if you must know."

"So that's why you want to go to the police. To turn me in?" Calpurnia snorted. "And what are you going to tell the police my motive was? I can see why I might want to murder my husband, but why Candy and Al Fox?"

"This is a weird conversation." Audrey dug her fingers into the sand making five neat holes, pulled her fingers out, and examined her nails.

"Candy was an airhead," said Calpurnia. "Even Colley recognized that after a year of marital bliss. And Al Fox? He didn't have a hold over me the way he did with you."

"Just the eight-million-dollar trust fund."

"Colley can't touch the money and I get a good chunk of it when he dies. That's an excellent motive for my killing Colley. Before he runs off with Joy. Unfortunately, he's still alive."

Audrey glanced at Calpurnia. "What did Colley do with the four hundred fifty thousand he got from Ambler?"

"I have no idea. He's close-mouthed about the money. I know your thugs frightened him, which is when he went to Al Fox to get a loan from the trust."

"Did he buy real estate?"

"I doubt it. He'd brag about acquiring something like that. Anyway, four hundred fifty thousand doesn't go far if he spent it on Vineyard real estate." Calpurnia shrugged. "Forget Colley. I'm curious to know what you think my motives are for the two murders."

"Candy was sucking alimony out of Colley. And I understand Al Fox renegotiated an annual cost-of-living increase for her."

"Cost of living, ha!"

"Two motives right there."

"You think I'd trouble myself to kill someone over a mere forty or fifty thousand a year?"

"Frankly, yes," said Audrey.

Calpurnia stood up, brushed the sand off the back of her trousers, bent over, and picked up her sandals. "We're not getting anywhere with this conversation. Instead of going to the police, you know who we should talk to?"

Audrey, too, got up. "I was thinking the same thing. Victoria Trumbull."

When Victoria sat down in her usual armchair in the West Tisbury police station, Casey snickered. "I'm sorry, Victoria. I keep remembering Candy Keene dusting off that seat with her scented lace hanky."

Victoria scowled. "I came here to make a long-distance phone call. May I?"

"Where to?"

"Arizona."

"Police business?"

"It's a number Colley called recently."

Casey pushed the instrument toward Victoria. "Go ahead. I won't ask why."

Victoria dialed a number and waited. A disembodied voice told her she'd reached Sun Spa and demanded that she press one or two or three—up to seven—if she wanted the voice mail of one of the doctors, and to remain on the line to speak to an operator. Victoria raised her eyebrows and looked at Casey while the voice went through her options. Casey fiddled with a retractable ballpoint pen, snapping the point in and out.

Finally, Victoria got a live person. She said, raising her voice a quarter octave so she sounded like a young woman, "This is Mr. Jameson's secretary."

Casey opened her mouth to say something and glanced up instead at the ceiling, where a spider was building an intricate web.

Victoria continued in her girlish voice, "Could you confirm the date and time of his appointment?" Before the operator had time to demur, Victoria added, "He's terribly absent-minded, and didn't give me all the details, and I need to make his plane reservations."

Victoria listened and made a few notes. "Thank you so much," she said. "And that was Dr. Papadoupoulis?" One of the names she'd picked up from the automated voice. She nodded and glanced up at Casey, who was not looking at her.

"Thank you for correcting me. Mr. Jameson is absolutely impossible." Victoria had been holding her chin up to maintain the high pitch. "He had it all wrong. And Dr. Gurney is so wonderful. Mr. Jameson says so many good things about him." She cleared her throat and glanced again at Casey, who was still watching the spider. "Was it Harvard Medical School he went to?" She waited. "Mr. Jameson had that all wrong, too. You know what these vain men are like, I'm sure. Thank you so much. I'll correct his records and make sure he gets on the right airplane."

Victoria hung up, pushed the phone back to Casey, and sat back again in her armchair, with a self-satisfied smile.

"What was that all about, Victoria?"

"I know what Colley did with that four hundred and fifty thousand dollars. Can you find something for me on the Internet?"

"What?"

"The specialty of a Dr. Theodore Gurney, who graduated from Southwestern University Medical School."

Casey busied herself on the computer. Victoria stood up, went to the window, and watched the swans on the mill pond. Seven cygnets had hatched in the spring. Now there were only two. Snapping turtles had eaten the other five. She turned around when she heard Casey sigh.

"Did you find out anything?"

"How's this?" Casey moved her computer mouse around and the image on the screen shifted. "Dr. Gurney specializes in cosmetic surgery. Reversing the aging process. Skin tightening. Facial reconstruction. He's currently practicing at Sun Spa Clinic in Tempe, Arizona, with a Dr. Cornelia Siegelman, who specializes in tummy and fanny tucks, thighs and upper arms."

Victoria laughed. "That's what Colley did with his four hundred and fifty thousand dollars. A deposit on a complete makeover at the Sun Spa Clinic. Nonrefundable."

"I hope Mrs. Fieldstone's goons don't decide to ruin the job."

CHAPTER 24

Victoria was in the *Grackle*'s loft office talking to William Botts when the phone rang.

"Mrs. Trumbull? Yes, she's here," Botts said. "May I tell her who's calling?"

Victoria sat forward.

"Yes, Mrs. Fieldstone. Certainly." Botts stood, edged around John Milton, and handed Victoria the phone. She put her hand over the mouthpiece.

"Did she say what she wants?"

"No, Madam Reporter, she didn't." Botts returned to his seat. John Milton thumped his tail.

Victoria said into the phone, "This is Mrs. Trumbull."

"Audrey Fieldstone, Mrs. Trumbull. I have a favor to ask of you."

"Oh?"

"Calpurnia Jameson and I need to meet with you. Today, if possible."

"May I ask why?"

"It's rather sensitive. We'd prefer to talk to you in person. Would this evening be convenient?"

"Not really."

There was a long pause. "We have to meet with you soon," Audrey said.

Botts took off his glasses and leaned back in his chair.

"Are you there still, Mrs. Trumbull?"

"I'm checking my schedule," said Victoria. "It would help if you gave me some indication of what you want to talk with me about." Victoria waited. "Does this involve the recent deaths?"

"I'd rather not say over the phone. We can come to your house."

"Just a moment." Victoria put her hand over the mouthpiece again. "She wants to meet me tonight. Will you be here, William?"

"I can be."

Victoria moved her hand away from the phone. "I'll meet you at the *Grackle* office around seven."

"We want to meet with you alone," said Audrey.

"That won't be possible. Mr. Botts will be here. Anything you need to discuss with me, you may say in front of him."

"We don't want anyone else involved, Mrs. Trumbull."

"Then I think you'd better find another confidante."

Botts swung his glasses by one earpiece.

Audrey took a breath. "Mrs. Trumbull, you're the only person on this island who has the background, the depth of knowledge, the wisdom, and the sensitivity to understand our situation. We need your advice."

Victoria patted her hair and cleared her throat. "I'll see you here at seven, but only on condition that Mr. Botts is present. He can be discreet."

Botts muttered, "If I try."

Audrey paused. "All right. Seven o'clock at the *Grackle* office?"

"You know where it is?"

"Everybody on the Island does, now."

Victoria handed the phone to Botts, who hung up. " 'Knowledge, wisdom, sensitivity,' " said Victoria.

"What on earth does she want?" Botts asked.

"They. Audrey *and* Calpurnia."

Botts had set his glasses down on the desk. He picked them up again and chewed on the earpiece. "That's a strange alliance."

"It is," said Victoria.

"Sounds as though I'm about to be caught in heavy crossfire."

Victoria smiled. "Quite possibly."

"What if I stop by your house a little before seven and pick you up."

"Make it six-thirty. You might get a good story out of this, William."

Botts murmured something.

"I didn't hear you," said Victoria.

"It doesn't matter," said Botts. "I'm regretting the loss of my innocence, is all."

"What is the matter with you, Colley? Stop pacing, will you?"

Calpurnia and Colley were having their predinner drinks in front of the fireplace.

Colley, still dressed in the coat and tie he'd worn to the newspaper office, had paced to the built-in bar at the end of the long living room. He turned and paced back again, his hands clasped behind his back. "I have a lot on my mind."

"I should think so. Have you thanked Mrs. Trumbull for saving your life the other night?"

"Victoria Trumbull doesn't need my thanks."

"I doubt if anyone else on the Island will thank her for saving you. Send her flowers, Colley. Better yet, a box of Chilmark Chocolates."

Colley had reached the fireplace end of the room, where Calpurnia sat in one of the wing chairs. He spun around. "I blame a lot of my problems on Victoria Trumbull. Damned if I'm going to acknowledge anything she allegedly does for me."

Calpurnia waved her hand airily. "She stopped the press the day you caught your tie."

"That never would have happened if she hadn't been in the press room—where she had no right to be." Colley resumed his pacing.

"Would you stop that? It's driving me crazy."

"Ha," said Colley, still pacing.

"I suppose Audrey's goons are putting the squeeze on you?"

"That's part of it."

"Pressure from the California girlfriend?"

Colley stopped abruptly. "What are you talking about?"

"I suppose she wants collateral for the money you plan to squeeze out of her? Did it occur to you to tell 'Joy' that you're already married?"

Colley spun around. "Who told you that?"

Calpurnia laughed. "We live on an island, or did you forget?"

"Joy is merely someone on the Internet."

"Oh, really?" Calpurnia turned and smiled at him. "A 'merely someone' with lots and lots of money, I understand. Let's see, you're meeting her, where? In Arizona, is it? You're so charming. What a pity thousands and thousands of women will never have the privilege of meeting you."

"Is that a threat?" said Colley.

Calpurnia's smile widened. "Speaking of money, are you going to tell me what you did with the four hundred and fifty thousand you got from Ambler?"

"No."

"Wonderful husband," murmured Calpurnia. "When you reach the bar again, get me another drink, will you." Calpurnia held up her empty glass. "Mrs. Trumbull found jobs for everyone you fired, including herself."

"For God's sake, I never fired her. She and Botts are putting me out of business with that sophomoric rag of his."

"Loosen up, Colley."

Colley poured another bourbon and water and took it back to Calpurnia. "Mind telling me where you're off to tonight?"

"That's my business."

"Wonderful wife," said Colley.

Victoria and Botts reached the loft office shortly after six-thirty. Botts lowered John Milton's basket to the floor of the barn, John Milton climbed in slowly, and Botts raised the basket up to the loft. He set a bowl next to the dog and filled it with water from a plastic milk bottle.

"What do you expect to happen tonight?" he asked after John Milton had settled himself next to the desk with a sigh.

"I don't know, William. Now I believe Audrey might have been the person who lured Colley to Chappaquiddick, intending to kill him there." Victoria shook out the bright serape that covered the chair cushion and put it back on the exposed spring.

"Why Chappy?"

"Chappaquiddick is out of the way."

"It certainly is, but why?" Botts asked.

"Audrey took her boat there for the Trustees field day, which isn't until this weekend. Two days early?" Victoria eased herself into the chair.

"She thinks ahead," said Botts.

"You know how desolate that area is, even at this time of year, don't you?"

Botts nodded.

Victoria continued. "She enticed Colley there, late at night so he'd couldn't go by ferry. That way, he'd have to use the beach route where no one would see him." She shifted to a more comfortable position, away from the covered spring. "If we hadn't been watching him, no one would have known where he'd gone. Once she'd killed him and disposed of his body, no one would know what had happened to him."

"If Colley had drowned that night, it wouldn't even have been her fault."

"She may have suspected the cut would happen that night, but I doubt if she counted on it."

"Looking back, it was a sure thing," said Botts. "A full moon, a high tide, heavy surf, and the vibrations of a vehicle on unstable sand to trigger the break. You ought to get a medal, Victoria. You saved him." Botts looked down at John Milton, then back up again. "Several things don't make sense, though. Why would Colley agree to meet her late at night in a remote area? And what reason would she have for killing him? Why would she kill him? I can imagine why she might kill Candy Keene and

Al Fox. I understand, the two planned a bit of blackmail. But why Colley?"

Victoria shifted position again. "Perhaps he saw her leaving Al Fox's office the night he was killed. Colley was meeting with Al Fox earlier that same day and I interrupted them. He may have been returning to finish his business."

"Maybe," said Botts. "You mentioned Calpurnia as a suspect. What possible motive would she have? And how could she convince her own husband to meet her at Audrey's boat?"

"I don't suspect Calpurnia alone anymore. She was in bed when we brought Colley home that night. There's no way she could have gotten home and in bed before we arrived. I'm beginning to think the two women collaborated in the murders." Victoria thought for a few moments. "Calpurnia inherits part of the Jameson trust fund only if she is still married to Colley at the time of his death." Victoria sat up straight. "I know what's happening now. The two women have worked together in the killings. Calpurnia couldn't have called Colley. He'd surely have recognized her voice. So it must have been Audrey who called." Victoria picked at a rough spot on the back of her hand. "What's strange is that Colley claims he couldn't recognize the voice."

Botts shook his head. "So he gets a call from a woman he can't identify and goes charging off down an unstable beach to meet with her?"

"Colley thinks he's invincible."

"That's true."

"He can also be stupid."

"Colley has a king-size grudge against you, you know." Botts looked at his watch.

"Why should he have a grudge against me?"

"Narcissists don't think they need rescuing and you've rescued him twice." Botts leaned back in his chair. "The *Grackle* has become his competitor, thanks to the money you finagled out of him. According to him, none of this is his fault."

"Colley has to face facts."

"He never will." Botts continued to chew on his glasses frame. "Ironic that he almost drowned, through no fault of the killer's, whichever one it is." He looked at his watch again. "I must say, Victoria, I'm a bit uneasy about this meeting with one or both of the killers. This office is not exactly high security. We need to make a plan of some kind."

"Before you picked me up, I called Casey. She'll keep an eye on us."

Botts rolled his eyes. "We'll be up in the loft with the killer while the police chief is watching the doors? I knew I shouldn't have agreed to be here tonight."

John Milton lifted his head. His ears perked up. Victoria heard a car drive past. Several minutes later, she heard footsteps on the stairs to the loft.

Botts looked at his watch again. "They're early."

"Victoria?" Casey appeared at the top of the steps. "I parked out of sight behind the house. Junior Norton will be here in another ten minutes."

"You'll need to stay out of sight," Victoria said. "Audrey agreed only reluctantly to have William present."

Botts opened a small low door behind his desk and peered into it. "I think you can fit into this storage space. You may have to crouch down. Not much head room."

Casey looked in. "That's fine. Before they get here, though, I have something to tell you, Victoria."

Victoria sat forward.

"The state police found the gun that shot Candy Keene. It was in the brook behind where the father and son were shooting. They've traced it to the owner."

"Who?" asked Victoria.

"Tom Dwyer's wife."

CHAPTER 25

Victoria struggled to her feet. "That can't be."

"There's no question about it," said Casey. "Mrs. Dwyer's father gave the gun to her as a high school graduation present more than twenty years ago."

"Have you talked to her?"

Casey sighed. "Victoria, the state police told me strictly out of courtesy. This case belongs to them."

"Then I'll talk to her."

"Not officially," said Casey.

"Hello?" Audrey's voice called from the foot of the steps. Victoria hadn't heard her car drive up.

Casey slipped behind the desk, bent down, and crawled into the storage space under the eaves, leaving the small door open a crack.

Victoria leaned over the arm of her chair and called down, "We're up here."

When Audrey and Calpurnia reached the top of the stairs, both glanced curiously around the loft, at the exposed rafters, water-stained ceiling, and stacks of books and papers.

Botts cleared a pile of papers off the kitchen chair and moved the chair next to Victoria. Then he turned a milk crate upside down. "One of you will have to sit on this."

Calpurnia took the chair. "You tell Mrs. Trumbull, Audrey. It's your show."

Audrey perched cautiously on the low plastic crate. "I don't like sharing what I'm about to say with anyone other than you, Mrs. Trumbull."

Victoria said nothing.

Calpurnia tilted her chair back. "Audrey intended to go to the police and blame me for the murders . . ."

"That's not true," said Audrey.

". . . which is when we agreed we needed to get your advice, Mrs. Trumbull."

Audrey leaned over and patted John Milton. "We're in an appalling situation." She stopped talking and continued to pat the dog.

Victoria nodded.

"The cat's got Audrey's tongue," said Calpurnia after a while, and laughed. She swept her hair away from her face. "Well, I'll tell you the story then, since she apparently can't. Audrey's husband, J. Ambler Fieldstone, and I had an affair that lasted for almost a year. He told me he was going to divorce Audrey and marry me."

Audrey looked up. "Never!"

"Shall I continue?" When Audrey said nothing, Calpurnia went on. "Ambler and I were cruising on his boat when I learned that he and Colley—my own husband, of all people— were buying and selling me like a piece of merchandise."

Audrey looked up from John Milton and smiled. "Raw meat."

"Exactly. Raw meat. That ended the affair. Humiliating. Especially since everyone on this Island but me seemed to know the situation. He had no intention of divorcing Audrey. Now I find out . . ."

Audrey broke in. "Calpurnia and I have never been on good terms. But when I learned that Ambler was meeting another woman . . ."

"Candy Keene," said Calpurnia.

Victoria raised her eyebrows.

". . . on Nantucket for a tête-à-tête, I called Calpurnia. *Miss* Keene wouldn't set foot on Ambler's boat because she got seasick, so she flew over to Nantucket. Her excuse was that she was consummating a real-estate deal."

"'Consummating,' ha!" said Calpurnia. "When Audrey called me to suggest we play a little trick on Ambler, I was going to hang up without talking to her. Then when I heard what she had in mind, I thought her little trick might be fun."

Victoria looked from Audrey to Calpurnia, her eyes hooded. "The 'little trick' was to run over him with his boat?"

Audrey shuddered. "The idea," she said, "was to intercept Ambler in Muskegut Channel in my Chris, tie up alongside, and board his Hatteras. I planned to start an argument with him while Calpurnia went up to the controls in the tower. I was going to shove him overboard in the heat of the argument, then Calpurnia was going to circle around . . ."

"With her boat tied alongside," said Calpurnia.

". . . and after he'd been in the water a good long time, pick him up and take him back to Oak Bluffs."

"Leaving Candy Keene alone on Nantucket," Calpurnia finished.

"But you ran over him instead," said Victoria.

Audrey turned away.

"Why didn't you report the accident to the Coast Guard right away?" Victoria asked.

"It was too ghastly," said Audrey. "We weren't thinking straight."

"People get killed by propellers more often than the public realizes," said Victoria. "You were foolish. The Coast Guard knows how to deal with boating accidents. It's not too late to explain to them what happened."

"We simply couldn't bring ourselves to face the authorities," said Audrey.

"Audrey won't take responsibility for her not-so-funny trick. She must have known he'd go under the props when she pushed him overboard," Calpurnia said.

"Calpurnia was the one who ran him over when she put the boat in gear," Audrey said. "Not I."

"Ambler's death has been puzzling me," said Victoria. "I couldn't imagine how he could kill himself by accident." She turned to Audrey. "Call the Coast Guard and make an appointment to meet someone at the station. Tell them what happened before this goes on much longer."

Both Audrey and Calpurnia were silent.

"Call them from here. You'll be in trouble for not reporting the accident immediately, but you'll be in worse trouble if it comes out that you never reported it."

Audrey and Calpurnia were both looking down, Calpurnia at her feet, Audrey at John Milton.

"There's another matter that needs to be cleared up," Victoria said. "The deaths of Candy Keene and Al Fox."

"What about their deaths?" Audrey asked.

Calpurnia continued to look at her feet.

"Both of you had motives for killing them."

Calpurnia looked up. "What are you talking about?"

"Someone killed those two people and thought he or she had a good reason," said Victoria.

"I had nothing to do with either murder," said Calpurnia.

Audrey's face flushed. "I certainly didn't kill them. She," Audrey said, pointing to Calpurnia, "is not telling you the whole story."

"Whole story!" said Calpurnia. "Who's not telling the whole story? Why don't you tell Mrs. Trumbull about Buddy, *Mrs. Fieldstone?*"

Victoria studied the two women. Botts toyed with his pencil.

Audrey turned on Calpurnia. "Strange, isn't it, darling, that a knowledgable boat captain like you would put a boat into gear just as a passenger falls overboard. Accident? I hardly think so, darling." She made a gesture with the side of her hand, as if to slice the air. "Buddy? I'll tell Mrs. Trumbull about Buddy. But first, you tell her about Colley's plan for his total body makeover to impress a sweet thing he met on the Internet who had a lot of money and who calls herself Joy."

Calpurnia stood. "What makeover?"

"That's what he's doing with the four hundred and fifty grand. Vanishing. Starting a new life with his new body and face and his new rich sweetie." Audrey laughed. "She may be worth more than his trust fund."

"That's a lie!"

"You think so, darling? I told you about Joy. What else do you think my goons have been doing, besides hasseling Colley for my money? He's not terribly good at covering himself. A total body makeover at Sun Spa in Tempe."

"Stop it, both of you," said Victoria. "Audrey, did you call Colley on your cell phone from Chappaquiddick the other night?"

"Certainly not."

Victoria turned to Calpurnia. "Did you ask Colley to meet you on Chappaquiddick?"

Calpurnia laughed. "You mean the night you brought him home half-drowned?"

John Milton lifted his head and made a low rumbling growl.

Botts stopped playing with his pencil and stared at his dog. "What's the matter, boy?"

John Milton looked quickly at Botts, then toward the stairs, and continued to growl. He got unsteadily to his feet. The fur on his neck was standing up.

Victoria, too, got to her feet. "All of you, get to the back of the loft near the hay window and lie down. Right away."

"What . . ." Calpurnia started to say.

Victoria moved behind her chair. "Casey," she called out softly.

Casey pushed the closet door open, crawled out, stretched her arms and legs, and put her hand on the back of her neck. She shifted her belt around so her holster was near her hand.

John Milton stood facing the stairs, feet apart, teeth bared, growling steadily, the fur raised along his back.

Victoria glanced toward the large window in the back of the loft. Low evening sunlight streamed through, right in her eyes, making it difficult to see the three people lying on the floor. She could barely make out Casey, hunched over with her back to the angled ceiling.

John Milton barked once.

The step near the middle of the stairway creaked. Victoria tilted her head to listen. She heard crickets in the field. A song sparrow sang a few bars of an aria. There was no other sound. She held her lilac-wood stick tightly in one hand and grasped the arm of the chair, ready to lower herself behind it, away from the open stairwell.

John Milton spread his feet apart, raised his head, and howled. Victoria had just enough time to consider that she and John Milton shared a primitive fight reflex when she saw a figure, head partly concealed by hunched shoulders, reach the top step.

Victoria took a deep breath.

"Colley Jameson! What are you doing here?"

Colley spun around. He was holding a gun and pointed it at Victoria.

Several things happened at once. John Milton lunged unsteadily for Colley's leg. Casey, her own gun in hand, shouted, "Hold it, Jameson!" Colley swung around and aimed his gun at the dog. Victoria, using every bit of strength she had, shoved the rickety armchair toward Colley. A chair leg broke, the chair tipped over, and caught Colley just above his knees. His gun fired. John Milton sank his old teeth into Colley's leg and Colley, with a shriek, dropped his gun.

Casey stepped forward, held her gun on Colley, flipped him over one-handed, holstered her gun, twisted his arms behind his back, and handcuffed him.

"Can we get up now, Madam Reporter?" Botts called out from the back of the loft.

"It's over," said Casey.

Victoria looked for a place to sit and catch her breath. She settled onto the kitchen chair.

Colley swore. "If it weren't for you, Victoria Trumbull . . ."

"Shall I call the state police?" Victoria asked Casey.

"Yeah," Casey muttered.

While Victoria was on the phone, Casey maneuvered Colley to his feet and followed him down the stairs, holding her gun at his back.

"Where's my sergeant when I need him?"

"Here," Junior Norton said from the foot of the stairs.

"Take care of Mr. Jameson until the state guys get here, will you? Victoria needs to explain something to me."

"Not now," said Victoria, leaning heavily on her stick. "Tomorrow morning. At my house."

"Right," said Junior.

In the loft, Botts got down on his knees in front of John Milton and rubbed his head. "Ground filet mignon for you tonight, old friend. Triple ground." John Milton licked his face. "Your teeth must hurt."

CHAPTER 26

Victoria woke up late. Elizabeth had already gone to work but had left a freshly baked coffee cake and a full pot of coffee.

William Botts was the first to arrive. Casey and Junior came together in the police Bronco.

"Where's Matt?" Victoria asked.

"At the hospital," said Casey. "With his wife and a brand new eight-pound baby girl named Rowan. Born at two this morning."

Victoria smiled. "How's his wife?"

"Glowing. So's Matt."

They helped themselves to coffee. Botts carried the coffee cake and plates into the cookroom and Victoria seated herself at the table with her back to the window. Casey sat across from her and Junior and Botts sat on either side.

Victoria smoothed the red-checked tablecloth and helped herself to the still warm coffee cake. "Where's Colley now?" she asked Casey.

"Temporarily incarcerated in the county jail. They'll take him off Island later today." Casey leaned forward, elbows on the table. "Okay, Victoria, now how about explaining yesterday's performance? Why did we have to go through all the theatrics?"

"I had no idea we'd end up trapping the killer," Victoria replied. "Audrey and Calpurnia wanted to tell me something and I thought you should be there to hear whatever it was they had to say."

McCavity entered the room, glanced around, climbed into

the wastebasket, turned around a few times, and began to clean himself.

Casey sighed. "I'd like to hear your version of whatever it was you knew. Or deduced."

Victoria took a sip of coffee, narrowing her eyes in the steam. "It's hard to know where to start. We were dealing with three deaths, Ambler Fieldstone's, Candy Keene's, and Al Fox's."

Casey scowled but said nothing.

"Ambler's was the most puzzling. Last night when Audrey and Calpurnia explained what happened, it cleared up that part of the puzzle. Ambler's death was a stupid prank that went wrong. An accident."

"Accident, my foot," Casey muttered. "We'll see about that. The Coast Guard will, I mean."

"I never suspected Colley. He couldn't possibly have run over Ambler with Ambler's own boat. And, of course, he didn't."

"The false obituaries threw everyone off," said Casey.

Victoria nodded. "They seemed to point to Colley as victim, not perpetrator. I assumed the killer was writing them to frighten Colley."

Botts had taken a small spiral-bound notebook out of his pocket and was scribbling notes. He looked up. "The obits succeeded in frightening Colley enough to pay you to track down the writer's identity. How did you know the writer was Tom Dwyer, by the way?"

"The last obituary was Tom's private joke. You know how upset he was about the beaches being closed to fishermen during the nesting season."

Junior laughed. "Gotta try his recipe sometime."

"Don't use piping plovers," said Botts.

Casey was tapping her fingers on the table. "Go on, Victoria. I've got to get back to work."

"Tom realized his obituaries were not amusing to anyone," said Victoria, "and worst of all, that they were confusing the hunt for the killer. But he couldn't resist sending a last one.

When Colley showed it to me, I held the note up to the light and saw the watermark." Victoria smiled. "The paper was twenty-four-pound Plover Bond."

"Where in hell did he find that?" said Botts.

"Go on, Victoria," said Casey, tapping her fingers.

"I knew Tom wasn't the killer, so I eliminated the obituaries as clues."

"At that point you were left with Audrey and Calpurnia, who actually did kill Fieldstone." Botts set his notepad down and helped himself to more coffee cake. "This stuff is great. I'd like the recipe."

"Bisquick," said Victoria.

Botts licked his fingers. "Seems to me both of them had motives and opportunity for killing Candy and Al Fox. They'd killed once. Why not a second and third time?"

Victoria nodded. "I suspected them almost from the beginning and decided they might have been working together, only pretending their hostility. One or the other could have lured Colley to Chappaquiddick, planning to kill him and take his body out into Nantucket Sound in Audrey's boat, which was conveniently at Dike Bridge. But I was wrong. Colley planned to kill Audrey. That's why he risked driving along the beach."

"Calpurnia too, I suppose," said Botts. "Ironic that Colley would have been swept out to sea and drowned if you hadn't saved him."

Casey sighed and looked at her watch.

Victoria continued. "Candy Keene's shooting puzzled me too. At first I was afraid that the boy, who was target shooting in the hayfield near Candy's house, had shot her by mistake, just as she feared."

Junior shook his head. "They were practicing with rifles. She was shot with a hand gun."

Victoria broke off a piece of her coffee cake and held it while she continued. "At the *Grackle* office last evening Casey told me the police had found the gun in the brook."

"Stupid way to dispose of a weapon," said Botts.

"I supposed the killer needed to get rid of it in a hurry and simply tossed the gun toward the brook. After all, the boy and his father must have been nearby." Victoria set her coffee cake down, uneaten, and sipped her coffee. "When Casey told me the gun belonged to Tom's wife, Phyllis, I began to think that Colley might be the killer."

"Yeah?" Casey leaned forward on her elbows. "How did you make that leap? The state cops suspected Tom Dwyer."

Botts shifted slightly. "Why suspect *him*? He had no reason at all to kill anyone."

"The gun belonged to his wife," said Casey. "The state guys figured Tom had access to it."

"That doesn't make any sense at all," said Victoria.

"That's cops for you." Botts bowed his head at Casey. "Present company excepted, Madam Chief."

Victoria pushed her plate to one side. "I couldn't believe that Phyllis still owned the gun. I thought she might have left it behind when she divorced Colley."

"The gun was a high school graduation present," said Casey. "You wouldn't leave something like that behind."

"I would," said Victoria. "She certainly had no sentimental attachment to it."

Casey shook her head. "I always loved guns. As I kid I'd have thought I'd died and gone to heaven if my old man had given me a gun."

Victoria looked at the chief warily, thinking Casey had made a joke. But Casey tended to be literal, so Victoria let the comment about heaven pass.

Botts licked the point of his pencil. "But why would that make you suspect Colley?"

"I thought, if Phyllis left the gun behind when she divorced Colley, he had access to it," said Victoria. "Right after Casey told me about the gun, I recalled seeing a letter opener the other day on Colley's desk. The letter opener looked very much like the one I'd seen on Al Fox's desk that turned up missing."

Casey sat up straight. "Why didn't you tell me that right away? The letter opener could be the missing murder weapon."

"I didn't put things together until last night, and then everything happened at once."

"Why on earth would Colley keep the weapon and flaunt it?" asked Botts, raising his shaggy eyebrows.

"Textbook example of narcissism," said Junior. " 'Fox deserved what he got. I did the world a favor by killing him.' Probably never occurred to Colley to get rid of the weapon. 'Why should anyone suspect *me*?' "

"You were saying, Victoria?" said Casey.

"Colley was outraged at Al Fox, who was delivering alimony in person to Colley's ex-wife in Majorca. Vacationing with Colley's money and, probably, getting to know Colley's ex-wife. The souvenir letter opener on Al Fox's desk must have been the last straw for Colley."

Casey set her elbows on the table again. "Go on, Victoria. You guys stop interrupting her."

Victoria smiled. "Last night when John Milton growled, I was prepared for the killer to show up. By then, I thought the killer might be Colley."

"But why did he kill Candy?" asked Botts.

"Colley had a handsome income from the newspaper, but most of it was going to those three, the Majorcan ex-wife, Al Fox, and Candy. He felt they were bleeding him."

"How did he manage to shoot Candy?" asked Botts. "She must have known he was there."

"We'll have to ask Colley, but I think it's likely she contacted him first. Perhaps to insist that he write an editorial in the *Enquirer* about the target shooting. You can imagine the rest. She invited Colley to her house on the afternoon the boy and his father were shooting and took him to the edge of the hayfield. He waited until her back was turned and shot her, figuring the sound of the rifle shots would cover his."

"Why didn't she say something at the hospital when she was recovering?" asked Botts.

"She had been expecting a wild shot from the boy, despite all Casey's assurances that they were using every safety precaution. While she was in the hospital, she was talking to Al Fox about suing the town."

"I suppose Colley made the divinity himself," said Botts.

"It's not a difficult recipe," said Junior.

Casey looked at her watch again. "One more thing, Victoria, then I got to leave. Why did Colley show up at the *Grackle* office at that exact moment?"

"He and Calpurnia argued last evening and she refused to tell him where she was going. So he followed her. I don't think he knew what to expect. When Audrey showed up right after Calpurnia and the two went up to the office together, he realized he was in trouble. He reparked his car where it wouldn't be seen, then came up the stairs after them."

"Toting a gun," said Botts.

"His own," Casey said. "Was he planning on killing all four of you? And the dog, too?"

"I doubt if he was thinking clearly," said Victoria.

"Typical narcissist," said Junior.

About a week after the dust had settled, Victoria called on Botts. "William, I have some bad news for you."

Botts looked up. "What now?"

"According to the terms of the Jameson Trust, control of the *Enquirer* has been turned over to Lynn Dwyer, Colley's daughter. Lynn has asked her mother to serve as editor. Phyllis says she intends to reinstate all the staff members that Colley fired and plans to start paying summer interns."

"Good," said Botts.

"That means you'll lose Katie and Matt, probably Tiffany and

Wendy, too. Including Lynn, that's five out of eight staff members, leaving only you and your wife. I'll stay with you, of course."

"Victoria," said Botts, getting to his feet, "I can't think of a better revenge on Colley than for you to go back to writing your column for the *Enquirer*. As my farewell gift, I'll donate to the *Enquirer* all four hundred and seven of my subscribers."

John Milton got up from his bed of newspapers and lifted his front paw. Botts bent down and scratched the dog's head. He removed the bright serape from Victoria's chair, shook it out, folded it in half, then half again, and set it down on top of the newspapers.

"You can have your blanket back, old friend."